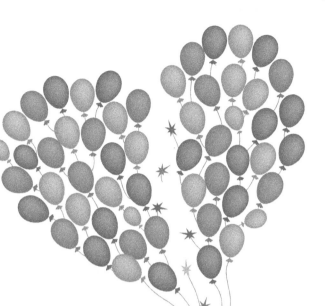

17 WEDDINGS

MARK CAMERON

Published in Canada by:
Catch Our Drift Productions Inc.

www.catchourdrift.ca

info@catchourdrift.ca

ISBN 978-0-9940953-3-6

Cover design by Kristin Summers, *Redbat Design*
Interior design by Mark Cameron
Copyedit by Sheila Cameron

For Sheila
(and the best wedding ever)

March, 2015

WEDDINGS

Bernard Kirby

I ALWAYS THOUGHT IT WAS COOL TO BE INVITED TO A WEDDING. As a kid, weddings were all about *dessert*. The all-you-can-eat buffets of cheesecakes and profiteroles and chocolate cream pies that made even the most boring nuptials enjoyable. I gorged on wedding treats even more once we discovered that my little brother had Celiac disease. At least I'd had ten years to develop a taste for proper dessert—six before Bruno came along, and another four before we learned that gluten was turning his small intestine into a warzone. After that, mom promptly replaced at least half the Kirby menu with two new food groups—pasty slop and particle board.

In my teen years, weddings were about dessert and *girls*. Weddings were the only occasions when I could get a girl to dance with me, notwithstanding my brief glimpse of popularity in grade nine, when my unrequited crush, Tamara Turnbull, invited me to her house party. Ignoring the fact that Tamara had always treated me as something between a pet and a pest, I accepted the invitation and trusted her intentions. After all, Tamara was *pretty*, and pretty always gets in the way of proper judgment.

I had a blast at Tamara's party, demonstrating some over-the-top dance moves that I'd learned at weddings—like a Russian crab dance and some seriously-70's disco steps—which got the whole crowd of popular kids chanting, "Bernie! Bernie!" It was all fun and games until Tamara's twin brother, Teddy, announced that the only reason she'd invited me was to win a bet with him. Teddy—star point guard for the Pearson Junior Pumas and lead singer of Rigid Cookie, his ridiculous excuse for a Limp Bizkit cover band—was my arch-nemesis. I should have known that he would use the party to remind me—and everyone else in attendance—that Tamara was way out of my league.

When Teddy called out his sister's intentions, Tamara's face turned redder than a candy apple—and I must have turned as pale as Marilyn Monroe's dress in *The Seven Year Itch*. After a humiliating exit from my moment of fabricated popularity, my reputation for crowd-pleasing antics stuck ... so I embraced it and became the class clown everyone expected me to be. I was never sure whether people were laughing *at* me or *with* me, but once I got a taste of attention, I stopped caring where it came from.

Anyway, back to weddings ... once I hit nineteen, *alcohol* greatly enhanced my enjoyment of marital festivities. In the decade since then, I've learned to appreciate weddings as invitations into people's inner circles—which are much easier to penetrate when you're drunk.

During one of my earliest drunken wedding episodes, at my second-cousin Jerry's nuptials in Saskatoon, I invented a party game called *Where's Uncle Bob?* It turns out that just about everyone has an Uncle Bob, or a Great-Uncle Bob, or an *almost* Uncle Bob—someone named Rob or Robert or Bobby or Roberto, or failing any actual Bob-like name, someone who just *seems* like an Uncle Bob. Nobody who has imbibed at least three drinks can resist a game of *Where's Uncle Bob?* Which is why—and how—I met Stephanie Hansen.

When I met my cousin Fiona's maid of honour on March 14, 2009, Stephanie stood above me in every way. A Thompson Valley farm girl with Scandinavian roots, Steph was tall, beautiful, fit, and capable of drinking me under the table. Two years older than me, she already had a college diploma, a career in business administration, and a basement suite of her own. Her perfectly-proportioned five-foot-seven body—a full inch and a half taller than mine—was accentuated by a teal bridesmaid dress that turned her into a princess. As she jigged and jived and two-stepped across the tiny dance floor at the Granville Island Hotel to celebrate her friend's special day, I half expected a fairy godmother to show up and whisk her away in a pumpkin-carriage.

I am forever in debt to Fiona for inviting Stephanie and me to be in the same place at the same time. And I am infinitely appreciative of Fiona's aunt, Roberta—the only person at Fiona's wedding whose name, face or demeanour (in her case all three) resembled a *Bob*—for allowing me to meet the mischievous woman hiding inside of Stephanie Hansen's flawless physique.

In hindsight, I understand the forces that brought Stephanie and me together. As we shared a bottle of wine and countless cans of Kokanee, it became clear that we had a lot in common: a passion for dancing like lunatics; an appreciation for the social networking game, Peace Warrior; a diabolical sense of humour, which culminated in some very politically incorrect observations about Aunt Bob; and the clincher for me—a shared history of watching Canadian football.

When Stephanie suggested that we step outside for some fresh air—to continue a talk about football, of all things—I couldn't believe my luck. Finding a CFL fan in Vancouver is rare enough. Finding a CFL fan in Vancouver who is a *girl* is like winning coffee for a year from your *RRRoll Up the Rim to Win* cup at Tim Hortons. Finding a CFL fan in Vancouver who is an unbelievably *attractive* girl is like winning Lotto 6/49—with the Extra.

I was surprised when Stephanie pecked me on the cheek after some other partygoers spilled out onto the patio and interrupted our discussion—but it kinda made sense. Apart from some questionable humour and a few loud beer belches—all of which seemed to amuse my new female friend—I'm pretty sure I acted like a gentleman.

By the time Stephanie's chariot arrived—a yellow taxi that would carry her away with two other bridesmaids to some princess-only after-party—I was starting to believe that we had potential for a real connection. When she wrote her phone number on a cocktail napkin and blew me a kiss before hopping into the cab—leaving me to wind down the wedding with a handful of fellow piss-tanks—I knew that I'd made a half-decent first impression.

What I never quite understood was why Stephanie stuck around. Maybe I never truly believed that she did. It was no small miracle that she returned the phone message I left two days after Fiona's wedding. According to my best friend at the time, Jonathan Donaldson, I was committing a grade-A faux pas by calling a woman within three days of first contact. Truth be told, I would have called Stephanie the morning after the wedding if my head hadn't felt like a cracked-open watermelon.

When I mustered the courage to call Stephanie, I was disappointed to reach her voice mail—and relieved that I didn't have to get my words right on the first try. I erased at least half a dozen botched messages before leaving a borderline-acceptable request for her to call me back. Not only did she return my call moments later—she waited patiently while I jumbled my attempt to ask her out for hot chocolate. And when I finally completed the question, she actually agreed to meet me at The Big Bean on Kingsway. After our first date—when I discovered that: (a) Steph was even *more* attractive than I'd remembered; and (b) I could make a pretty girl laugh *without* the assistance of alcohol—Stephanie started calling me. She invited me for second, third, fourth and fifth hot chocolate dates at The Big Bean—all within two weeks of our first outing. Then, on our fifth date, she suggested with a sultry voice that we go back to *her* place. I froze, too stunned to answer. I knew that *my* house was no place for a fifth hot chocolate date to end—not with my parents, teenage brother and toy poodle there to chaperone us. But the thought of going to Stephanie's place, where she lived alone—where she slept and showered—roused feelings that were almost too intense to bear.

I must have nodded my head, because next thing I knew we were riding in her brand-new Ford F150 to *her* place—a basement suite on West 26th Avenue, at the epicentre of Vancouver's stratospherically-overpriced housing market. The moment we burst through the door, she grabbed me by my t-shirt, guided me to her couch, and set a standard for physical pleasure that far exceeded anything I had ever achieved on my own. That was the day I learned what it meant to be alive.

I hadn't expected Stephanie to return my first phone call—or to invite me on four more hot chocolate dates. I certainly didn't expect her to invite me back to *her* place and cause me to lose my virginity three times on the same day. And I was utterly amazed when, after not quite a full year of dating, Stephanie looked up from the little cardboard box where I'd asked the waitress to plant an engagement ring under a chocolate pizza—the regular ending to our weekly Friday night Boston Pizza date—and said *yes*. There were even tears in her eyes. Before long, I was a blubbering mess.

On July 24th, 2010, four-and-a-half months after she agreed to be my *fiancée*, Stephanie Hansen walked down the aisle of St. Patrick's Catholic Church beside her father, Earl, to become my *wife*. Stephanie was wearing the most stunning wedding dress in the entire universe—a short, white number that showed off her shoulders and her amazing calves. She looked like a cross between Audrey Hepburn and Rita Hayworth, only prettier.

Earl, whose full name is Earl John Wayne Hansen, is a giant, scary Viking-rancher from Kamloops. He told Stephanie that if she insisted on getting married to *me*, and if she wanted *him* to pay for it, then we would at least get married in a Catholic church. I knew that Steph had some doubts about God and Jesus being the same almighty being, but she didn't let that stand in the way of a Catholic wedding—or admit her religious misgivings to Father John, our frail, balding priest who looked like he'd time-travelled from the eleventh century. Father John doted over Stephanie like she was a perfect Catholic girl, but he seemed entirely unimpressed with my lack of knowledge about the Holy Trinity. He only agreed to marry us so long as we planned to raise our kids Catholic. We didn't want kids anyway—a fact that we were smart enough to conceal from both father Earl and Father John.

At the front of the church, Stephanie's dad gave her a big hug, whispered something in her ear, and looked at me like he was nauseous. I never warmed up to Earl, and he never warmed up to me, but I kinda felt bad for him on our wedding day. I think he might have had food poisoning or something, because he didn't look quite right all day.

Standing at the altar, Stephanie turned to her woozy-looking father and said, "It's okay, Dad. I want to do this. I love him." As I stared into my fiancée's amazingly blue eyes, my emotions got the better of me and I started blubbering like I had at Boston Pizza. When Stephanie and I said our vows in the company of *our* inner circle—with a bar full of Kokanee and a gluten party of desserty goodness waiting for us to wrap up the religious mumbo-jumbo—I felt almost holy. At twenty-four years old, I finally felt like a real man.

When Stephanie said *I do*—when she agreed to make *her* place *our* place—I could tell that I was in for an amazing life full of Peace Warrior, pizza, Canadian football, and mind-blowing sex.

Or so I thought.

For most of my life, weddings were happy places for me—raucous celebrations, bursting with dessert and girls and alcohol and dancing—and I cherished every opportunity to witness the union of two kindred souls.

But that all changed when I received the wedding invitation from Hell.

THE BIG BEAN

Arnie Ganesh

When Bernard asked me to meet him at The Big Bean, I sensed that something was wrong. I thought I had finally weaned him off that place. He'd been making progress for the past few months, taking baby steps toward accepting his status as a divorcee—such as feeding his hot chocolate addiction at places that didn't remind him of Stephanie. It helped that she was no longer playing Peace Warrior regularly, meaning Bernard couldn't stalk her in his favourite online community. He was getting out a bit more, too—he'd even joined me and my cousins at a Barenaked Ladies concert at the Commodore Ballroom, where he spent hours dancing and chatting with my cousin Riya. I found out the next day that Bernard had talked about Stephanie the whole night—he'd just been happy to find a sympathetic ear. I was actually relieved that there was no spark between Bernard and Riya—having him as an extended family member would be a nightmare—but I was also disappointed that he was still hung up on Stephanie.

"What's up, B-man?" I asked, sitting across from Bernard at his favourite table by the window—the one he'd always shared with his wife.

He handed me an envelope and gave me his classic mopey look—his forehead wrinkled into huge folds, and his chubby cheeks drooping like a St. Bernard. His mom, Blanche, must have told me a dozen times that he'd had that same expression when he was born. That he'd seemed grumpy at the doctor for pulling him out of his perfectly comfortable hot tub—never mind that he was already fifteen days past due. Blanche had planned to name her firstborn Austin, but she says he named himself the moment he was born.

I looked at the envelope and recognized that it was a wedding invitation—no small trigger for my divorced friend. When I opened it and read the introduction, I realized the full gravity of the situation:

> *You are cordially invited to witness the union of*
> *Stephanie Hansen and Jonathan Donaldson at two*
> *o'clock in the afternoon on August 22nd, 2015*

"Man," I said as I looked at the invitation, "that really sucks."

"Balls," Bernard added.

"You know you can't go, right?"

"Oh, I'm going," he said. "And I'm gonna get really, really wasted."

"I'm sure that'll turn out well."

"I can't not go."

"Why not?"

"Because if I don't go, I can't rescue the bride from a life of misery with Mr. More-Looks-than-Brains."

I've always liked Stephanie. Everybody loves Steph. But as Bernard's personal break-up counsellor, she presented a unique challenge in the fine art of getting over someone. Ever since their break-up, she'd invited Bernard on countless outings as a third wheel—gatherings that B-man referred to as "Strangulation by Triangulation," even though he accepted every invitation Stephanie tossed his way.

Steph liked having Bernard around, and B-man liked to pretend they were still together. Even after Stephanie sweet-talked Bernard into signing divorce papers after she and Jonathan took him bowling, Bernard continued to act as if he and Stephanie were just taking a break.

It must have driven Jonathan crazy that Steph invited B-man to join them for dinner, movies, football games—you-name-it. But I also think Jonathan took some perverse pleasure from the expression on Bernard's face whenever Stephanie snuggled up to her new lover. I only joined the twisted trio a few times, because I hated watching Bernard writhe in agony whenever his ex-wife went home to sleep with his ex-best friend.

I looked at the invitation again. "Do you plan to save Steph before or after you get wasted?"

Bernard shrugged. "I dunno. Maybe a six-pack before their nuptials would get me lubed up for the job."

"Sounds like a brilliant idea," I said. "Why don't you pick a fight with Earl, too?"

Bernard's eyes widened, suggesting he hadn't factored King Earl John Wayne Hansen into his plans to rescue Princess Stephanie. I jumped at the opportunity to disrupt his heroic game plan. "He'll kill you with his bare hands if he has to."

"Death before dishonour," Bernard snapped.

It was not going to be easy to talk Bernard out of attending Stephanie and Jonathan's wedding. He hadn't invited me to The Big Bean to talk him out of anything—he just needed to share his bad news with someone. But I put on my stern counsellor expression and said, "Seriously, man, you can't go. Have you even been to another wedding since Steph …" I stopped before finishing my sentence—we still hadn't reached the stage of Bernard's recovery where I could talk openly about his divorce.

B-man shook his head.

I thought about our childhood—about The Three Amigos, as Bernard, Jonathan and I used to call ourselves. "It's kind of hard to imagine Jonathan married, isn't it?"

"Yup," Bernard grumbled.

Our school years together seemed like a sitcom: Bernard was the joker; I was the academic; Jonathan was the charmer. I never quite understood what girls saw in Jonathan, and I only hung out with him because he was Bernard's best friend—and I wanted to be Bernard's friend, too. I was both fascinated and repulsed by Jonathan's boasting about how many girls he dated during our late teens and early twenties. Living vicariously through Jonathan was as close as I came to having a love life of my own.

When Bernard met Stephanie, I should have known that Jonathan would not be able to keep his hands away from her. From the day she entered our life until the day she left B-man, Stephanie considered Bernard, Jonathan and me to be her three boys. She dragged us all up on the dance floor together, shared our food and drinks without asking, borrowed our toques when it was cold and our umbrellas when it rained. I always felt like the fourth wheel—I had the weakest relationship with Stephanie, by far. In hindsight, I believe my sole purpose in that strange four-some was to keep the Kirby-Hansen Express from going off the rails. It worked for a while.

When the crowd counted down to midnight at the Planetarium on December 31, 2012, the love triangle I had been watching develop suddenly seemed obvious, inevitable. I had repeatedly shrugged off Stephanie and Jonathan's flirtations as playful friendship, but deep down I'd known better—and I'm quite sure Bernard had, too. That night, when the jazz band stopped playing and their frontman told the audience to pucker up and find their soulmates before the clock struck midnight, I saw the glance that Stephanie and Jonathan shared before she reluctantly embraced Bernard.

New Year's Eve is painful enough for a perpetually single guy like me, but that night when we ushered in 2013 was excruciating. Not only did I have to watch every other person in the room make out like the world was ending, it also felt like I experienced the unravelling of Bernard and Stephanie's marriage in slow motion. Their last kiss was awkward and brief—Bernard was obviously expecting a big smooch, but Stephanie just pecked him on the lips and then moved on to Jonathan. She pecked him, too—then stopped and stood about six inches from his face. I couldn't turn away ... it was like a magnet was pulling my eyes toward Stephanie and Jonathan ... and an even stronger magnet was pulling their faces together. Next thing I knew, they were kissing passionately, giving in to their pent-up attraction—despite the fact that Bernard was standing beside them, frozen in disbelief. The band resumed, and people started dancing all around us, but they just kept on kissing. When Stephanie finally pulled away from Jonathan, she looked as shocked as Bernard did. Then she found my face in the crowd, pulled me in for a hug, and held on for dear life. After many long seconds, she muttered into my ear, "Oh Arnie, what have I done?"

Five days later, B-man called to ask me for a ride to his parents' house—and the day after that, he invited me to The Big Bean so he could pour out every high point and misstep of his relationship with Stephanie Hansen. That would become our regular meeting place, where Bernard would pretend that Stephanie wasn't really gone—while she continued to treat him like a BFF while sleeping with the guy who had been his best friend since kindergarten.

More than two years after that fateful New Year's Eve, there I was sitting at The Big Bean again, wondering how I could talk my best friend out of making the biggest mistake of his life—again.

BRiNGiNG Up BABY

Bernard

"Here you go, Scout." Dad handed me a microscopically small bowl of popcorn and took his place on the couch with Mom while I lounged on the chaise. Bruno sat awkwardly in the beanbag chair he'd outgrown many years ago—long before he'd become the tallest member of our family at a towering five feet, nine inches. It was a reunion of sorts—a rare Friday when Bruno came back to watch a movie with the rest of the family instead of hanging out at the bachelor pad he shared with two of his buddies.

"Thanks, Dad," I said, "but you do know I'm not six anymore, right?" My miniature movie snack would last no longer than five minutes, but Dad—a man of serious rituals—had been serving popcorn in the same small bowls for as long as I could remember.

"You're welcome to make your *own* next time," Dad groaned as he sat down and fumbled with three different remotes. Our family room—a small, cozy space with a U-shaped couch and plush grey carpet—looked pretty much as it had when I was a kid, except for the 60-inch TV that Dad had recently bought to reward himself for a promotion at the architectural firm where he and Bruno worked. I was looking forward to watching life-sized football on the massive screen, but it was proving to be a terrible fit for classic movies, most of which were filmed in grainy black and white or blotchy technicolor. The larger the screen, the worse some of those films look—but I must admit that was the first TV that did justice to the busty goddessness of Marilyn Monroe and Jane Russell in *Gentlemen Prefer Blondes*.

Once Dad finally got the movie going—he'd chosen a classic comedy, *Bringing Up Baby*—I had a hard time keeping my mind on it. I kept thinking about the invitation to Stephanie and Jonathan's wedding, which got me thinking about everything that had happened since I'd met Stephanie six years earlier. Classic films had been a tradition for my entire life—and they were especially awesome when Stephanie was part of the family. Movie nights were her favourite part of being in the Kirby clan—she'd even had her own miniscule popcorn bowl. I missed cuddling with her in my parents' family room almost as much as I missed making love with her on the couch in our own basement suite.

No matter how hard my dad tried to make movie night feel like old times, it was impossible to appreciate when such a big piece of my heart was missing. Mom understood that better than Dad—and she was a lot more supportive than him about my temporary relocation to my childhood home. Mom and I have always had that kind of bond, while Dad and Bruno developed more of a we're-somehow-cool-despite-being-total-nerds connection that I've never related to.

Watching Katherine Hepburn and Cary Grant bumble their way through one of the zaniest movies ever, I found the romantic aspect of the story hard to stomach. It dawned on me that the movie was about a guy coming to his senses just in time to avoid marrying the wrong person. It was a clear message to my broken heart that no matter how crazy and hopeless things seem, the right ending is always possible.

That night, when I went to bed, I ruminated with my toy

poodle, Fluffball—who has a knack for being there when I need someone to talk to—about the movie's key message. I flip-flopped back and forth between optimistic prognostication and utter helplessness, and Fluffball toggled his head back and forth in sync with my mood swings. I reminisced about good relationship role models, like my mom and dad; and lousy ones, like my own personal Uncle Bob—my dad's older brother—whose witch of a wife left him for her boss at the Credit Union. Bob hadn't held down a steady job ever since, and I had come to understand his lack of motivation the minute I joined him in the formerly-married department. Without someone to love and support you, it's hard to generate sufficient motivation to be a self-sustaining adult.

Lounging with Fluffball in my single bed that I thought I'd left for good in 2010, I started thinking about weddings—about my own wedding; about classic movie weddings; and about all the weddings I'd ever attended. I wondered what had happened to all those couples I'd seen tie the knot. Who had stayed together, and who had drifted apart? In most cases, I didn't know. I'd lost touch with over half the couples—which seemed weird, because I'd been close enough to each of them at some point in my life to witness their nuptials.

That's when I thought of The Plan.

THE PLAN

Arnie

"I HAVE A PLAN," Bernard said, taking a swig of hot chocolate that left a whipped cream moustache on his round face.

"A plan …?" I tried not to grimace at words that sounded all too familiar.

"Yeah. If I can help it, there's not even going to be a wedding."

I was glad to see that B-man had recovered some of his usual energy after receiving the wedding invitation, but I was nervous about being implicated in yet another hair-brained Bernard Kirby scheme. "Okay," I said, "enlighten me."

"I've been thinking—"

"That's a start," I interrupted.

Bernard raised his eyebrows and continued. "As far as I can remember, I've been to sixteen weddings in my life—counting my own and not counting one where my mom had to carry me when I was still a parasite."

"A parasite?"

"Yeah, you know, an infant. Kids are narcissists, and babies are parasites."

"And twenty-eight-year-olds living at home are …?" I regretted saying it the moment it slipped out of my mouth, but Bernard just scowled at me and took another gulp of hot chocolate. "Sorry, that was offside. So, what's your plan?"

Bernard set down his mug and said, "Well, some of those marriages must have turned out okay, right?"

"Probably. Some do."

"Well, out of the sixteen weddings I attended, one was my own; three couples have divorced; one separated; three are still married; one person is dead; and the other seven couples are un-accounted for."

"You've done some detective work. So how does this relate to your plan?"

Bernard sat up straight and beamed, his teeth standing out against his darkly-stubbled cheeks. "I've only done a cursory analysis. I'm planning a case-by-case assessment of relationship status—I'm going to interview each couple, noting positive and negative attributes and correlating them with relationship out-comes."

For as long as I've known Bernard Kirby—which goes all the way back to fourth grade—he has been the smartest dumb guy I know. Or maybe the dumbest smart guy—I'm not sure which. "So, let me get this straight," I said. "You're planning to find out what happened to everyone you ever watched get married, and somehow use that information to ... sorry, to do what?"

"To win back Stephanie!" Bernard barked. "I read somewhere that every path forward goes through the past."

"Ah," I said.

"It was written by one of those relationship guru dudes. The only way I can fix what happened to me and Steph is to figure out what went wrong for us, and the best way to do that is to study what worked and didn't work for other couples."

"Right," I said, "because studying has always been your strong suit."

Bernard scowled at me again.

"Couldn't you learn about you and Steph by reading those books ... you know, by those relationship guru dudes?"

Bernard was undeterred. "For your information, love isn't some cold, hard thing you can just read about. It's a totally human state that you need to feel in your heart."

"But I thought you were planning to do a statistical analysis of your data."

"I don't see it as analysis. I'm looking for pattern recognition. I read this book by the guy who invented Peace Warrior—he's a Danish dude who seems to know everything about everything, and he was awesome enough to make a game about it. He says that we do our best learning through pattern recognition, not from old-school analysis. We correlate information in our sub-conscious based on our observations, and if we can bring that forward into our conscious mind then we can act based on what we've learned. Even the military does that now. It's not about data—it's about insight."

"So, you figure ... if you talk to fifteen couples, you're going to see some patterns."

"Exactly!" he said, almost shouting. "Well, fourteen, unless I consult the Ouija board for my great-aunt Aggie."

"And how is this going to help you win back Stephanie?"

"I have no friggin' clue," he said, "but I'm gonna find out."

I was so happy to see Bernard excited that I felt a tinge of support for his ridiculous project. I wondered if it could provide a worthwhile distraction from his preoccupation with Stephanie. Then I came to my senses and realized he would surely find some way to sabotage his own plan—which couldn't end well. Leaning back in my seat, I crossed my arms and shook my head. "B-man, we really need to get you a date."

"Yeah, what do you know about dates?" he said.

"Oh, gee, look …" I glanced at the clock behind the counter. "Time for me to go."

I was not about to let Bernard turn the conversation about his tortured love life into an exploration of my own non-existent one.

THE LIST

Bernard

My mom said The List was a crazy idea, but I could tell she loved it. While we drank coffee at the kitchen table, she and I studied the sheet of paper containing the names of sixteen couples—complete with wedding dates—that she had helped me compile:

Nancy & Chris Pendleton — June 13, 1992
Bob & Shirley Kirby — Oct 9, 1993
Johnny & Sophia Lievenchuck — June 10, 1995
Reg & Lorna Mortenson — April 19, 1997
Clyde Barnsworth & Cheryl Moore — Sept 16, 2000
Agatha & Leonard Smith — Sept 8, 2001
Prakash & Meera Ganesh — July 23, 2005
Jerry & Jordan Young — May 6, 2006
BJ & Jasmine Duggan — Dec 1, 2006
Cheyenne Walls & Devan Johnson — Aug 11, 2007
Joey & Cecilia Yang — Oct 18, 2008
Fiona & Marcus Pfyffer — March 14, 2009
Sabrina & Mike McDonald — June 13, 2009
Bernard Kirby & Stephanie Hansen — July 24, 2010
Tamara & Tracy Spencer — April 16, 2011
Amanda & Dave Carson — May 19, 2012

"Remember your Aunt Agatha's wedding?" Mom asked.

"Yeah," I said. As if anyone could forget my great-aunt Agatha's wedding, which took place when I was fifteen. It was memorable enough for the fact that Aggie was like a hundred when she married Leonard, who was no older than my dad. My second-cousin Jerry told me that Aggie had lots of money from her fourth husband—some oil guy from Calgary—and that she'd been dating younger men ever since he died. Leonard was the dorkiest groom I can recall—Jerry said that Len was marrying for love *and* money, and I could believe it. Watching Aggie and Len dance was like some geriatric reality TV show, but they were enjoying themselves. They actually seemed to be in love.

Aunt Aggie's wedding was a breakthrough in my ability to interact with girls. I spent most of the night dancing with cousins, and I even slow-danced with Fiona to Elvis's *Can't Help Falling in Love*. That seems kinda creepy in retrospect, but at the time it felt like an important teenage milestone.

The exact timing of Aggie's wedding—a few days before 9-11 happened—was impossible to forget. When I came down for breakfast on September 11th, my parents were watching the news. I just walked up and watched with them in stunned silence. Then my mom turned and said, "I have some bad news."

"Yeah, that's kinda obvious."

"No, not this. It's about Aggie."

"What do you mean?"

"She died last night, on her honeymoon."

It turns out that Aunt Aggie died with a smile on her face at Harrison Hot Springs, forty-eight hours after her wedding and less than twelve hours before those airplane-flying idiots screwed up the family trip we were planning to New York. Rumour has it

Aggie and Len were going back and forth between the hot pool and their hotel room, and her ticker just stopped—probably in the middle of a copulation session. Maybe she wasn't ready for another reminder of how evil people can be, so she checked out while the world still seemed like an almost decent place.

My mom's fingers tapping on The List brought me back to the kitchen table. "What do you think happened to Leonard?" she asked.

"I don't know. Jerry said last time he heard about Len—maybe ten years ago—he was enjoying the octogenarian dating scene in Palm Springs."

I looked down and wrote B beside Leonard's name, to signify that he was a lower priority. I marked four other couples as B: my deadbeat uncle Bob and his ex-wife, Shirley; my older cousin Clyde and his high-school sweetheart, Cheryl, whose marriage lasted all of ten months; my dad's childhood friend, Johnny, who left his wife Sophia to be with a woman half his age in the Philippines; and my friend Cheyenne, who was already on her third husband at the ripe old age of twenty-eight (I made such an ass of myself at her first wedding that I wasn't invited to the other two). Recognizing Cheyenne as a special case—she epitomized the philosophy of *if at first you don't succeed, try, try again*—I scratched out her B and changed it to an A.

"Why don't you start with people who are happily married?" Mom asked.

My dad, who popped in to retrieve a repulsive blackish-green smoothie drink from the fridge, let out a cynical laugh and said, "That'll make for a short list."

"Oh, hush, Karl," Mom replied. "And which category would you and I fall into?"

"The happily married one, of course," Dad said, stopping to peck my mom on the cheek before wandering back out of the kitchen.

"Are you taking notes?" Mom said. Then she added, "So what have we got to work with?"

I looked at The List again. There were eleven couples on my A-List. Easy-peasy. Except that I had lost contact with most of them. I thought about how once people get married, they stop hanging out with their single friends. After they have kids, they stop hanging out with anyone who doesn't have kids. And when someone becomes a divorce victim, he's voted off Married People Island altogether.

"Why don't you start with the people you've seen in the past year?" Mom suggested.

"That's only three couples," I said.

"You have to start somewhere."

"I suppose." I scanned my list again. Fiona and Marcus had been in Switzerland for almost a year—they moved there so Marcus could take a banking job with his dad's firm. Fiona had known Stephanie forever—they grew up together in Kamloops—and she was the one who introduced me to my bride-to-be. I wrote down *VIP* and *Skype* beside their names.

Next was Jerry and Jordan in Saskatoon. To my knowledge, they hadn't voted me off their island yet—though I was probably on probation after my Roxy incident the previous summer. It was time to see if the J's still considered me a tolerable single dude, so I wrote *Road Trip* beside their names and made a mental note to repay my debt to the Roxy once my part-time White Spot job was upgraded from bus boy to waiter.

The third married couple I had seen within the past year was my high-school crush, Tamara, and her football-player husband,

Tracy Spencer. I'd felt a hint of envy when Stephanie and I watched the T's get married in 2011, though at that time I was happy enough in my own newlywed life that I only felt a mild pang. I vaguely recall rambling some passive-aggressive warning to Tracy—during the peak of my inebriation at their reception— that he'd better treat Tamara like she deserved to be treated. I don't think he was particularly concerned about my warning— Tracy never seems concerned about anything I say or do. The guy is built like Atlas, runs like Usain Bolt, and has the patience of Buddha—which is a totally inequitable combination of traits for one human to possess.

It was cool to be invited to a wedding where I was surrounded by a few of the lesser-known BC Lions—Tracy was on their practice roster back then before he was upgraded to third-string quarterback. It was Stephanie who got us invited, because she and Tamara worked together in the administration department at the children's hospital.

I'd last seen Tamara and Tracy a few months back, at Stephanie and Jonathan's New Year's Eve party at Joe Fortes—a memorable event that left me hungover, broke, and slightly regretful about my motor mouth. In hindsight, my attempt to toast Stephanie and Jonathan on the second anniversary of their first kiss was a questionable judgment call. Everyone dispersed after that. And in my New Year's Day fog, I realized that a few people were probably happier *not* knowing what had happened when Stephanie swapped me for my best friend.

"Bernard," Mom said, pulling me out of another vortex of self-loathing, reminding me that I was still sitting at our kitchen table on Victory Street.

"Yeah?" I replied.

"Are you okay?"

"I'm fine, Mom." I took a sip of coffee and realized it was cold. I'm not a huge fan of coffee—although I have to admit that whatever magical enchantment Tim Horton's puts on its coffee makes a Timmy's double-double taste almost as good as hot chocolate. My mom's home-brew is lousy, but it makes a half-decent delivery system for cow fat and sugar.

"What are you thinking about?"

"Coffee," I said, getting up from the table to pour myself the last dregs from the carafe on the counter. I realized that no amount of cream and sugar could make it drinkable, so I walked over to the sink and dumped the slurry of half-cold sludge from my mug.

"Any idea who to start with?" Mom asked.

I watched the coffee-like substance ooze down the drain, and it dawned on me that aside from my family and Arnie—and in some strange and twisted way, Stephanie and Jonathan—I didn't have any other friends left.

"I guess Jerry and Jordan," I said, wondering if even my second-cousin and his wife would be happy to see me anymore.

THE ROOF FORT

Arnie

B-MAN IS EASILY DISTRACTED. He once stopped building a snowman halfway through rolling its head, because he wanted to watch reruns of The Simpsons. His bedroom is littered with unfinished projects—ranging from a one-winged model airplane to a half-painted picture of Gandalf. And his garage, much to the chagrin of his father, contains at least three partially rebuilt bikes from the time Bernard decided to start a bicycle refurbishing business. But for all his false starts and unfinished projects, I have seen the persistent side of Bernard Kirby.

I learned how determined Bernard can be back in eighth grade, when he came up with the grand idea of building a fort on his roof—for no other reason than to see if he could get away with it. His plan was to build the fort, use it for a few weeks, and take it down before his parents noticed. Like most things B-man has ever done, the roof fort project did not go quite as intended.

I remember our first planning session for the project, in our high-school lunchroom, when Bernard explained how the trees would shield the fort from the neighbours across the back alley from his house.

"What about Mr. Brown?" Jonathan asked, thinking of how much trouble we'd get into if Bernard's grumpy next-door neighbour saw the fort.

"How's he going to see it?" Bernard responded.

"I'll bet he has X-ray vision," Jonathan said. "He's probably a retired supervillain."

"What if we fall off the roof?" I asked.

"We'll use my dad's climbing gear," Bernard replied.

"Awesome!" Jonathan said. "Maybe we can set up a bungee jump, too."

Ignoring both Jonathan's suggestion and my apprehension, Bernard laid out what seemed like a solid plan—so I pushed aside my spidey sense and went along with it.

The three of us worked on the fort two days a week, when Bernard's dad was still at work and his mom took Bruno to soccer practice. We all became obsessed by the project—Jonathan tracked time and kept an eye out for B-man's parents while I acted as Bernard's safety advisor, helping him rig up his dad's rock-climbing apparatus before he ventured onto the roof. The project was amazingly smooth, especially by B-man standards. I thought he would actually complete this one—until one afternoon around late May or early June, when Bernard made a catastrophic mistake.

For weeks, I'd been looping Bernard's harness around the leg of his bed, then leaning out of his window and pitching the rope up over a turbine roof vent—one of those spinning metal contraptions that looks like a crown. Bernard would catch the rope from his brother's window and attach it to his dad's rock-climbing belt. We'd tested the harness by having all three of us yank on the rope, but back then we didn't understand how much force a real-life falling B-man could generate.

On that unforgettable afternoon in May, Bernard leaned over to grab a board from me—Jonathan and I also tag-teamed to bring a few boards at a time from Mr. Kirby's stash at the side of the house. Bernard had become increasingly confident in his harness, but that day he reached just a little too far for gravity to ignore. I watched in horror as B-man tried to maintain his balance, throwing his arms out straight like a tightrope walker, then waving them frantically as he struggled to stay upright. Bernard tipped over sideways ... and reached down to brace his fall.

It probably took three seconds for Bernard to go over the edge of his roof, but it felt like he stumbled and bounced down it for three minutes. I still remember the whole sequence of events like it happened yesterday. I was helpless as I watched him go down ... down ... and over the edge, head-first.

What I remember most was the snap! For a second, I thought it was the rope breaking, and I almost died on the spot. Then I saw the turbine vent—which had broken off at its base—bouncing and rolling down the roof, following Bernard over the edge.

The rope snaked its way down the roof. Suddenly, a grinding screech from behind caused me to spin around—then a loud "Oof!" turned my attention back to the window. It took me a few seconds to calm down and scan the scene, and a few more seconds to understand what had happened. The rope, after it snapped off the turbine fan, had caught on the frame of the roof fort—and the sudden increase in tension had jolted the bed, moving it by a foot or so before it dug into the floor and held its ground.

Next, I heard the full volume of Bernard's voice screaming, "Arnie! Jonathan! Heeeeeeelp!"

I sprinted out of the bedroom to see what had become of my friend—and ran smack into Jonathan at the top of the stairs.

"What's going on?" Jonathan said.

I muttered a bunch of disjointed words as I ran down the

stairs. Jonathan followed, trying to make sense of my confused explanation.

As we emerged from the back door, Bernard was spewing a stream of complaints laced with profanity. When I saw him hanging halfway down the first storey of his house, dangling in his harness like a spider on a single strand of web, I looked over at Jonathan and we both started to laugh.

"He bungeed without us!" Jonathan yelled.

B-man exploded in rage, screaming insults about my spotty record as a safety advisor. Jonathan and I shared a moment of hilarity at our friend's expense—until Mr. Brown stormed through the side gate and spoiled the party. Needless to say, the project was terminated prior to completion.

Looking back on the roof fort incident, I'm impressed about how my parents and Bernard's parents handled it. Although they couldn't admit it at the time, I think all four of them found the situation quite amusing. They put on a show by grounding Bernard and me for a month—but they were lax about enforcing it.

Jonathan took the brunt of parental backlash for our ill-advised project. He never said exactly what happened—he wasn't one to talk about his home life—but he got a lengthy grounding and an earful from his stepdad. I sometimes wonder if he took more than verbal abuse from the jerk his mom chose to live with through our early teen years. Jonathan's home life was always tumultuous—his real dad left when he was five, and his mom went through a string of boyfriends and one mean stepdad before finding Dale, a nice guy she's been with for the past decade or so.

The look in Bernard's eyes when I met him again at The Big Bean took me back to eighth grade—it was the same look of roof-fort determination that told me there was no way to talk him out of hunting down every one of the couples whose weddings he'd attended. He would probably fail on his own—spectacularly, if past projects were any indication—but I would not be able to talk him out of trying. And if I wanted to have any chance of talking him out of attending Stephanie and Jonathan's wedding, I would need to understand his plan. So I asked Bernard how I could help.

"I need you to go with me to Saskatoon," he said.

"To see your cousin?"

"Second-cousin," he corrected.

"Why can't you call him?"

"I'll get more out of Jerry and Jordan if I see them in person—communication is way more than words, you know—and besides, I haven't visited them in ages."

"Why do you need me to go with you?"

"Well, first of all, I need a car. I was kinda hoping we could use yours."

"I don't think so," I replied, mildly offended that he was more interested in my vehicle than my company. "I'm saving up for new tires—my rear ones are almost bald."

"Then I'll need a second driver," Bernard said, undeterred. "I can use my dad's Jetta, but not until after some site visit he has on Monday afternoon—so timing will be tight. We need to get to Saskatoon, interview the J's, and be back in time for my White Spot shift on Wednesday night. That's about forty-eight hours, and it'll take at least thirty-six hours to drive there and back, including stops to eat and crap."

I knew that Bernard knew my schedule—I had four days off from my nursing shift at Burnaby General Hospital, which I'd been planning to spend cycling, reading, and watching movies with B-man. There was no way out. "Alright," I said with a re-signed sigh—not wanting to admit that, as usual, Bernard was injecting some much-needed excitement into my life.

Still, I should have known better than to join Bernard on an overnight trip to Saskatoon.

THE EGG

Bernard

I SHOULD HAVE KNOWN BETTER than to let Arnie pick the route to Saskatoon.

Arnie was convinced that the roads would be clearer on the Yellowhead Highway through Jasper and Edmonton than the Trans-Canada through Banff. I'd said, "It's an extra 98 kilometres that way," but the know-it-all research department in my passenger seat insisted my dad's all-season radials were no match for the mountain passes on the shorter route.

It's not entirely Arnie's fault that we wound up in the ditch. God—or Mother Nature—or whoever dreams up the inexplicable concept of snow in late March—also needs to shoulder some responsibility. March is springtime, no matter what Arnie and my dad say, and it's not supposed to snow in the friggin' spring. But it *was* Arnie who talked me into taking a detour through Vegreville so we could see the largest friggin' Easter egg in the universe. How's a guy supposed to keep his eyes on the road when you're passing a 31-foot tall *egg*? I mean, I kinda wanted to see it too, but I had a schedule to keep. I know I was driving a bit faster than I legally should have, but we had to make up time because Arnie's undersized bladder made us stop at every stupid little town between Vancouver and Edmonton—and there are a lot of stupid little towns between Vancouver and Edmonton. I thought we were going to make some headway after Edmonton, but then Arnie started telling me about that friggin' egg.

"Who put a town *here*, anyway?" I asked, as we surveyed my dad's Jetta for potential damage. Fortunately, somehow, after a 360-degree spin on black ice, I'd maintained enough composure not to hit anyone or anything—except a snowbank. Unfortunately, we were stuck in a major way, and there was no chance that Arnie and I could dig the Jetta out of the snow ourselves.

I called my dad's roadside assistance plan, but with the snow-storm they'd had overnight—and the fact that Vegreville is in the middle of the bald prairie with too many icy roads and not enough tow trucks—we had to wait over an hour for our rescuers to arrive. It had already taken us fifteen hours—a full hour more than I'd allotted, thanks to Tiny Bladder Man—so we were way behind schedule.

While we waited for the tow truck, we went across the road and studied the egg. That pysanka *is* pretty amazing, and if I hadn't been so angry at Arnie and God and the egg itself, I might have seen it as a highlight of our trip. It's made of a zillion trian-gles and hexagons, and it turns in the wind like a weather vane. The software they created to cut the egg's tiles was even used for the space shuttle. Still, we were wasting precious hours and I was pissed off, so at the time it seemed like a really big, stupid egg. A big, stupid egg that I would grow to detest even more within twenty-four hours.

It was no small miracle that Arnie got us to Saskatoon without any more stops—he drove the next four hours from Vegreville so I could get some much needed shut-eye, ignoring numerous bladder warnings because he didn't want to wake me up. When he stopped at Tim Hortons on the way into Saskatoon, I forgave him for the egg detour by treating him to an apple fritter and a double-double dark roast.

As we drove through Saskatoon, my mind flashed back to my last evening with Jerry and Jordan, during their visit to Vancouver the previous summer. I still wasn't sure what had prompted me to climb up on stage with the house band at The Roxy and grab the bass guitar during a cover of *Learn to Fly* by the Foo Fighters. The bass guitarist let me take it—I think he was too stunned to react—and the band was real professional, continuing to play despite the discontinuity of their rhythm section. But before I managed to butcher a full chorus, three huge-ass bouncers converged on me, forcing me to jump off the stage—with the bass guitar in hand. I narrowly missed landing on an entire stagette of tiara-wearing girls drinking from penis glasses. It's weird that I can remember all that, because after I landed like a pancake and most likely concussed myself, I forgot most of that night—except a vague memory that I broke some sort of consumption record for *She Ran Over My Heart with a Bulldozer* shooters.

It's like some cruel and unusual karmic punishment that I remember every detail about my brief moment of cover-band stardom, including the part where the princess bride-to-be looked up from her dick glass—milliseconds before I was forced to leap from the stage—and yelled, "Hey Fatboy, you suck!" I thought that was rather hypocritical coming from a woman drinking from a penis.

I hadn't even spoken to Jerry and Jordan since the morning after I learned to fly—when they checked on me to make sure I was still alive, and to inform me that I owed the Roxy house band one very expensive bass guitar.

Dinner with the J's wasn't as informative as I'd hoped it would be, but at least they didn't mention the Roxy incident. I asked them about a hundred questions, and the main thing I observed from their answers was that even after almost nine years of marriage, they didn't seem to have much in common.

"I *hate* hockey," Jordan said when I broached the subject of Jerry's favourite sport. "It's like war on ice."

"It's way more graceful than that," Jerry argued, "and the camaraderie of a hockey team is unrivalled."

Jordan scoffed at Jerry's assessment of hockey, and though I offered my two cents worth—that hockey pales by comparison to football—they were more interested in arguing with each other than carrying on a civilized analysis of team sports. Arnie ate quietly while I stuffed my face with flavourless versions of chicken chow mein and ginger beef.

Jordan started talking about dancing, and it was Jerry's turn to scoff. I remembered that even at their own wedding, Jordan could hardly get Jerry up on the dance floor. Not that I could blame him—their middle-aged DJ had apparently purchased his entire collection of one-hit wonders during a brief period in the early 1980s. Bored by his unreasonable facsimile of music, I'd discovered how much fun it was to track my very drunk Uncle Bob, who toggled between dancing like a maniac and disappearing frequently to smoke, pee or puke. Despite its humble beginnings, that game of *Where's Uncle Bob?* eventually led to my relationship with Stephanie Hansen—so I've always remembered Jerry and Jordan's wedding with a level of nostalgia that it probably didn't deserve.

Throughout dinner, Jerry and Jordan argued about everything. I asked about Peace Warrior—Jerry had once shared my passion for it—and Jordan put her hand to her mouth in a mock yawn. That led to another argument—Jerry said, "Oh yeah, well even a game of Pong would be better than another round of euchre with your parents"—and I began to think a divorce was imminent.

"So," I finally interrupted, "as far as I can tell, the only two things you have in common are disco bowling and bland Chinese food."

"Yeah, pretty much," Jerry said.

"Well, that and the hot tub." Jordan smirked.

Jerry returned Jordan's smirk, and it made me feel queasy. Suddenly, it was like they didn't care how little they had in common—and like they couldn't wait for me and Arnie to leave so they could ravage one another in the hot tub on their back deck. I felt jealous—and sad.

I couldn't wait to get out of the J's place after dinner. The thought of them having sex in their hot tub got me thinking about the ski trip Stephanie and I took to Sun Peaks during our first year of marriage—when we'd spent most of the weekend frolicking in the private hot tub on our patio. Then my memory snowballed, and I couldn't get Stephanie out of my mind.

I couldn't believe we ran out of gas right in front of the friggin' egg—like it hadn't given us enough grief already! I'd meant to fill up the gas tank in Saskatoon, but I was so depressed after dinner that I suggested we stop for a movie before heading home. *Paddington* was showing for half price, and I thought a light family movie would cheer me up. It turned out to be super emotional in my volatile state—which made me forget that we only had half a tank of gas in the Jetta—and Arnie didn't remind me to gas up like a competent wingman would have.

In fairness to Arnie, you would assume there'd be one 24-hour gas station close to the Vegreville Egg—I mean, it *is* their biggest tourist attraction, and Vegreville *is* on a major trucking route. I pulled off there—about half an hour after the gas light came on—because it seemed like my best option for refuelling.

By the time we walked all around Vegreville—no thanks to their signage, which was as pitiful as their snow-clearing infrastructure—we eventually found a Shell station where I could buy a jerry can full of fuel. It was then five AM and we were still well over twelve hours from Burnaby—not counting Arnie's need for hourly pit stops.

We'd left Saskatoon in what should have been plenty of time. If it hadn't been for the curse of that blasted egg, I would have made it home in time for my evening work shift. As it was, I thought of calling my boss about a hundred times, but I kept putting it off because I wasn't sure how to explain my situation. When five PM rolled around and we were only in Kamloops, I decided it would be better to tell my boss about my travel misadventures after the fact.

When I returned my boss's multiple calls the next day, she didn't accept my justification for missing *another* shift, and she said that even though she *adored* me as a person, she couldn't cut me any more slack as an employee.

That's how the Vegreville Egg, with help from Arnie and Mother Nature and Paddington Bear, cost me my job bussing tables at White Spot. I knew that my unemployed status wasn't going to make it any easier for me to win back Stephanie Hansen, so I was quite dejected following the trip to Saskatoon. But after a few days, I realized that I just had to try harder.

T⊦E ROADMAP

Arnie

B-MAN CAN BE SUCH AN IDIOT SOMETIMES. I couldn't understand why he was mad at *me* for running out of gas and losing his job.

More than a week after he'd suggested that I was partially to blame for his most recent firing, Bernard called to invite me to the International House of Pancakes on Kingsway.

When I arrived at IHOP, I was hoping for an apology. I should have known better. In typical B-man fashion, Bernard dove into explaining his new strategy for completing The List. "I have 136 days until Steph's wedding, and I want to allow a month to consolidate results and finalize my wedding derailment plan. I have ten more couples on my A-List. That gives me about ten days per couple."

"Okay ... what's next?" I asked, resigned to putting our latest disagreement behind us.

"Well," he said, "I think we made a strategic error in our approach to visiting the J's."

I took offense to the words *we* and *our*, but I bit my tongue and said, "Are the J's an A or a B? It sounds like algebra."

"The J's are an A," Bernard said. "The problem is that we didn't go deep enough in our interrogation. They played us like violins. Fortunately, I already know them better than most of the other couples, so I was able to glean some insight despite the apparent failure of our questionnaire."

"Okay," I said, "what insight did you glean?"

"The J's are attracted to one another because they're different. And they wanted to have sex. Visiting with us was like mental foreplay."

"You think they were using us to get aroused?"

"Eww," Bernard said, scrunching his face in disgust. "Jerry's my second-cousin. No, we weren't making them horny. It's just that we were standing in the way of their hot-tub date. It's like the more they argued about all the stuff they didn't have in common, the more they wanted each other—which is really screwed up. I mean, Steph and I always liked the same stuff, and we never argued like that—but the longer we were together, the less she seemed to want me. Toward the end, she just wanted to cuddle most of the time. I don't get it. I was so much better in bed than I'd been when we first met. I'd mastered the cunnilingus alphabet and built up some serious stamina. But for some reason that I don't understand—because I'm a guy, I guess—she'd wanted me more back when I was a lame-o in the sack."

Bernard was speaking more loudly than required, and I could tell that others were looking at us—one particularly well-dressed elderly couple was scowling at B-man, which caused me to sink into my seat. He was oblivious, as usual, and carried on talking.

"The other problem with our trip to Saskatoon was that we didn't have a roadmap," he continued. "We were making it up as we went, which left too little time to mentally prepare for the interview—and cost me my job. The problem with The List is that it's *just* a list, which could lead to more Vegreville Eggs if we're not careful."

"*We?*" I finally said. "How are *we* supposed to be more careful about *your* ridiculous plan?"

Bernard glared at me for a moment, then pulled out a small stack of paper. He unfolded a diagram that covered six pieces of paper, all taped together, and said, "This is The Roadmap. It's meant to augment The List and provide more of a framework for our investigation. I need you to help me stay on it—with no more diversions to idiotic landmarks."

The Roadmap was an impressive piece of work, containing a complex array of coloured lines and shapes. There were green boxes for each of his A-List couples; orange boxes for the B-List couples; a black triangle for deceased Agatha and her widow, Len; a silver hexagon that read "Bernard and Stephanie – July 24, 2010"; and a red circle with a line through it that read "Stephanie and Bonehead – August 22, 2015."

Most of the green boxes contained contact information, along with a date range for interviewing each couple. The Roadmap resembled a Gantt chart, with a calendar along the top and weeks separated by dotted lines.

"Wow," I said, "I'm impressed. I still have no idea how this is supposed to pry Stephanie and Jonathan apart, but I'm impressed all the same."

"You're my wingman," Bernard said. "You have to keep me on track. No more Vegreville Eggs."

"Gotcha. I'm on the lookout for giant Easter eggs."

"I'm talking metaphorically," Bernard said. "I'm going to be too emotionally invested in this to objectively assess all situations and avoid unnecessary obstacles. I need you to be like a second set of eyes—you've gotta help me keep track of the details so I can focus on pattern recognition. And I need you to be a better navigator than you were on the Saskatoon trip."

I sat back and stared at Bernard. The more he talked, the less I understood him. I was also getting hungry—we'd only been given a glass of water and a pitcher of coffee upon our arrival at IHOP—so I waved down a waitress, who gave me the "just a minute" head nod. Then I turned back to Bernard and asked, "What's next?"

The waitress arrived before he had a chance to answer. "I'm sorry," she said. "We're short-staffed, and I'm all in a tizzy." We locked eyes momentarily, and my whole body went warm from the inside out. Her straight, shoulder-length black hair was tucked neatly behind her ears, and her whole face seemed to smile while she talked. I glanced at her name tag—*Loretta*—before looking down at my menu. "What would you two boys like for breakfast today?" Her voice was sweet, almost childish—and it suited her perfectly.

I forgot I was hungry. It took me a while to focus, and to realize that Bernard had already ordered. I gathered my wits and ordered an omelette.

When Loretta left to put in our order, Bernard looked at me and grinned. "Are you blushing? Is it possible that Arnie Ganesh might actually be eyeing up a date?"

"I don't know," I said. "She is cute."

"I'm all in a tizzy," Bernard said, chuckling as he looked back down at The Roadmap. "Where were we before you went all googly-eyed?"

"I was asking you what's next." I was happy for the change of subject.

"Right," he said. "I'm going to interview Joey and Cecilia Yang. They've been married almost seven years, which my mom says is a notoriously tough point in most marriages—so I want to get a deep understanding of the challenges they've overcome. I know they have a couple of little Yangs running around, which, if left unchecked, will totally interfere with the interview. I need you to keep the offspring occupied while I interrogate the parents."

"So, you want me to babysit?" I asked, still trying to find a full breath.

"Call it what you will. How's Saturday at eleven AM? I've already confirmed their availability, and I know you're off shift then."

I looked over at Loretta, who was serving the table beside us. I couldn't stop staring at her, and when she set down the last of her plates, she returned my glance. She smiled before I had a chance to turn my head back to Bernard.

"The Yangs live near Royal Oak," he said. "We can meet—uh, let me see … cute waitress … Arnie in love … how about … here?" Then he hollered over to Loretta, who was serving another table, "Hey, are you working Saturday morning?"

Loretta paused to think, and then she nodded. "Yes, I am."

When Loretta was gone, Bernard turned back to me and said, "Let's meet here at 9:30. That'll give you an hour and twenty minutes to schmooze with our cutie-pie waitress before we head over to the Yangs' place."

"Okay," I replied, feeling embarrassed … and more excited than I'd felt in years.

YOKO ONO

Bernard

ARNIE HAS ALWAYS BEEN EASILY EMBARRASSED, and I was starting to recognize what a hypocrite he was, too—telling me *I* needed to find a *second* true love when *he'd* never even been to first base. (Arnie has long argued that lip-locking is a sufficient measure for a single, but I've always insisted that you're not safe on first until you've tagged tongues.)

When we met at IHOP on Saturday morning to finalize plans for our interview with Joey and Cecilia Yang, I was just trying to be helpful. I do like IHOP, but I went there the second time for Arnie's sake. I knew that *he* needed a date even more than he thought *I* needed one. While I was ordering my breakfast combo from Loretta—I made sure we got a seat in her section—I told her, "My friend thinks you're hot," at which point Arnie practically slithered under the table.

While Arnie and Loretta exchanged increasingly awkward glances, I briefed him about my relationship with the Yangs. I'd been in some classes with Joey Yang in high school, but I'd never hung out with Joey and Arnie at the same time. Joey started dating Cecilia in grade eleven, and I helped him write love letters to Cecilia during our spare period, while we ate french fries at Wendy's. I guess Joey felt some loyalty to me, because he and Cecilia invited me to their wedding four years after we graduated, even though I'd hardly seen them since high school. Their special day was nothing to write home about—they had a long Christian ceremony and a huge meal of mostly inedible seafood dishes, followed by a brutal dance party with some one-man-band dude butchering cover tunes on a synthesizer. I'm pretty sure I went home around ten PM, only slightly buzzed.

It was almost painful to watch Arnie dance around the obvious attraction between him and Loretta. I could already see their annoyingly adorable Indo-Chinese parasite babies, but even after I accelerated the process for them, he could only manage to look at her for a few seconds at a time. When Arnie and I paid our bill and walked out of the IHOP without him asking Loretta for a date, I wondered aloud if my friend would *ever* get to first base. Then he got all grumpy and suggested that I could have used the word "cute," because "hot" made it sound like he was a testoster-one-driven misogynist. I said he was hung up on semantics, and besides, I could tell that Loretta took it as a compliment.

Arnie and I didn't talk on the way to the car, or on the short drive to the Yangs' townhouse on Royal Oak. Then we made small talk as I parked the car and we walked up to the front door, determined to put our breakfast spat behind us.

The minute we walked into the Yangs' place I could smell poop, which made it hard to proceed with the interview—but I focused on my mission and soldiered on. It didn't seem to bother Arnie at all. With three younger siblings, I guess he'd built up a strong resistance to the smell of crap.

Fortunately, Joey went off to change their one-year-old daughter's diaper—which he had to do again in the middle of the interview. If I learned anything from my meeting with Joey and Cecilia, it's that baby Yang is a professional poop factory—

and Joey Yang's life has decayed to that of a professional diaper changer. Joey said that it was only fair for him to change diapers whenever he was around, since Cecilia had to do it when he was at work. I thought Joey was a glutton for punishment, and I couldn't understand his eagerness to get up close and personal with baby feces, but it sure seemed to make Cecilia happy.

Arnie spent most of the interview playing Lego with Jimmy Yang, who had received the world's largest Lego collection for his fourth birthday. I had to admit that Jimmy was a cute kid—and the contrast of his bowel control to that of his sister made him seem positively angelic—but I was still glad to have Arnie along to manage the little narcissist. Kids seem to think they should get everything they want, all the time. Jimmy Yang was no exception. Each time Arnie started to build a cool Lego contraption, Jimmy would insist on taking an important piece of Arnie's invention. I would have said, "Chuck you, Farley," but Arnie fed the kid's self-absorption by giving him whatever piece he wanted.

I was ready for the Yangs to report some seven-year breakdown, especially given the hardship of having two kids. I had prepared some tough questions about the challenges of work-life balance and the difficulty of raising two toddlers while paying for a mortgage in the most expensive city on Earth. But Joey and Cecilia kept looking at each other with puppy dog eyes, and it was almost making me ill.

"It's difficult," Cecilia confessed at one point, and for a second I thought I was going to bring some dirt to the surface.

"It must be," I said. "You must find it really hard to have any intimacy with a kid hanging off your breast all the time, eh?"

Joey shot me a brief look of disapproval. Cecilia raised her eyebrows and said, "No, I'm way more in tune with my body now than I was before kids."

I wasn't sure where to go after that. Cecilia's answer was way outside of the mental flowchart of potential responses I'd drawn up in my head. I had expected some sort of negativity that I could exploit for deeper investigation.

"I find Cici even more beautiful now that she's a mother," Joey added, reminding me of the fake maple syrup I'd slathered all over my pancakes at IHOP.

Later, I was thankful for the positive tone of my interview with the Yangs, glad that I had a successful marriage to analyze. But at the time, I felt some combination of disappointment and nausea—only part of which could be blamed on baby Yang's full diaper.

The weirdest part of my interview with the Yangs was that it negated everything I thought I'd learned from Jerry and Jordan. Whereas my second-cousin and his wife seemed to revel in the fact that they had *nothing* in common, Cecilia and Joey seemed to have *everything* in common. They were both chamber musicians— Cecilia on flute and Joey on violin; they both hated team sports, which I found particularly disturbing; they had gone to the same church since they were teenagers; and so on. For every question I asked, Cecilia and Joey gave compatible answers. It was as if they never argued, even though they insisted they sometimes did.

After two interviews, pattern recognition was proving more challenging than I'd expected. So much for my budding theory that marital success was rooted in contrast. Other than my assumption that Cecilia had a vagina and Joey had a penis, I almost thought the Yangs could be the same person. In retrospect, I'm kind of impressed with how happy they seemed throughout our interview, despite the poop show and constant interruptions by

Jimmy to show them Unidentified Lego Objects. They reminded me of my best times with Stephanie—when we seemed happy just to be together, like there was nothing else we needed.

Unfortunately, that day was the first real crack in my relationship with Arnie. He told me he was super embarrassed by some of my questions, and that he thought the Yangs were really classy with their replies. What sucked most about that day was that Arnie started to act like he was better than me. We kept meeting at IHOP and when he finally scraped together the courage to ask Loretta on a date, he started talking about her like she was more special than anyone else's girlfriend had ever been. He stopped appreciating my jokes about his virginity—a topic that had provided us with boatloads of laughter before Loretta came along—and he wouldn't even tell me what base they'd made it to.

As far as I'm concerned, Arnie broke the bachelor communication code. I started to feel like I was Paul McCartney and Arnie was John Lennon … and I'd gone and introduced him to Yoko Ono.

FATMAN SCOOP

Arnie

THE IHOP SESSIONS WITH BERNARD were both embarrassing and exhilarating. Each time Bernard and I went for breakfast, Loretta stayed at our table a little longer, and it became easier for me to talk to her. But it was impossible for me to ask her on a date without Bernard constantly chirping about what a cute couple we'd make. On our fourth breakfast with Loretta as our server, I found an opportunity—when she came to fill my coffee while Bernard was in the bathroom—to squeeze out the words, "Would you like to go for coffee sometime?"

Loretta beamed at me and said, "I thought you'd never ask."

After her shift that day, Loretta and I talked for hours at The Big Bean. I could tell right away that I was heading into uncharted territory—and I should have seen that such a big change would not be easy for Bernard to accept.

I give B-man credit for making sure I didn't miss the best opportunity of my life. I've always been nervous around women I'm attracted to—my usual pattern is to avoid them—and Bernard wasn't about to let that happen with Loretta. So I owe him thanks, even if he turned into a complete jerk the second I did what he'd been egging me on to do.

As soon as I started seeing Loretta, B-man began to give me a rough time about focusing all my energy on her. Then one day, when I met him at IHOP to plan his next interview, he really ticked me off.

"Where's Yoko?" Bernard asked.

"Her name's Loretta," I said. "And she's off today."

"I should have known ..." Bernard began, then stopped to see my reaction.

"What? Should have known what?"

"That once you found a girl, you'd forget about your best friend."

"Give it a rest. I'm just—" I realized Bernard was baiting me, so I took a deep breath and said, "Who's next ... the next couple? Who are we interviewing?"

"Prakash and Meera," he said, referring to the cousin I had always looked up to, and his wife who had never forgiven me for inviting Bernard Kirby to be my guest at their wedding ten years earlier.

I cringed at the thought of sharing space with Bernard and Meera for the first time since the infamous Fatman Scoop Cake Incident.

I could tell that Meera was being overly polite when we first arrived at their massive new house in North Burnaby. Interview Meera was not the same person who had been avoiding me at family gatherings for the past decade.

I only overheard some of Bernard's questions to my cousin and his wife as I moved between playing foosball with their seven-year-old son, Aidan, and playing dolls with four-year-old Emma. At first, I was impressed with Bernard's professionalism. His questions seemed intelligent, and he shut up for long enough to hear Prakash and Meera's answers. I wondered briefly if Meera's attitude toward B-man—and toward me—might finally soften. I was surprised that she had even accepted the interview request, though in hindsight I think she was expecting a long overdue apology from Bernard—which explains why she was acting so sweet when we arrived.

As well as the interview seemed to be going, I wasn't prepared for the side of Meera that emerged when Bernard asked, "How would you compare your feelings toward one another on your wedding night with your feelings today?"

Aidan scored about a dozen goals on me while I listened to Meera unravel herself trying to answer B-man's question about her wedding.

Prakash and Meera's wedding took place at a golf club in Langley, just after Bernard reached the legal drinking age of nineteen. The wedding combined a traditional Hindu ceremony with a typically Canadian dance party. Bernard was reasonably well behaved during the rituals, except when he laughed during prayers to Lord Ganesh—no relation to me—and blurted out, "Does that make you Lord Arnie?" I'm sure Bernard thought he was whispering, but his idea of a whisper is what most people would consider a shout.

At the reception, B-man fully embraced his status as a legal consumer of alcohol. He became increasingly abrasive as the DJ shifted from slow love songs to upbeat hits. When *Lose Control* came on, Bernard yelled out, "Here comes the Fatman Scoop"—referring to the rapper who accompanied Missy Elliot on her hit song—and he started dancing like a wild man. Although he'd had some experience drinking prior to his adult status, I'm sure he at least doubled his previous record that night. I don't know what possessed Bernard to act like a ballerina on speed, but the result was that he actually did lose control—and spun into the table containing Prakash and Meera's wedding cake. The table was no match for a spinning Fatman, and the cake was no match for gravity.

The wedding cake exploded as it hit the floor, and Meera exploded too. At first, she wailed. Then she screamed. Then she wailed again. Prakash eventually ushered her out of the room, and we didn't see them again that night. Once the cake was cleaned up, the DJ tried to carry on ... but the wedding was essentially over.

The next time I saw Prakash and Meera, almost a year later, I apologized about Bernard's presence at their wedding. Meera's expression told me that I should never mention it again, so we swept it under the rug and talked about the Vancouver Canucks. I suspected that Meera's wedding wound would never heal, and I was quite sure that I would never become as close to Prakash as I had often hoped to be.

When Bernard asked Meera about her wedding, she launched into a tragic recap of her life—starting with the spiral of depression and self-doubt that she had suffered since the Fatman Scoop Cake Incident spoiled the biggest day of her life. In fairness to Bernard, I thought a stubbed toe might have triggered her descent into misery, given what a crappy life she'd had. I hadn't realized that Meera's father abandoned her family when she was nine, or that her mother was forced to work two jobs while raising six kids; that their move from Burnaby to the only house her mom could afford, in the troubled Whalley district of Surrey, led to a life of drugs and crime for her two oldest brothers; or that the wedding cake was probably the nicest thing Meera's mom had ever made for her.

It wasn't Bernard's question that ticked me off—it was his selfishness after that which caused my blood to boil. I've always thought of Bernard as a caring and generous person, but he was so caught up in his own agenda that he didn't give Meera any space to grieve. He allowed her to talk while he scribbled notes, but he gave no hint that he was sorry, or that he cared about her emotional state. He kept muttering "Mm-hmm" as he took notes about her family history, and when she ran out of words, he marched on with another unrelated question. By that time, she was fully spent, and Prakash was in protective-husband mode, shutting down the remainder of the questionnaire and escorting us out the door as quickly as possible.

As we walked from my cousin's front door to the Jetta, Bernard said, "Well, that sucked."

"Yeah," I agreed, though I suspected we thought it sucked for different reasons.

"I hardly got any useful info before Meera melted down," he said, stopping on the sidewalk in front of the car.

"You think?" I said, my voice bristling. "If you were paying attention, you might have learned a thing or two." Bernard shrugged as if he didn't have a clue what I was talking about.

For all his stupidity, I have always appreciated Bernard's heart. I appreciate that he cries like a baby almost every time we watch a movie, and that he has a knack for giving me thoughtful, cool gifts every birthday and Christmas. Bernard has always had a generous streak. But that day, standing on the curb of Dundas Street while my cousin was inside trying to comfort his wife for a lifetime of sorrows, Bernard could only think of himself.

I was about to tell Bernard how selfish he was being when he stepped onto the boulevard and picked up a small stick. Then he knelt on the road and used the stick to pick up a caterpillar. As he walked over to a nearby shrub and placed the caterpillar out of harm's way, I sighed at what a paradox my lovable idiot of a friend could be.

TAMARA

Bernard

I'M PRETTY INTUITIVE ABOUT PEOPLE, so I could tell the last couple of interviews had been challenging for Arnie. The pattern-recognition skills that I'd been honing since I began working on The List helped me see the common denominator between those two interviews: *children*. Arnie must have been having a harder time with childcare than he wanted to admit.

I decided to interview Tamara and Tracy Spencer next. They didn't have any bambinos, so I could go without a wingman and Arnie could recharge his babysitting energy. I didn't want Arnie there when I interviewed the T's anyway, because I still found it hard to be composed around my high-school crush and her almost-famous husband.

Tamara had always known I was attracted to her. Once she became friends with Stephanie at the children's hospital, the two of them talked about my infatuation with Tamara. Steph even admitted that they joked about having a ménage-a-quatre—which both aroused and disturbed me. It's funny how some crushes don't really go away; they lie dormant like the chickenpox virus and come back in weird ways later. I'd always felt like my lifelong attraction to Tamara could pounce on me like a case of shingles. Those old feelings had me worried on my way to Tamara and Tracy's apartment in downtown Vancouver.

Tamara buzzed me up to their seventh-floor apartment and greeted me in a super cute t-shirt and jeans that hugged her small curves perfectly. I loved how her straight blonde hair fell just past her shoulders—even after all my years of knowing her, she was still the second most gorgeous woman in the world. Standing in her doorway, I felt kind of funny all over.

Tamara greeted me with an intense hug. Then she stood back, looked me in the eyes and said, "How are you doing?"

"I'm okay." I was trying not to give away how nervous I felt. "Where's Tracy?"

"He got called into a team meeting. It's just you and me."

I felt both relieved and excited about being alone with Tamara. She led me into her living room, which has an awesome view of English Bay, and put on some soft music. Then she took me by the hand and led me to her loveseat. "So, what *is* this interview, exactly?" she asked, sitting down beside me.

I felt like I might hyperventilate with her so close to me, but I managed to say, "I'm trying to learn about love."

"What exactly do you want to learn?" she asked, and I realized I hadn't chosen my words very well.

"I'm, uh …"

"Are you okay?" Tamara smiled, calming me down a bit.

"Yeah," I said. "I'm … well, I'm trying to figure out what makes some relationships work and others fail."

"This is about you and Steph, right?"

"Yeah."

"I know it's been hard for you watching her … and Jonathan …"

I nodded, not sure what else to say. Between the music and the softness of Tamara's yellow-brown tiger eyes, I felt like I was in a sensuous dreamland.

"You know what women say about breaking up?" Tamara asked. I shook my head and she said, "That the best way to get over someone is to get under someone else."

I shifted uncomfortably, feeling my body temperature rise quickly.

"It's cheesy, but ... there's truth in it."

"I wouldn't know," I said, glancing out the window at the gorgeous view. Then I felt Tamara's hand on my thigh, which caused my chest to constrict right up into my throat. I turned toward Tamara and tried to say something, but I could hardly breathe.

"It's okay, Bernie," she said.

I feared that Tracy Spencer was going to appear any minute and see his wife's hand on my lap, and his Buddha-like patience would snap—as in, snap *me* like a twig. "But ..." I choked, "Tracy ..."

Tamara smiled and said, "You want to understand what makes some relationships work and others fail?"

"Uh-huh," I squeaked.

"Well, I believe jealousy is toxic ... and that people are meant to love one another. That we aren't meant to put boxes around our relationships." Tamara removed her hand, as if she could feel my fear. "I'm sorry, Bernie. Am I making you uncomfortable?"

"Kinda."

"In a good way, or a bad way?" she asked.

"Kinda ... mostly good."

Tamara turned her body and gazed straight into my eyes. I couldn't look away—it was like I was Odysseus and she was a siren. "You don't need to be shy with me," she said. "We've known each other a long time."

I tried to talk again, but nothing came out.

"Have you kissed a girl in the last two years, Bernie?"

I shook my head.

"Would you like to?"

I froze solid. After a few seconds I tried to nod, though I'm not sure if my head actually moved.

"What do you want to learn about love, Bernie?"

"I don't know." Tamara's calm tone was starting to relax me.

"Have you heard of polyamory?" Tamara asked.

"You mean … those Mormon guys who marry a bunch of women and have dozens of kids?"

"No," she laughed. "That's polygamy."

"Then, no, I guess not."

"It's when you love more than one person, each in their own unique way. How do you feel about love, Bernie?"

I noticed that my interview had been turned around. Tamara was asking all the questions, and I was struggling to come up with any answers.

"I feel love for you, Bernie," she said. "I have for a long time."

"Whoa," I said, and the sense of calm that I'd been feeling evaporated, leaving me all tingly again.

Tamara Spencer leaned over and kissed me on the lips. Then she kissed me again, and my lips started to respond. She sat back and looked at me. Next thing I knew, she was sitting on top of me and we were full-on necking.

As Tamara and I made out like I'd dreamt of doing since junior high school, our hands wandering up and down each other's back and shoulders, I felt emotions jabbing into me from everywhere. Love. Arousal. Joy. More arousal.

And then I felt a tinge of shame.

Suddenly, all I could think of was Stephanie. I must have stopped moving my lips, because Tamara sat back and said, "Are you okay, Bernie?"

Part of me wanted to keep kissing Tamara—and to live out my lifelong fantasy of making love to her. But something also felt totally wrong about being there together—alone—in her apartment.

Tamara, still straddling me, one knee on either side of my legs that were clenched together, pressed her chest against mine and rested her head on my shoulder. Then she said in a super sultry voice, "I've always wanted you too, Bernie."

Being so close to a woman made me think about Stephanie—and Jonathan. They were always snuggling up close to one another at movie theatres, bars, restaurants … even at the bowling alley. They would tease one another in front of me, and it would eventually lead to them leaving without me. It didn't matter how much fun we'd had together—it always ended the same way. Stephanie and Jonathan going home, no doubt to have sex, while I went back to my parents' place to play video games or watch movies.

My mind wandered to The Offspring … to recent memories of my dad playing *Self Esteem*, pretending to be cool while delivering a thinly-veiled message to yours truly. He likes to belt out the line, "The more you suffer, the more it shows you really care," like an aging rock star playing one of his hits from yesteryear. Every time he sings it I want to tell him that suffering *is* a sign of commitment, and that I have every intention of suffering my way back into Stephanie Hansen's heart. But Dad wouldn't understand, because he never lost a girl. Mom was his first and only love.

There on Tamara and Tracy Spencer's love seat, straddled by a woman I'd wanted since puberty, I felt the full weight of my suffering. I sat there like a statue, thinking about my ex-wife and my parents and The Offspring, until I felt a tear roll down my cheek. Another tear followed, and then another. Soon, I was bawling.

As my chest expanded and contracted involuntarily—I was taking in huge breaths of air, sobbing like an infant—Tamara sat up and looked at me. Then she said, "Oh, Bernie ... sweet Bernie," and she smothered me with a hug. She wrapped her arms around my neck and nestled her head beside mine, saying in the softest, sweetest tone, "It's okay, Bernie, it's okay."

At that point, years of pent-up desire for Tamara converged on my pelvis in the form of a raging erection—which was really uncomfortable because my penis was stuck down one of my pant legs, and the pressure from Tamara's thighs wouldn't allow it to escape. I sat there in agony, horny and crying at the same time. Tamara held on for what seemed like an eternity, until my passion faded and sadness took over again, allowing my trouser snake to soften and escape Tamara's death hold.

After a few minutes, when my wailing finally stopped, Tamara climbed off the loveseat and invited me into her kitchen for tea. We talked for two hours, mostly about Stephanie and Jonathan and my feelings, and about polyamory—which sounded really complicated to me, even though Tamara seemed to think it was the most natural thing in the world. She said that she had always felt love was abundant. Tracy grew up in a conservative southern family and was slow to embrace life "outside of the monoga-box," but he warmed up to the idea once he understood that it was more of a philosophy than a lifestyle. I couldn't quite understand the difference myself, but it was cool to talk about such a deep and personal subject with Tamara.

She had misunderstood my reason for visiting her that day. I guess I'd been too vague, saying something about wanting to become more worldly in the love department. She thought it was time to share a bit of her love with me—which was really awesome, even though I wasn't ready to accept it.

When I left Tamara's place, we agreed to talk again sometime. We had a lot in common—more than I'd known. I also discovered that even though I'd lusted after Tamara for years, I didn't really want to be more than friends with her. It felt weird to know that you can find someone super attractive—inside and out—and still not want to be in a relationship with them.

SABRINA MCDONALD

Arnie

AFTER THE INTERVIEW AT PRAKASH AND MEERA'S PLACE, I didn't see Bernard for a while. When he finally called, he invited me back to The Big Bean. Over a mug of hot chocolate, he told me that he'd gone to see Tamara—but he was unusually tight-lipped about the Spencers' marriage.

As much as B-man had been driving me crazy lately, I was surprised to feel a twinge of resentment for being excluded from his most recent interview. All I'd gleaned from him was that Tamara was a very kind person and a good listener. "Bernard," I said, "if you want my help with this stupid project, you're going to have to fill me in on the details."

Bernard's reply was terse. "It's not a stupid project, dickwad."

"Did you just call me a dickwad?" I asked.

"Did you call The List stupid?"

"I guess."

"Then I guess, too."

It felt like we were back in grade four, arguing about who had the grossest lunch. I took a sip of my coffee and looked out at a small traffic jam on Kingsway. Then I gave in. "Okay, your list's not stupid."

"You're still a dickwad," he replied without a trace of humour.

"Why won't you tell me what Tamara said?"

"Because it was a very personal conversation."

"Fine, whatever." I realized this conversation was stupid, so I changed the subject. "Who's next?"

"I was planning to go for one of the golden oldies—either my Aunt Nancy and Uncle Chris or my parents' friends, Reg and Lorna ... but they're both away right now. So I spent some time in research mode and found out where Sabrina and Mike Mc-Donald live."

"Who are they, again?"

"They were the first wedding I attended with Stephanie, in 2009—a few months after we met. Steph went to college with Sabrina, and they were good friends for a while. But after Sabrina got married, she and Mike moved to Fort McMurray so he could work."

"What?! In Alberta? You're not planning another road trip, are you?"

"No—as much as I'd like to visit that friggin' egg again." He shuddered. "I did some sleuthing on the Internet. Sabrina's an office manager for some oil company, so I called there and found out she's on mat leave. The receptionist said that she and Mikey are staying at her parents' place in North Burnaby. I sweet-talked her into giving me Sabrina's e-mail address, and I closed the deal this morning. We're on for an interview tomorrow."

"What's my role this time?" I asked.

"I might need baby assistance."

"How am I supposed to help with a baby?"

"Maybe you could breastfeed the kid." Bernard smirked. "I don't know. Just find a way to be useful."

When we stepped through the small gate in the brown picket fence at Sabrina's parents' house, the whole place seemed too perfect. The yard was well maintained, the house freshly painted, and a baby bouncer hung from the ceiling of the porch, beside a double-seated swing.

Sabrina's mom greeted us with a stiff smile. "You must be Bernard," she said. "And who is your friend?"

"This is Arnie," Bernard said. "He's my wingman."

I nodded and followed Bernard up the stairs and into the small foyer, where Sabrina's dad appeared from the kitchen wearing a light jacket and gardening gloves. He greeted us cheerfully as he stopped to put on his gum-boots.

We were guided into the living room and seated in two chairs, where we sat for at least five minutes studying perfect furniture, perfect ornaments and perfect photos. Most of the photos were old, but there was one picture of a young couple—which I assumed to be Sabrina and Mike—holding a baby. The room felt like the cancer wing in the hospital. It felt like grief.

I relaxed a bit when Sabrina's mom reappeared with her daughter, who was carrying a sleeping child that I guessed to be about six months old. Sabrina looked a lot less proper than her parents, with short, messy red hair and loose clothing. She was cute in a plain way, with full lips and the greenest eyes I had ever seen.

"Hi, Sabrina," Bernard said. "Remember me from your wedding?"

"Of course," Sabrina smiled. "Who could forget Bernard Kirby? You were the life of the party."

"It was a lot of fun. You had a great band."

"Yeah," Sabrina said, sighing the word.

"Who's the bambino?" Bernard asked.

"This is Mikey," she said, moving the receiving blanket to give us a better view of his face.

"Huh," Bernard said, hardly even looking at the boy. "Mikey Junior. Just to confuse the little bugger, eh?"

Sabrina didn't reply. She just stared at Mikey.

"Where's Senior?" Bernard asked.

Sabrina continued to look at Mikey, and her mom looked down without replying.

"Where's Mike?" Bernard persisted. "Your hubby."

"He's … gone," Sabrina said, almost whispering. It took me a moment to understand what she meant, but then the grief in the room suddenly made sense to me.

"Gone?" Bernard said, his voice still booming. "You mean … out?"

"No," Sabrina replied. "He's gone."

"Gone?" Bernard said again.

"I thought you knew," she said, finally looking at Bernard. "Your e-mail … you said you wanted to talk to me about my wedding. I assumed …"

"Knew what?" Bernard asked, then added with a goofy voice, "I think someone forgot to include Bernard on the cc: list."

"Bernard," I said, trying to get his attention so I could motion for him to shut up. But he kept looking at Sabrina with a stupid expression. Then he opened his notebook and flipped pages until he found what he was looking for.

"I guess we'll have to start without him," he said.

"Bernard," I said again. "I think what Sabrina's trying to say is …" I looked at Sabrina again, who was now crying. I hadn't even introduced myself to her yet, but years of nursing experience helped me to navigate the situation. "How long? If you don't mind me asking."

"Three months," Sabrina said. Then she sat down on a couch across from us, and her mom quietly left the room.

"What are you—" Bernard began to ask, looking up from his notepad.

"He was working in the field," Sabrina said. "The roads were icy ... a bunch of guys were fooling around after work. They were on a beer run ... Mike was driving ..."

"I'm sorry," I said. "I'm so sorry."

Bernard's eyes widened as the lightbulb in his head finally turned on.

Sabrina kept talking about the day of Mike's accident ... about what a hard day it had been at home on her own with a colicky baby ... about how frustrated she had been that Mike hadn't come straight home from work ... about the knock on the door ... about how she opened the door to find an RCMP officer standing on her front step, and it felt like she was in a movie. She knew at that moment that Mike was gone.

B-man stared into space. Then, when Sabrina ran out of words and slumped into her seat with a sigh, Bernard leaned forward and said, "What was the best thing about your marriage?"

It seemed like an innocent question—and Bernard's tone was sensitive.

"It was the day Mikey was born," Sabrina said without hesitation. "That was my highlight. Mike was unusually tender that day, and completely focused on me and our son—for a few hours. It didn't last long ... I don't think Mike was cut out for parenthood, or marriage for that matter. But on that day, I thought ... maybe ... he'd changed."

Bernard jotted down Sabrina's reply. Then he looked at her and asked, "What was the biggest challenge in your marriage?"

I was concerned about Bernard proceeding with the interview, but Sabrina nodded and pondered his question before replying, "Mike's drinking was always a challenge. You probably remember how drunk he got at our wedding?"

"Oh yeah," Bernard said. "He was even more drunk than me. I remember helping a couple of his friends pick him up and carry him onto the dance floor. He wanted to dance, but he couldn't support his own weight."

Sabrina laughed gently, bitterly. "Yeah, that was Mike, alright. He was a lot of fun for the first few beers ... then he turned into a mess. But he was a good provider. He somehow always managed to get up in the morning and go to work—and from what I heard, he was a hard worker."

Bernard proceeded with his interview, his wording more sensitive than usual, and Sabrina answered each question with grace. It was clearly therapeutic for her. She even managed to smile on a few occasions.

When Bernard asked Sabrina how she had met Mike, she recalled with a smile how he'd won her heart during a very drunk enactment of *The Unicorn Song* after seeking her out in a crowd at The Blarney Stone. Then Bernard dropped a bomb.

"How was your sex life with Mike?" he asked. This was Bernard's reserve question—the one I had recommended he strike from The List altogether. Why he thought it was a good idea to ask a widow such a personal question about her dead husband, I'll never know. But he asked it, and Sabrina's smile vanished.

"That's—" she began. "I'm really ... that's hard to answer." Mikey stirred, as if on cue, and Sabrina began nursing him. Although she tried to be subtle about it, we briefly saw her full, engorged breast—a sight which Bernard's moronic brain couldn't help commenting on.

"Breastfeeding," Bernard said, "wasted on the young."

I gritted my teeth and stared at Bernard, but he looked back at Sabrina and said, "Speaking of breasts, what was Mike's strongest attribute in bed?"

Even after a lifetime of Bernard Kirby moments, I was quite certain that was the most uncomfortable he had ever made me feel.

"I think we should go," I said to Bernard. "And let Sabrina get on with her day."

"I was trying to lighten the mood," Bernard said. "I mean, we can go, but ... it's not like that's going to change anything."

I hated Bernard right then—I hated his lack of couth and his history of pushing things too far. I hated his stupidity—and his intelligence—and how the two never quite fit together. I stared at Bernard, wondering how I'd managed to stay friends with him for so long, through so many painfully awkward situations. I was about to get up and leave without him when Sabrina's voice broke the silence.

"Sex with Mike was awful," she said.

I turned toward Sabrina and froze. She was wearing an ironic smile as she continued to speak.

"The truth is ... Mike was an asshole. He killed himself and two other men because he was an asshole. He was always selfish, except for that brief moment in the hospital room when he held Mikey for the first time—I'll always remember the look on Mike's face that day, because it's the only time I ever saw it.

"Yeah, Mike drank too much—always—and he said things that hurt me. He hated it when I was pregnant—he told me he didn't like me fat, and my nipples were too large. He was mean to me. He was mean to just about everyone, and I don't know how much of it was the alcohol because I never saw him sober for long enough to judge him without it.

"So, you want to know how he was in bed? He was horrible. Like screwing a robot. A selfish asshole of a robot. And it feels good to say it. I'm sick and tired of holding it in and pretending to be the perfect grieving widow."

Tears were flowing down Sabrina's cheeks as Mikey pulled away from her breast and started to wail. She sat there for a few seconds, her breast hanging out while her baby cried. Then she looked down at him and pulled him up to her shoulder, cradling him gently. "It's okay, Mikey," she said, rocking him back and forth. "Your daddy was an asshole, but you're an angel. You're the best thing he ever did for me."

When I closed the passenger door of the Jetta in front of Sabrina's parents' house, Bernard held up his notepad and said, "It'll take me a while to sort through these notes."

"It was ... pretty intense," I replied, holding back what I really wanted to say.

Bernard pulled away from the curb as I did up my seatbelt. He began to ramble about the interview, and there was a hint of glee in his voice—as if he'd just hit the jackpot. I let him talk for a while, but when he turned in front of a pickup truck onto Boundary Road—the driver had to hit his brakes and gave us a long horn to voice his displeasure—I lost it.

"Shut up!" I said.

"What?" he asked with his St. Bernard voice.

"You just about killed us! And you humiliated the hell out of me back there."

"What do you mean?"

"You treated Sabrina like some sort of psychology experiment."

"Well, it ... kinda is."

"Whatever it is, you need to learn some situational sensitivity," I said

"You used to have a sense of humour," he snapped.

As Bernard drove, I thought about the interview. I cooled off somewhat, because despite B-man's best attempt to humiliate me, Sabrina had handled herself extremely well. She actually thanked us for coming and said she'd like to talk again sometime. It was obvious that she'd had a lot of anger and grief bottled up inside, and it took Bernard's bluntness to let it out. Once she started talking, she went on for ages. We learned that Mike McDonald was a self-centred jerk whose only saving graces were that he earned a decent income and that he had never physically abused his wife. Sabrina met Mike shortly after breaking up with her high-school sweetheart—she said that she could have fallen for Attila the Hun at that stage of her life, and it sounded to me like she had. We also got a glimpse of the spirit-crushing home Sabrina had grown up in. Though her parents were sweet and well-intended, she confirmed that they were both uptight perfectionists who were incapable of talking about matters of the heart. I felt sad that she had to sort through her grief in such a suffocating environment.

As Bernard turned onto Rumble Street, my thoughts drifted back to him. I felt a strange combination of anger and pity, and I felt a rare need to tell him what I was thinking.

"Look, Bernard," I said, "I don't want to be mean, but ... I think it's time for you to grow up a little."

"What the hell?" He turned toward me, clearly hurt, then turned back to face the road. "Not you, too ..."

Bernard turned onto McKay Avenue and pulled up in front of my house. When he stopped, I spoke again, trying my best to carry a constructive tone. "You're fun to be around, B-man ... most of the time ... but you don't know when to shut it off. It's like you're still in eighth grade. You were lucky back there—lucky that Sabrina needed to vent. But that doesn't take away from the fact that you were way offside with your questions. And that breast comment—come on, man—really? For all the times you've embarrassed me—and you've embarrassed me a lot—that was the worst I've ever experienced."

Bernard looked down at the steering wheel and sulked. We sat there in silence for a long while, the Jetta idling.

"You're like Peter Pan, Bernard. The boy who never grows up. You're a man-boy."

I immediately regretted voicing the thought that had crossed my mind a thousand times—the thought that I'd always swallowed before, somehow understanding that once I said it, I'd never be able to take it back. Speaking my mind in B-man's language was a dagger straight to his heart.

Bernard's neck tensed, and his hands tightened on the steering wheel. Tipping his head up to stare straight ahead through the windshield, he said with the most serious tone I'd ever heard him utter, "Fuck you, Arnie Ganesh. And get the hell out of my dad's car."

SiERRA LEONE

Bernard

I ALWAYS THOUGHT ARNIE WOULD HAVE MY BACK, but when he *stabbed* it in front of his house after the Sabrina interview, I realized he was just like all the others who had walked away from me. Every grade and every job brought new temporary friends, but most people didn't appreciate me for long enough to stick around. Arnie had always been different; he understood me when others didn't—or so I thought.

Arnie's betrayal brought up my whole history of failed relationships like a rancid meatloaf. I puked up memories of John Chang, who seemed destined to be a fourth amigo at the start of junior high school—until his father took offense to me calling his Sunday church commitment a weekly prison term. I barfed up memories of Polly Wilson, who came over to my house almost every day in grade one before deciding that she liked playing dolls better than video games. I gagged on memories of Teddy Turnbull, who was actually my jungle-gym recess buddy until grade two, when he turned to more sporty activities like capture the flag and basketball—and picking on me. And I regurgitated memories of Jonathan, which always ended in resenting him for committing grand theft wife.

After acknowledging my complete lack of friends, I spent most of May playing Peace Warrior. I didn't go online to stalk

Stephanie, like I had for a while after our separation—I was pretty sure she'd quit playing anyway. I played because Peace Warrior was the one community where I could put on a mask and be someone else. In Peace Warrior, I was a dashingly handsome man-god whose *weapon* was water—specifically, solar-powered desalination systems that I distributed to places in developing countries where fresh water was scarce.

I made Hero status by late May for my work along the west coast of Africa. After a successful run in Ghana and the Ivory Coast, I rolled the dice in Liberia—barely surviving malaria and walking unscathed through an Ebola zone. I received a lot of Kudos—one of the game's most important assets—from the people of Bensonville, a small city south of the country's capital. I considered settling there; as a Settler, I could gain a lot of Kudos in a short period. But there were other regions that needed the water I could provide, so I kept moving. In my real life, I seemed to be stuck in one place. But in Peace Warrior, I was *Bernard the Great—Digital Aqua God*.

I had just left Liberia when my dad came into the room and asked, "Hey, Scout, where are you now?"

"Sierra Leone," I replied, ignoring the stupid nickname he'd been calling me ever since I'd tried half a year of Beaver Scouts when I was six.

"What can you tell me about Sierra Leone?" Dad asked. Fluffball ran over and jumped up on my lap, then stared at the screen as if he wanted a geography lesson, too.

I hovered my mouse over the Country Stats icon and read aloud. "Area: 27,699 square miles; population: 6.2 million; main industries: agriculture and mining; religion: Muslim majority with a significant Christian minority—with little or no religious violence."

"Well, I'll be," Dad said. "If this game had existed when you were growing up, I might have agreed with your mom's idea to homeschool you."

"I wish," I replied, thinking that a video game education would have been better than real school, with its cliques of jocks, geeks and artists—none of which ever accepted me as one of their own.

"Son," Dad said with that tone that told me he'd been talking to Mom again—the tone that said she was worried and he was angry. Fluffball jumped off my lap and ran out of the room, no doubt to avoid the drudgery of a Karl Kirby lecture.

"Yeah?" I grunted.

"When's the last time you were out of the house?"

"I dunno."

"I don't think you've been out this week. And it's almost summer-like."

I stared at the screen, waiting for the bus that would take me from Sulima to Freetown. Peace Warrior can be boring sometimes—they make it as lifelike as possible—and my dad has a talent for asking questions when I have no excuse for ignoring him.

"Come for a hike with me and Bruno—he's coming by in a few minutes."

"Nah," I said. "I've got lives to save in Sierra Leone."

"Maybe you should focus on your own health for a change." His voice had an edge to it—I could tell that he was on the brink of eruption, so I forced myself to come up with a benign response.

"I just don't feel like going out."

Dad took a deep breath and sighed, and I could hear his frustration at not understanding me. He and Bruno have always been kindred spirits—they hike and bike and ski together, and they'll only eat things they can pronounce. They even work together—

Bruno was a summer student at Dad's firm as he raced through a university degree in a sickeningly-fast four years, then joined the firm full-time as soon as he graduated. I've always felt judged by my male family mates for preferring video games and pizza and varied employment to exercise and kale salad and a full-time job. I've always known that my life has been one big disappointment to my dad and my brother.

"It's your life," Dad said, perfectly on script, "but you need to do *something* to shake yourself out of this rut. Why do you think I let you use my car so much? I want to get you *moving* again. Even getting back to that crazy list of yours would be better than locking yourself in the house and monopolizing the office."

"The List is on hiatus," I mumbled, trying to ignore his why-I-loan-you-my-car-and-when-will-you-stop-monopolizing-the-office guilt trip. It was true that Dad offered me far more transportation support than Mom did—which was ironic given his unfathomable preference for cycling whenever possible. It also didn't help that Mom had grown very possessive of her recently-purchased Volkswagen Beetle—which she drove whenever and wherever she could justify driving.

"Then maybe you can embrace moving on with your life," Dad said. I was sure he was going to launch into another diatribe, but to my great relief he held back. He looked over my shoulder at the screen while I waited for my bus, which was already way late and seemed like it would never arrive.

"Well," he said, "how about a beer later?"

"Maybe," I replied. I knew that he was trying to speak my language, but when it comes to beer, we've always spoken different dialects. Dad's the kind of guy who savours every sip of a craft brew, talking about malt and hops and purity laws. I'm more of a dozen Kokanees kind of guy. It's funny, because my dad probably drinks a beer four or five times a week, but I don't think I've ever seen him drunk. I've wondered sometimes if a good father-son piss-up could help us find more things in common.

I was passing through Gandorhun—a small town that produces a lot of diamonds—when Mom walked into the office. I braced for another round of parental annoyance, but she just said, "Stephanie's on the phone."

I perked up at the sound of Stephanie's name, but I didn't want to admit that to my mom—or acknowledge my shock that someone had actually called me. The only family member who received less phone calls than me was Fluffball—even Bruno, who had moved out almost a year ago, outnumbered me ten-to-one in the call-reception department.

I stared at the picture of Gandorhun on my screen. It looked like an exotic place, but the red dirt road and ramshackle buildings told me it wasn't likely to be on my holiday destination list.

"Are you going to take the call?" Mom asked. "Or should I tell her you'll call her back later?" Then she whispered, "Or not at all?"

I kept staring at the screen, but I was thinking about Steph. The last time I'd spoken to her—almost a month earlier—had been unusually awkward. I'd called her the day after Arnie betrayed me, hoping for a sympathetic ear, attempting to talk about Peter Pan metaphorically—but I've never really understood metaphors, so my rant probably came out sounding like a Leonard Cohen song. Anyway, Steph had listened to my Cohenesque Peter Pan tirade, half-heartedly interjecting words like "Uh-huh" and "Yeah" with her *my-poor-Bernie* voice, before telling me she had to go do some wedding stuff with Jonathan.

"Bernard …" Mom said, holding the phone between my face and the screen.

"Yeah, yeah," I grumbled, finally taking the phone from her.

I paused the game and waited for my mom to leave the office. Then I put the phone to my ear and said, "Hi."

"Hi, Bernie," Stephanie said, and my heart melted. She dragged her "Hi" a little—just long enough to make it seem like that was all she was going to say—then her voice softened as she said my name all sultry-like. The one thing that had never changed since the first time I talked to Stephanie on the phone was the way she greeted me. It always made me feel like we were still together, like nothing had changed.

"What's up?" I asked, trying to sound nonchalant.

"What are you up to this afternoon?"

"I'm installing water stations in Sierra Leone. You?"

"I need a shopping partner."

"For what?" I asked.

"My wedding dress."

I felt like I was receiving a hug and a kick in the balls at the same time. Stephanie could do that—she could make me feel super important and all used up with the same words.

"Why me?" I asked. "We've hardly spoken—"

"You've always had a knack for helping me pick out clothes."

"You mean … Mr. Perfect doesn't have fashion sense?"

"You know that's not his strong suit."

"Pun intended?"

Stephanie laughed. "It would be nice to catch up. We're overdue."

"Who else is going?" I asked.

"Just you and me."

I tried to remember the last time I'd spent an afternoon alone with Stephanie—without Jonathan—and I couldn't think of one. As far as I could remember, we had not been alone—not once— since she'd left me.

"Why?" I asked. "Why me? Why now?"

I heard Stephanie breathe into the phone. Then she said, "Because you understand me. Sometimes I think you're the only person who ever has."

I gulped hard and said, "I know what you mean."

After an oddly comfortable silence, Stephanie said, "I'll pick you up in an hour, 'kay?"

"'Kay," I replied. Then I shut off Peace Warrior, walked casually past my mom in the kitchen, and went upstairs for a shower—my first in three or four days. Given my first opportunity in almost two-and-a-half years to spend an afternoon alone with Stephanie, I was planning to look and smell my best.

OLD FRIENDS

Arnie

LORETTA STRETCHED ACROSS THE COUCH in one of my t-shirts, her head on my lap. I sat in my housecoat and smiled down at her, reflecting on the past hour of intimacy we had shared. Loretta had proven to be both a patient and knowledgeable teacher in bed—and more adventurous than I would have guessed, given how innocent she seemed.

Inexplicably, my mind shifted to Bernard swearing at me. The more I'd tried to chase those thoughts away, the more they'd consumed me—his words becoming more toxic with each passing week. I leaned back and stared at the ceiling, willing my mind to return to the pleasant images I'd been thinking of moments earlier.

"You're thinking about B-man," Loretta said matter-of-factly.

"Yeah," I replied. "He's an idiot, but ..."

"You miss him."

"A bit."

"He's your best friend. Of course you miss him."

"He was my best friend," I replied. Bernard had been a total jerk to me when I called him out for his selfishness after the interview with Sabrina McDonald, and he was even worse when I called him a few days later.

"I thought I told you to F-off," Bernard had said when he picked up the phone.

"Hello to you too."

"Did you phone to apologize?"

"No."

"I hope you don't expect *me* to."

I had wanted him to accept some responsibility for our fall-out, but our discussion went nowhere—so I offered him an olive branch. "I thought maybe we could grab breakfast."

"Will Yoko be there?"

"You don't get it, do you?"

"Well," he said with a mock British accent, "will she, John?"

"Get a life, Bernard."

"Right back atcha," he replied and then hung up. I hadn't spoken to him since.

"You two are like the fox and the hound," Loretta said. "Even though you're totally different, you need each other."

I wasn't sure I agreed with her anymore. In the weeks since I'd last seen Bernard, I had relived my friendship with him and begun to truly understand the dynamic between us. I was Bernard's wingman. I had always played second fiddle to him, played the straight man to his clown act. I was always there to help him pick up the pieces after he humiliated himself and anyone in his vicinity. But he wasn't always there for me. When my dad fought through prostate cancer when I was twenty, Bernard came up with a nickname—Fred Astaire—for the catheter my dad had to use after his surgery. Fortunately, my dad found that funny—but I still thought it was insensitive. And Bernard didn't even acknowledge when my grandma died in high school—it was like he had no capacity for dealing with life-and-death matters.

"No," I said to Loretta while I stewed over my one-sided friendship with Bernard Kirby. "He's a self-centred jerk."

"But he's your best friend," she said.

"Not anymore."

"Don't be silly."

I looked into Loretta's face, and she hypnotized me with her big brown eyes. "Not the eyes," I said. "How am I supposed to turn down the eyes?"

"You're not," she smiled, continuing to stare me down.

"But he called you—"

"Yoko?"

"Yeah."

"So?"

"Doesn't that bother you?"

"No," she said, as if her answer required no explanation.

"You're … how did you get so nice? Okay, fine … I'll call him."

Loretta reached over to the coffee table and picked up my phone, handing it to me without moving her head from my lap. I dialled Bernard's home number, since he'd shut down his cell phone plan when he lost his job at White Spot.

"Hello," Bernard's mom answered.

"Hi, Blanche. Is Bernard there?"

"No," she said, and I could tell by the tone of her voice that something wasn't right.

"Let me guess … he's working on The List?"

"No," she said. "The List is on hold. He's mostly been playing Peace Warrior all month. But Stephanie called today."

"Oh. Do I want to know?"

"They're shopping for a wedding dress."

"Oh no," I groaned. "That's a brand-new low for Steph."

"Yeah," she sighed. "It's a wonder they haven't driven me to drink. Those two still act more like a married couple than most married people."

"I know. It's crazy."

Blanche and I have spoken often over the years, whenever I've visited their house or called looking for Bernard. Somewhere in my twenties, she insisted that I start calling her by her first name—it was awkward at first but grew increasingly comfortable.

Sometimes, even when Bernard has been home, I've spent more time talking to his mom than him. She's nice to a fault—especially to her big baby of a son. Her spoiling of Bernard—which has included loans that were never paid back, a free pass on household duties, and defending Bernard's move back home to her husband, Karl—has surely led to Bernard's leisurely pace of maturity. But she's lovable and generous, and I know she's tried her best to raise a very challenging human being.

"I should have known that I'd never understand my son," Blanche said. "I tried so hard to figure out every crazy thing he did, and each time I found myself a bit more puzzled—as if I'd given birth to an alien. If I had a dollar for every time a friend or family member offered me a diagnosis of Bernard—I've heard 'em all—but nothing ever seemed to fit. He was just ... Bernard. And even now, as he's off helping his ex-wife shop for a wedding dress so she can marry another man, all I know how to do is love him. Underneath that crazy shell, his heart is as pure as anyone I've ever known."

"Yeah," I said. I knew what she meant. But I was starting to wonder if Blanche Kirby and I had fallen under the spell of

Bernard's quirky charm—and if his heart was still as pure as we'd remembered it being, or if it had been forever scarred by Stephanie Hansen.

"Well, I have to run and pick up Karl from the Skytrain," she said. "I'll tell Bernard you called. It was so nice to hear your voice—we've hardly heard from you lately. Bernard told me you have a new girlfriend—I'm sure that's keeping you busy. I'm happy for you, Arnie."

"Thanks," I said, looking down at Loretta, who flashed me the eyes again and made me temporarily forget about my complicated relationship with B-man. "I'm happy, too."

WEDDING ATTIRE

Bernard

FOR ONE AFTERNOON, I got to feel like Stephanie was my girl again. She'd gone upscale since we were together—I'm sure Jonathan's income added some nice padding to her parents' cost-of-living-in-Vancouver subsidy—but other than having more expensive taste, she was the same Stephanie I'd fallen in love with.

We hit up four stores downtown, quickly establishing a familiar shopping pattern. We'd always been compatible with stuff like that, because I was happy to spend time with Stephanie and would go anywhere she wanted to. Once, when we were married, we'd spent an entire day shopping for shoes at Metrotown, and I hadn't minded a bit. It was worth it—it was always worth it—and shopping for wedding dresses felt *almost* the same. I tried to forget that unless I got my ass in gear in the wedding derailment department, Jonathan Donaldson would be the one who got to help Stephanie remove whatever dress she chose.

After shopping downtown, we headed over to West 4th Avenue. That's when things got all awesome and stupid at the same time.

Stephanie picked out three dresses and went to try one on. I was hanging outside the change room, waiting to trade dresses with the store clerk who called herself a *Wedding Attire Consultant*—I nicknamed her the *WAC*—when Steph said she needed my help. Steph opened the door to let me into the change area, which was way too small for a wedding dress store, then closed it behind me and showed me the problem. There was a long zipper that went up the length of her back, and it had snagged on her bra. It looked like a simple problem, but when I tried to unsnag it, I realized one of her bra clips was hooked on the little flappy part of the zipper. I guess she'd applied too much pressure trying to get it unstuck, so it was fused together into a single bra-dress. We probably should have called the WAC to fix it, but we were determined to solve it ourselves.

Stephanie faced the mirror while I tried to extricate her from the dress. It was an elegant, knee-length, off-white beauty, but it had one hell of a stubborn zipper. It was worth more than a thousand dollars, so I tried to be gentle—even though I really needed a pair of pliers. As I stood there trying to wiggle the zipper free from the bra hook, Stephanie started to giggle—which made my job even harder because she couldn't stand still.

"Are you okay in there?" the WAC asked from outside the door.

"We're fine," Stephanie said. "I just need a little help with this one." She was bending down a bit so I could work on her dress, which allowed me to look over her shoulder and see her face in the mirror. She looked radiant, as always.

For the next few minutes, Stephanie and I got more up close and personal than we'd been in years. She was giggling a lot, and I was feeling both romantic and aroused as she leaned into me.

"Try undoing my bra," Stephanie said when it was clear that I wasn't making any progress. I wasn't going to argue, so I did as I was told and exposed the whole top half of her back. At that point, she could have solved the problem herself—at least getting out of the bra-dress so the WAC could fix it—but she didn't ask me to leave. Instead, she pulled one arm out of the bra-dress and then, holding it against her breasts with her free hand, she asked me to pull off her other sleeve. I held the end of it—just below her elbow—while she twisted her shoulder and pulled her arm out.

Stephanie stood tall in front of the mirror, both of her shoulders exposed as she held the wedding dress up against her goddess breasts. I looked at her bare back, and it took all my self-restraint not to reach out and touch it.

"I guess I should do the rest on my own, huh?" she said.

"I guess," I said, reluctantly.

"Thanks for helping me."

"Uh-huh." I stood there, looking up at Stephanie in the mirror, and I wondered why I was there. I understood why she hadn't asked Jonathan. What I couldn't figure out was why she'd asked me. It was kind of awesome and cruel at the same time. I knew I'd start crying if I stayed there any longer, so I smiled weakly at Steph and then exited the change room.

As I stood outside the change room, the WAC looked over at me and said, "She's going to be a beautiful bride. You're a lucky man."

I nodded, then turned away and muttered under my breath, "Stupid WAC."

Stephanie needed to order some minor alterations to the dress— she'd decided it had chosen her, so she chose it back—and it took the WAC at least ten minutes to free the dress from the bra. While we waited, Steph's uncontained nipples poked through her thin green blouse, completely messing with my head. After she finally got her bra back and popped into the change room to re-harness her breasts, we went to a funky little restaurant for caffè mochas.

"Thanks for coming with me today," Stephanie said as we sat down at a small table near the window.

"Yeah, no problem," I replied.

"I needed some Bernie time."

I didn't really know what to say. I wanted to tell Stephanie that she was making a huge mistake, and to tell her about The List and about my plan to save her from her own wedding—a plan that I'd taken a break from after Arnie met Yoko Ono and went postal on me. Losing Arnie was similar and different from when I'd lost my other best friend, Jonathan.

That was the first time it struck me that maybe Stephanie was the real thief, or at least Jonathan's accomplice. Maybe *she'd* stolen *him* from me, rather than the other way around. Who could resist Steph—and how could I blame Jonathan for wanting her? Suddenly I blurted out, "You trampled my heart, you know."

Stephanie stopped smiling—she'd been smiling all afternoon—and her face dropped into a pout. "I know," she said. "I'm sorry."

"I shouldn't be here."

"I'm glad you are."

"I just want to spend time with you. That's why I always accept your offers to join you and Jonathan, even though it kills me to see you with him."

"I'm sorry, Bernie." Stephanie looked sadder than I'd ever seen her, and it made me want to hold her and tell her everything would be okay. But two-and-a-half years of anger boiled to the surface, and her sadness made me angrier. What right did Stephanie have to be sad? She had run over my heart, again and again, while she slept with the guy who had been my best friend since kindergarten. Now she wanted *me* to feel bad for *her*? I felt my face harden as I watched hers get softer, like we were heading in opposite emotional directions.

I stood up and looked at my half-finished mocha. Then I looked Stephanie straight in the eyes and said, "Fuck sorry. Have a nice wedding ... and a nice life."

I walked out of the coffee shop and turned west—the opposite direction from my pathetic life in Burnaby. I walked for half a block, then turned around. I'm not sure if I was more relieved or disappointed that Stephanie hadn't followed me. I couldn't believe I'd walked out on her—I'd even sworn at her—and I almost went back to apologize since she was my ride home. But I couldn't bring myself to do it, so I continued walking west for ages. Eventually, when my legs were tired, I turned north toward the water.

Under a clear blue sky, I walked until I reached the end of the beach—past Jericho Pier all the way to the Spanish Banks concession, where I bought myself a hot dog and doused it with ketchup. Then I sat on a log and watched a bunch of families and couples frolic in the summer-like weather, remembering all the times Stephanie and I had gone to the beach together. Sitting there alone, I felt like I had nowhere to go and nobody to turn to. I'd lost my wife and my two best friends, and at twenty-eight I was too old to be living at home. I hated to admit it, but Arnie was right. I *was* Peter Pan—the boy who never grew up. The problem was, I didn't know how.

F-OFF

Arnie

I WAS SURPRISED TO HEAR STEPHANIE'S VOICE. I don't think she'd ever called me before.

"Hi, Arnie," she said. "How's Bernie doing?"

"Beats me," I replied.

"What do you mean?"

"I haven't seen him in weeks."

"But, you … you always see Bernie."

"Not since he told me to F-off."

"You too?"

It took me a moment to process what Stephanie said. "What happened?" I asked.

"I took him wedding dress shopping."

"I heard. What were you thinking?"

"I just … missed him."

"Yeah." I missed him too, but I wasn't about to admit it. "Things alright between you and Jonathan?"

"Yeah, I think."

"What do you mean, you think? You're marrying him in three months, right?"

"Yeah," Stephanie said. "I just wonder … I'm scared of failing again."

I didn't know what to say, so we sat in silence until Stephanie spoke again.

"I really thought Bernard and I would make it ..." she finally said.

"You might have been the only one who did," I said. "I don't think even B-man believed it, as much as he wanted to."

"I don't like what we did to him," Stephanie admitted, her voice cracking. "Me and Jonathan ... we just ... it just happened."

"I know," I said. "But I think I always knew that might happen. Didn't you?"

"Maybe," she said. "I was attracted to Jonathan since the first time I saw him. I just thought he was a distraction, a test. I thought the good little Catholic girl in me was stronger than that, but ... here I am, a divorcee getting ready to marry again."

"Why are you marrying him?" I asked, voicing the question I'd wondered about ever since Stephanie and Jonathan had decided to tie the knot. "What makes you think it will work this time?"

Stephanie was silent for a very long time. Then she sighed and said, "He's kind of ... everything Bernie's not. He's serious ..."

"And good looking?"

"Yeah. Bernie's good looking too, in a different way. But Jonathan has ambition, focus ... he'll make a good father."

I wondered if Stephanie was right. Jonathan had worked hard to establish a solid career, and it seemed like Stephanie had tamed the womanizer within him. But thinking of Jonathan as a father—and Stephanie as a mother—still seemed like a stretch. "I didn't think you wanted kids," I said.

"I didn't either. But that thing about the biological clock ... it's true. I think it was already going off when ... when I left Bernie."

"Did you ever tell him?"

"No."

"I think he wants kids, too," I said. "He seems to detest them … but I know him well enough to read between the lines. I think … if you'd wanted kids with Bernard … he'd have been there with you."

"Yeah," she said. "He would have. It's just …"

"Just what?"

"I felt like I already had a child in the house."

"Yeah," I said. "So, what do we do about the guy?"

"I don't know. Could you check on him? I think I should probably leave him alone for a bit."

"I'll try."

"Thanks."

I sat on the couch in my basement suite, holding my cell phone and thinking about Bernard—wondering how I could help him without feeding his victim complex. I thought of him watching movies and playing video games—I was sure that was how he was spending most of his waking hours—and I felt a newfound appreciation for The List. At least it gave him something to focus on. And maybe he was learning something—about humans and love, and about himself—by interviewing everyone he had seen get married. Maybe that was just the therapy he needed. And besides, how was I going to help Bernard get a date if he sat inside playing Peace Warrior all day?

CEASEFIRE

Bernard

MY MOM WALKED INTO THE OFFICE with the phone in her hand. It felt like déjà vu.

"Let me guess ... it's Stephanie calling to invite me flower shopping."

"No, it's Arnie," she said.

"Hmm ... guess number two ... he wants to take me out to buy a Peter Pan outfit." I was flipping through pictures of Freetown—the capital of Sierra Leone—which seemed to be half beach resort and half post-apocalyptic disaster zone. I stopped at a picture of a young girl holding a shell, sitting on a beach under an ominous grey sky. There were dozens of men and boys beyond her, working with a huge net to catch some sort of seafood. The girl was black as night, but she was smiling the whitest smile, looking up at the photographer.

"Bernard," my mom said, "are you going to take the call? Or should I tell him you're too busy playing video games?"

"Tell him I moved to the International Space Station."

"Bernard," she sighed, "he's your best friend. The least you can do is take a call from him."

"*Was* my best friend," I replied. "I don't have best friends anymore. They keep betraying me."

Mom moved closer to me and looked at the photo over my

shoulder. I was studying every bit of it: the bluish-grey ocean with frothy whitecaps lapping onto the shore; the city backdrop on the other side of the bay—with hillsides full of run-down buildings and cranes; the dismal haze that fell over the whole picture; and the girl, who was smiling through it all.

"Wow," Mom said. "That's a one-of-a-kind shot."

"Yeah," I agreed. Peace Warrior is cool that way—it forces people to think about other people, and to appreciate their own life a little more. That's why, when my mom reminded me again that Arnie was on the phone, I stopped loathing him for a moment and remembered all the nice things he'd done for me. I decided to take his call.

"Hey," I said when I finally took the phone.

"Hey," he replied. "You know I heard all that, right?"

"Am I wrong?"

"You're wrong about my reason for calling … and about not having any friends. Are you still doing The List?"

"No. It was a stupid idea."

"No, it's … quirky, and … quirky's alright. Anyway, if you decide to pick it up again, I'm still willing to be your wingman."

"'Kay."

"Well, let me know."

"'Kay," I said again. Then we bid each other civilized goodbyes and hung up.

Prick, I thought, annoyed at Arnie for being so likeable.

JASMINE DESLAURIER

Arnie

BERNARD WAITED THREE DAYS TO RECOMMENCE THE LIST. It was early June—a little more than two months before Stephanie and Jonathan were scheduled to get married.

I was kind of hoping he wouldn't call, but Loretta kept telling me I'd be glad when he did. "He'll come back to you on his terms," she said—and she seemed to know that he'd call eventually.

B-man dove back into The List headfirst. There were no apologies or explanations. He just called and said, "I need a wingman again. Childcare assignment." And, falling back into my supporting role, I went along with his plan.

He picked me up in the Jetta. He looked over and gave me a head nod—which was Bernard's way of expressing some combination of gratitude and apology for everything that had passed between us. Then he updated me on The List and handed me The Roadmap to study while he drove.

Bernard had completed five interviews so far, and he'd identified four couples as lower priorities. That left six high-priority interviews to schedule: Bernard's Aunt Nancy and Uncle Chris; family friends Reg and Lorna; Amanda and Dave Carson—Stephanie's friends who were married shortly before Bernard was dumped; Fiona and Marcus in Switzerland; Cheyenne and her husband-of-the-month; and the Duggans—Jasmine and BJ.

"We're going to see Jasmine," Bernard said as we drove east along Kingsway toward New Westminster. "Her and BJ aren't together anymore—he's gone back to Port Alberni, where he's from."

"They're divorced?" I asked.

"Yeah. They made the A-list before I realized that. She gets a free pass on divorce for attempting to live with someone named BJ. Imagine *those* expectations! Man, if I was called BJ, I'd change my name to Fellatio and introduce myself with a Shakespearean brogue. 'Hello, my name is Fellatio ... and this is my mate, Omelette.'" Bernard chuckled at his version of an old-English accent—which sounded more like a failed attempt at French.

"Can you give me some background?" I said. "You told me there are kids involved."

"Yup, two rugrats. By my calculation, Jasmine and Blowjob had a shotgun wedding—they must have shared more than a BJ—then they made the unwise decision to procreate again and split before number two was born. BJ's still in the picture—he *comes* to the mainland—hah! I kill me!" Bernard laughed at himself again, then continued, "Anyway, he visits them three or four times a year." Bernard kept chuckling at his juvenile sense of humour.

"You've done some reconnaissance," I said.

"Yup. Jasmine's a chatty one."

"Do you have names and genders for the kids?"

"Yeah. Nicholas is eight, and Zoey's six. Oh, and Jasmine's gone back to her maiden name—Deslaurier."

"Where do you know her from?" I asked.

"BJ and Jonathan were pals for a while, so I tagged along with Jonathan to BJ's stag. Then BJ invited me to their wedding while we were stumbling down Granville Street half cut, freezing our asses off because the dude's overactive sperm caused him to have a December wedding.

"When Jonathan and I got to the wedding, BJ didn't remember inviting me. But it was basically a house party with some nuptials thrown in, so I could have walked in off the street and nobody would have noticed. Everyone was super touchy-feely—I think a bunch of them might have been on Ecstasy—so I got a quick buzz on with some homebrewed beer they were pouring out of growlers. It was like sucking on an alcohol-infused tea bag, but it helped me to find my inner hippie for a few hours. The food was mostly unrecognizable, but the music was great and the vibe was kinda awesome. I also started the best game of *Where's Uncle Bob?* ever. We couldn't find anyone who resembled an Uncle Bob, so we all took turns acting like one."

"What does an Uncle Bob act like?" I asked.

"I dunno," Bernard said. "Like … an Uncle Bob."

I let the subject drop, and we rode in silence until we reached Jasmine's place—a suite in one of the few stand-alone houses on Agnes Street, up the steep hill from New Westminster Quay. The apartment was very artsy inside—Jasmine made her living as a painter and art teacher. I could tell instantly that I was going to like her. She looked like a petite Beyoncé—I actually did a double-take when she opened her door—but she was super down-to-Earth and natural with her kids. Bernard was impressed, too—especially by the Motown music playing in the background, and by the small collection of classic books and movies on the shelf above a small, old-fashioned TV.

"Would you like some kombucha?" Jasmine asked as we studied her bookshelf.

"Sure," I replied.

"Komwhatcha?" Bernard asked.

Jasmine began to explain the basics of fermented tea. When she mentioned the SCOBY culture used to make kombucha, Bernard launched into a monologue about *Scooby-Doo*, which included a disturbingly accurate imitation of Scooby's sidekick, Shaggy. Jasmine seemed genuinely entertained by his portrayal of the legendary slacker.

I got down on the floor of her living room to meet the kids. Nicholas and Zoey were both shy at first, playing quietly with a set of wooden blocks and ramps. I helped them build a large chain-reaction structure that included dominoes and ramps, spirals and rails, and marbles that looked like bloodshot eyeballs.

"It's a Rube Goldberg machine," Nicholas said, reaching over to the coffee table to pick up an old digital camera. "At the end, I want it to take a picture."

Zoey was the quieter of the two, but she warmed up to me quickly and started handing me materials to build a tower that would act as a starting point for the marbles—a little higher than a tower Nicholas had already constructed.

Jasmine and Bernard sat on barstools on the other side of a tall island that separated the kitchen from the play area. At first, Jasmine looked at us almost constantly. But as she grew more comfortable with my childcare, she focused more on her conversation with Bernard.

For the next hour or so, I worked with the kids to find cool ways to take pictures, while Bernard and Jasmine talked and took turns selecting soulful classics on her laptop.

I kept waiting for Bernard to drop a bomb and say something stupid—to embarrass all of us with some off-beat comment about oral sex. But he acted like an adult the whole time, and we left on good terms.

Bernard was quiet for much of the drive back to my house. "She's cool," he finally said.

"Yeah," I agreed. "Cool kids, too. So, what did you learn? I was pretty focused on those Rube Goldberg machines."

"I dunno. Mostly that she's totally dedicated to her kids. She's homeschooling them, and she makes a living from her art. She has a business partner who helps her juggle work and kids."

"Has she been single all this time?" I asked.

"I dunno. I kind of forgot about the interview. We mostly talked about other stuff—art and music and movies. I also told her about Peace Warrior, which she seemed really interested in. She didn't mention any other guys—but I did ask her why she and BJ had split, and she told me there wasn't enough mutual attraction. I was thinking, *how could BJ not be attracted to her?* but I figure it was more the other way around—even though he looks like a supermodel, too. Maybe they just didn't have enough chemistry, so it didn't matter how good looking they were. Anyway, she said BJ is a good dad, and he sends money from his mill job out in Port Alberni. It's kinda sad, 'cause it seemed like they had it all, but they still couldn't make it work."

"Strange, isn't it?" I said. "We think other people have it all, and we assume couples are attracted to one another. But our feelings are so much more complex than that. Sometimes when I look at Loretta, I wonder what makes me so attracted to her. Physically, she's so different than the women I grew up idolizing—yet she's the most beautiful woman I've ever met."

"Yeah," Bernard agreed. "Like, take Jasmine ... she's totally different than Stephanie. Jasmine's tiny and exotic and alternative looking, whereas Steph's a full-bodied Caucasian goddess. But they're both super gorgeous."

That was probably the most grown-up discussion Bernard and I had ever had. And his admission that he found Jasmine attractive was surely a step in the right direction.

PEACE WARRIOR

Bernard

WHEN I WALKED IN THE DOOR from an impromptu interview with
Aunt Nancy and Uncle Chris, I saw a note on the counter that
said, "Stephanie called." I set my dad's car keys beside the note, and
Fluffball started jumping up on me like a pompom with legs—the
little dude was seriously overdue for a shave. Nobody else was
home, so I fought off the pompom-dog and rooted around in the
fridge until I found a leftover bean burrito, which I put in the
nukrowave to appease my hunger.

I hadn't learned a whole lot from Nancy and Chris, though
I was a bit surprised that they'd had any relationship troubles at
all. I was only six when I attended their wedding—I vaguely recall
doing *The Bird Dance* with my parents, and I remember that my
mom was super pregnant with Bruno. There were some great
desserts, too—I'm pretty sure my dinner was at least fifty percent
strawberry shortcake.

Nancy said that at one point when their kids were little—
my cousins James and Sophie were now grown up and off to
college—they'd had a tumultuous year when Chris was off selling
software all over the world, and Nancy was stuck at home trying
to keep up with the chaos of two energetic bumpkins. They
wouldn't admit to having considered divorce, even though I must
have asked them twenty times to make sure they weren't glossing

over deep cracks in their relationship. They kept looking at me like they'd never heard the 'D' word. Anyway, they were one of the happiest couples I'd interviewed, and they reminded me of my own parents, who just seem to belong together. I guess it must run in my mom's family, because my dad's kinfolk have a more typical history of marital misfortune.

Removing my smoking hot burrito from the nuker, I looked at the note again. I was reluctant to return Stephanie's call—I was re-committed to The List, and the world's collective opinion was that I would have a better chance of winning back my ex-wife if I wasn't available every time she wanted some *Bernie time*. That was easier said than done. I wanted so badly to talk to her—to help her try on dresses and drink hot chocolate with her, then take her home and make long, slow love before asking her to marry me again. But that last part seemed unlikely, and the rest of it seemed kind of pointless without that critical piece. So, using all the willpower I could muster, I actually talked myself out of returning a phone call from Stephanie Hansen.

I put *Roman Holiday* in the DVD player and plopped myself down on the couch. Fluffball jumped up and sat on my lap. Even in grainy black and white, Audrey Hepburn was stunning—and the backdrop of the Italian capital was nice, too. My family had never travelled much—we'd been to Hawaii and Disneyland when I was young, and we went to Puerto Vallarta once, which was cool until we all came down with food poisoning. After that we'd stuck close to home, so I did my travelling vicariously through movies and Peace Warrior.

Right in the middle of my favourite part of the movie—the slapstick restaurant scene where Joe keeps dumping stuff on Irving to keep him from blowing Joe's cover—the phone rang. I didn't want to answer it, but then I thought maybe it was Stephanie again, and even though my left-side brain didn't want to talk to her, the rest of me did. So I paused the movie and got up to grab the phone—sending Fluffball scrambling to the floor.

"Hello," I answered.

"Hi. Is this Bernard?" I knew the voice—silky and kind of sultry—but I couldn't place who it belonged to.

"Uh, yeah."

"It's Jasmine. Jasmine Deslauriers."

"Oh." I suddenly felt lightheaded.

"That was a nice visit the other day," she said. "And my kids had a ton of fun with Arnie."

"Yeah," I said, trying not to sound as nervous as I felt. "It was ... I ..."

"I was wondering ... you know that game we talked about—Peace Warrior?"

"Yeah?"

"Do you think it would be suitable for Nicholas?"

"I ... yeah, I don't see why not. I mean, you can catch some awful viruses, and there's the odd troll who's out to undo your work—but ... yeah."

"It sounds like a good homeschool resource," she said, echoing what my dad had told me—and instantly validating all the hours I'd spent playing Peace Warrior.

"Yeah, it's totally educational," I replied. "It's like an interactive geography lesson."

"That sounds perfect. Nicholas is really into geography, and he's quite advanced for his age. I try not to shield him too much from real life."

We talked about Peace Warrior for five or ten minutes, until

Jasmine said, "I should run—Zoey's wanting my attention. When can we get together? And ... your place or mine?"

It had been a long time since I'd had to consider whether to host a pretty girl at *my* house—well, my parents' house—and even though Jasmine was only asking for a homeschool lesson, I felt funny inviting her into my childhood home. "I could come to your place," I said.

We settled on a time later that week. Then I hung up the phone and went back to finish watching *Roman Holiday*, feeling a strange buzz all over. Like I was a little tipsy. I remembered that feeling from my early days with Stephanie, and from pretty much every time I had passed Tamara in the hallway during my school years.

As I considered each word I could remember from my phone call with Jasmine, I wondered if I had been invited on a date.

BUTTERFLIES

Arnie

WHEN BERNARD ASKED ME TO MEET HIM AT THE BIG BEAN, he seemed both upbeat and anxious.

"What's up?" I asked, taking my seat at the corner table, where B-man was already sitting with a plateful of crumbs and a half-empty hot chocolate.

"I need you to keep me motivated."

"What do you mean?"

"The List. I'm worried that I might let it slip. The whole project feels kinda ... fragile."

"Why's that?" I asked.

"I'm feeling ... mixed-up. It's not like I'm questioning my love for Stephanie or anything, but ... I need your help to stay on track."

"Okay. How?"

"I've felt all kinds of things since this project started—sad, angry, horny, jealous, guilty—but the one thing I've never felt was doubt about my feelings for Stephanie. Whenever I've felt like quitting on The List, it's been because I haven't felt up to the challenge. Now I'm feeling something different, and it scares me. I'm ... kerfuddled."

"Kerfuddled? Is that even a word?"

"I don't know," he said. "Befuddled, kerfuffled, beheaded—

whatever it is, I'm confused."

"What does it feel like?"

"Like … butterflies."

"Okay." I waited to give him space to talk.

"Jasmine called me this afternoon, to ask if I'd show Nicholas how to play Peace Warrior."

"Ah," I said. "That's cool."

"Yeah," Bernard sighed, as if attraction to another woman was the worst thing that could happen to him.

"Why does that scare you?" I asked, putting on my break-up counsellor's hat.

"Because I know that Steph's my one true love, but I'm feeling something kinda … I don't know. I'm pretty sure this is a test."

"And you're worried that you'll fail it?"

"I dunno. It's not like when Tamara tried to seduce me."

"Tamara tried to what?!" I almost shouted.

"Oh, yeah. Tamara and I shared some polyamorous kissing in her living room, but then I started to cry, and we wound up having an awesome discussion."

I was too shocked to say anything. I wanted to hear all about Bernard's encounter with his long-term crush—and I didn't want to hear any of it. Kind of like I'd felt all the times Jonathan bragged about his romantic encounters while we were growing up.

"I finally figured out that I never really loved Tamara," Bernard said. "I mostly lusted for her, which is totally not the same thing, and it's kind of ironic, because now I think of her as a friend. But Jasmine and me … it's weird, because I don't usually dig her kind—she's hippie and funky and alternative at the same time—yet I found her totally intoxicating."

I took a big swig of coffee and let it swish around in my mouth before swallowing. Then I said, "Roll with it. If it's a test, like you think it is, then you'll learn a lot about yourself. And if it's more than that ... worse things have happened, right?"

"Are you serious?" he said. "Worse things than getting hooked up with a woman with two kids? It would be like a one-way ticket to Alcatraz!"

"Looks to me like the hardest part's already done. Those are two high-functioning human beings. They're cool kids, B-man."

"But what if ..." he began, then stared down at his mug before looking at me with his St. Bernard face. "How could I ever trust love if I let my feelings for someone else overshadow my love for Steph? She's my soulmate."

"Feelings ebb and flow," I said. "That's the nature of emotion. Just roll with this ... and stay positive. One way or another, I think it'll help you figure out what to do next."

Bernard nodded, but I wasn't convinced that he agreed with me. "Okay," he said, "I'll try. But you've gotta keep me on track, man. I set out to win back my wife, and I still plan to do that."

TREE-PLANTING

Bernard

WALKING UP TO JASMINE'S HOUSE, I felt nervous and uncomfortably formal. I was questioning my decision to wear the khakis and plaid shirt that my parents had bought me for Christmas—which felt like a lame attempt to look my best without trying too hard. Standing on the doorstep, my thoughts drifted back and forth between Jasmine and Stephanie. I recalled my just-as-I-was-dozing-off dream the night before, when I imagined myself in a threesome with the two of them. I woke up before the dream finished, doomed to lay awake for hours thinking about what the dream was trying to tell me.

I finally knocked on Jasmine's door and she answered quickly, giving me a big hug and inviting me into her house. She smelled spicy, like nutmeg and cloves—and she looked great, too. Her hair was a bit messier than last time I'd seen her, and she was wearing a dress that looked like a giant potato sack. But she still looked great.

Zoey was out somewhere with Jasmine's business partner, and Nicholas was already at their computer in the living room next to the kitchen. Jasmine had figured out how to install Peace Warrior, so I sat down beside Nicholas and showed him how to set up his character while his mom made tea.

Nicholas was a quick study. He was really smart and mature for his age. I was impressed that this little bumpkin with no formal

117

education could navigate his way around a computer almost as well as I could. Pretty soon, he was equipped with a backpack and a full set of travel supplies. He chose to be a white man in his late twenties—I wondered if he was modelling his character after me or his dad—and he chose Seeds & Saplings as his peace weapon.

Jasmine served all three of us almond milk chai lattes, which, to my surprise, tasted as good as she smelled. She pulled up another chair to watch Nicholas explore northern British Columbia. He'd chosen to start close to home, planting tree saplings in areas that had been clear cut within our home province.

"I planted trees for a few summers," Jasmine said as Nicholas's character battled heat exhaustion and hunger to complete a difficult patch of planting on a steep slope.

"Oh yeah?" I said, my nerves calmer now that I was focused on a familiar game. "Where was that?"

"Near Fort St. James. Smack in the middle of BC. Not far from where Nick's character is now."

"What was it like?" I asked.

"Hard. And life-changing. I was nineteen when I started. I made great money, which I used to travel during the winters. I miss those days, even though they were brutal at times."

"What was brutal?"

"Long days, heat, hunger. Just like the game … except there's no way to feel those things when you're sitting at a computer."

"Yeah," I agreed, even though I couldn't relate. Hard work wasn't my thing. I had to admit that I preferred to be comfortable—like exploring Africa on a computer while drinking hot chocolate, rather than joining my dad and brother for one of their gruelling hikes.

"The best part of tree-planting," Jasmine continued, "was the sense of community I felt. We worked on our own a lot—or in small groups—and we worked very long days. But we'd come together over meals, and sometimes we'd hang out late into the night, even though we had to get up early the next day." A warm smile formed on her face as she added, "I can thank those long summer nights for giving me Nicholas."

"Oh?" I said, looking back at the computer, feeling my face flush.

"One moment of weakness," she said, "which led to three years of emotional chaos. Funny things happen when you're getting over someone—but I have no regrets. That tree-planting gig led to the two greatest gifts I could have asked for."

"Huh," I grunted, not sure what to say. I wanted to ask Jasmine about all her past relationships, but I also wanted to pretend that she'd never had sex before. I know that was hypocritical of me, because I'd experienced three years of amazing bedroom Olympics with Stephanie, but I felt some jealousy about BJ and the two kids his little swimmers had helped to create.

Jasmine's mind drifted somewhere else, and she excused herself to catch up on chores while I helped Nicholas with his game. He didn't need much assistance, but I liked giving him hints—it was like playing wingman to another Peace Warrior, which I'd only ever done with Stephanie back when she was into the game, too.

After about an hour, Jasmine told Nicholas he'd have to wrap up soon. She told me the only things she was strict about were screen time and diet. The latter seemed a bit extreme to me, as she wouldn't let her kids eat two of my favourite food groups— sugar and dairy.

I was hoping that Jasmine would ask me to stay longer, but

she had to go pick up Zoey. When we were standing at the door, I thought of some things I'd rehearsed on the way to Jasmine's house—"Want to go out sometime, just you and me?" or "When can we do this again?"—but all I could say was, "Thanks for the tea."

"Thank you," Jasmine said, looking down at Nicholas, who smiled without saying anything—he hadn't said much the entire time I was there. Then she added, "It's good for him to get some guy time—he doesn't get enough of it in this estrogen zone."

"Yeah," I said. "Well ..."

"We'd love to have you over again," Jasmine said, "if you're up for it."

"Yeah," I nodded. "There's a lot more trees to plant."

"I'd like to go to Africa," Nicholas said, breaking his silence. I'd told him about my most recent escapades in Peace Warrior, and he seemed really interested in the continent where he obviously had some roots.

"Let's do it," I said. "Just ... call me."

"I will," Jasmine replied, and I was pretty sure she meant it.

She gave me another hug, and then we stood there until I started to feel awkward. "Well, see ya," I said, and I went out the door and walked the few steps to the sidewalk that ran along Agnes Street. I turned back to wave as I reached my car, and they waved back at me as they were putting on their own shoes.

Driving home in my dad's Jetta, I felt confused again. Jasmine had been nice to me, but I couldn't tell if she really *liked* me, or if she only wanted to be friends. I didn't know what I wanted, either. Our conversation had been comfortable, but different than the first time I was there. Hearing about her and BJ and their copulation in the middle of nowhere got butterflies fluttering around not only my stomach, but in my pelvis, too. My feelings about Jasmine seemed to be getting stronger—even though she had two kids—maybe in part *because* she had two kids—which I couldn't quite make sense of, given how I'd always felt about children.

THE CLUB

Arnie

I WAS SURPRISED THAT BERNARD WANTED TO MEET ME AT IHOP. He told me he wanted to get to know Loretta better, and true to his word, he was a gentleman whenever she served our table.

By the time I finished breakfast, Bernard's unusual politeness was making me anxious. "You're like a different person today," I finally said, crossing my arms and watching him dip the last piece of his waffle in a pool of syrup. "What's up?"

"Why does something have to be up?" he asked before stuffing the waffle into his mouth.

I raised my eyebrows and said, "Come on, B-man. Something must be up. You're acting far too … normal."

"Let's get back to work," he mumbled between bites.

"On The List?"

"Uh-huh. It's extra important right now. I'm definitely being tested."

"So, your time with Jasmine went well?"

"Yeah, kinda. It wasn't like a date or anything. I just played Peace Warrior with her kid."

"But you felt a connection with her?"

"Yeah."

"How do you think she feels?"

"I don't know. She's easy to talk to, but hard to read. Look, I don't want to talk about secondary romantic opportunities. You need to keep me on track, remember?"

"Of course." I was cautiously optimistic, but I didn't want it to show. "So, what's next?"

"I have four couples left on the A-List: Amanda and Dave Carson; my parents' friends, Reg and Lorna; Cheyenne and husband number whatever; and Fiona and Marcus."

"Not bad," I said, "and you've still got two months left."

"Yeah." I could see that he was struggling to process everything.

"Where are you at with this? I know you're confused ..."

"Of course I'm confused," he said. "Women were put on this earth to confuse men. Aren't you confused?"

"Not really," I replied. "Well, not about my feelings. Yours, on the other hand ..."

Just then, Loretta reappeared to bring us our bill. "How are my two favourite customers?" she asked.

"I don't have a friggin' clue," Bernard said. "You're part of the club. You tell me."

Loretta looked to me for clarity. "Apparently," I said, "B-man has noticed that you're a girl."

"Thanks for clearing that up," Loretta beamed. "What feminine wisdom can I bestow on thee today?"

I took a crack at explaining the situation. "Bernard thinks his love for Stephanie is being tested—because he's feeling attracted to a single mom he interviewed as part of his List project. He feels that if he falls for the mom and loses his feelings for Stephanie in the process, then he can't trust love at all." I turned to Bernard and said, "Is that a reasonable summary?"

"I guess," Bernard shrugged.

Loretta looked at Bernard and thought for a moment, then said, "Love is abundant. There's no limit to love—it's like energy—it just changes form sometimes."

"Abundant," Bernard looked at me like he'd cracked a secret code. "That's what Tamara said, too. I told you they're all part of the same club."

"Glad to be of service," Loretta said before leaving to serve another table.

Bernard took a swig of water and glanced at the bill, then retrieved his wallet from his back pocket. Pulling the billfold apart with his thumbs, he said, "Speaking of abundance … I hope your wallet is overflowing today, 'cause I got nothin.'"

I MET SOMEONE

Bernard

I never thought I'd try so hard to avoid Stephanie Hansen. She'd called four times in the week since my visit to Jasmine's place, and I'd been home every time. Mom and Dad were happy to support my avoidance strategy—they seemed almost gleeful telling Steph that I was unavailable—and the butterflies I was feeling for Jasmine made it possible for me to hold up my end of the plan. I knew it was good to give Steph a small dose of her own medicine, even though it felt strange turning down opportunities to communicate with her.

I was just sitting down to watch *Million Dollar Mermaid* when the phone rang, and then I could hear my dad talking to someone about me. I was hoping it would be Jasmine, but I was starting to doubt that she was ever going to call again. And I hoped it wasn't Stephanie, because my willpower was fading.

When my dad poked his head into the family room and said *Jonathan* was on the phone, I felt a twinge of hatred for my ex-best friend. Jonathan hadn't called me—not once—since he and Stephanie had crushed me like a bug. Stephanie was the only one who had called to ask me to join them—and I could always tell that he didn't want me there.

"Well," Dad said, "are you going to talk to him?"

"I don't know."

"What should I tell him?"

"I don't know. How about … that I'm circumnavigating the globe on a paddleboard."

Dad stood in the doorway with his best exasperated-dad look, and I sat there with the remote control trying to decide whether to start the movie. Finally, some weird mix of anger and nostalgia grabbed hold of me, and I got up to pick up the phone.

"Hey," I said.

"Hey," Jonathan replied.

"What's up?"

"Not much. You?"

"Why do you care?"

"I just …" he couldn't find an answer.

"So, why'd you call?" I said. "Did Steph put you up to it?"

"Yeah, she's got a gun to my head."

"Hilarious. What's up?" I asked again. It was like a telephone version of a staring contest—neither of us wanted to blink first.

"Steph said you haven't been taking her calls."

"I've been busy," I lied, not wanting to admit that I'd spent most of the last week watching movies and playing Peace Warrior.

"Want to come over for dinner tonight?" Jonathan said, unconvincingly.

I was tempted to accept his offer, in part because I knew that it would be an upgrade in the food department. (Jonathan had established himself as a grade-A foodie, whereas my mom was still cooking wheat-free gruel almost a full year after Bruno had moved out.) But a little voice inside of me said that I needed to stick to my avoidance strategy, so I said, "Can't. I have plans." In truth, I would be sitting in front of the TV watching my favourite Esther Williams movie for the umpteenth time, eating whatever insipid vittles my mom put in front of me.

"What about tomorrow?" he asked.

"Busy again."

"Oh, I get it. Too busy for us now, are you?"

"Yup," I replied.

There was a long silence before Jonathan said, "You know, I didn't plan … it just happened." After another painfully long pause, Jonathan continued, "I didn't mean to hurt you, Bernie. I know that was a shit thing to do, and I know I should have said this a long time ago, but … it was all too muddled in my head, and I've never known quite what to say, because I know that anything I say couldn't possibly be enough. I just … it's hard to say this, but … I'm sorry, man."

I wanted to tell Jonathan that his apology was two-and-a-half years too late, and that no words could ever make up for the douchebaggery of stealing your best friend's wife. I'd been waiting to hear him say the 'S' word ever since he and Stephanie shacked up and broke my heart, but I wasn't prepared to actually hear it. Now that he'd said the most difficult word in the male vocabulary, I felt a combination of appreciation and anger—which blended with my already mixed-up feelings about Jasmine to put me in a state of emotional bamboozlement.

We sat in silence for a while before I opened my mouth again. To my surprise, I said, "I met someone."

"Really?" Jonathan asked.

"Yeah, *really*," I said. "Hard to believe, huh?"

"No, I just … I didn't know. I'm happy for you, man. Who is she?" He sounded authentically happy, but I wondered if he was just relieved that he might finally shake the third wheel. "Seriously, man, what's her name?"

"Just someone I've known for a while," I replied. "It's not all that serious yet." I felt stupid for saying anything—Jasmine hadn't even called me in a week, I didn't know how she felt about me, and I had no idea if Jonathan was still in contact with BJ or Jasmine. I'd blurted it out because I hadn't known how to handle Jonathan's long-overdue apology—without thinking of the effect my news might have on Stephanie, or on my plan to win her back. I wasn't sure what I'd done, but I was too far in to back out. So I dug the hole a little deeper, adding, "We're just at the casual sex stage."

ROUND TWO

Arnie

I HEARD MY LANDLORD'S FAMILIAR TAP ON MY DOOR—four quick knocks—and I had to untangle myself from cuddling on the couch with Loretta. It didn't take me long to cross my small suite and reach the door.

"Hi, Arnie," Parvinder said. "How are you two lovebirds doing?" She peered into my suite and waved at Loretta, who rose from the couch to join me at the door.

"We're good," I replied. "Want some tea?" Parvinder—a lifelong friend of my mom—often stayed for a visit when she dropped off my mail.

"No, I just came to deliver this." She held up an envelope with fancy writing on it.

We hung in the doorway for a minute chatting, then I closed the door and went to my kitchen table.

"Real mail," Loretta said excitedly as we sat down. "I didn't think anyone knew you lived here," she added, poking fun at me.

"It's from Stephanie," I said, looking at the return address.

I opened the envelope and pulled out a small card, which caused a collection of shiny confetti to fall out of the envelope and drift to the table. "It's a wedding invitation," I said.

"Ooh ... for two?"

I looked at the invitation, which cordially invited me and a guest to the union of Stephanie Hansen and Jonathan Donaldson on August 22, 2015—less than two months away. "Yup," I said. "Who do you think I should invite?"

Loretta smacked me and giggled.

"I wonder why this came so much later than Bernard's."

"We're part of round two," Loretta said. "The people who get invited after some of the first invitees have said no."

"Ah, so we're second-rate guests?"

"Just think of us as more recently appreciated," she said.

I'd initially thought I might be invited by Bernard, but he was still in denial that the wedding was even real. I hadn't thought about a second round of invitations—about being a potential guest in my own right.

"I can't wait to meet them," Loretta said.

I thought about my indirect friendship with Stephanie and my long, strange history with Jonathan. Although we were more acquaintances than friends, we had shared a lot of experiences over the years—ogling girls at the food court in Metrotown during high school; attending Lions games at BC Place; enduring Bernard's horribly outdated taste in movies; and eating meals with the Kirbys like we were part of their family. Jonathan was kind of like a brother I could never quite relate to. He was smart, and he could be funny—in small doses. He had never been particularly secure, so when he realized in grade ten that girls found him good-looking, it went straight to his head. The one weekend we all shared in Whistler, when we were twenty, was a low point for my impression of Jonathan. He managed to bring home different women on consecutive nights, having noisy sex in the only bedroom we had—forcing me to share the pull-out couch with B-man, who snores like a jackhammer.

"I wonder if Jonathan has grown up," I said. "For Stephanie's sake, I hope so."

"From the little you've told me, they sound like a match," Loretta said.

"Maybe," I shrugged.

We went back to the couch to sit more comfortably. We both had the day off, and we were determined to waste it together. But we sat in silence until Loretta said, "You're thinking about B-man again."

"How do you do that?"

"Do what?"

"Read my mind."

"You project it, silly."

"I guess I'll never get away with lying to you, huh?"

Loretta smiled.

"Yeah, I was thinking about The List. Bernard zoned out on it this week … and I think it's because of Jasmine. Do you think she'll call him back?"

"What do you think?" Loretta had mastered the art of answering a question with a question, forcing me to think long and hard about Bernard's chances with Jasmine.

"I don't know," I said. "I was hopeful at first, but it's been a while. I think we'd know by now if there was serious potential. Then again, she is a mom, so she has other priorities. I don't know … I'd put money on him saying or doing something ridiculous to sabotage the whole thing."

"Maybe she's just a lily pad," Loretta said.

"What do you mean?"

"A place to pause and look at his reflection."

I didn't know exactly what Loretta meant, but even though she'd never met Jasmine and she hardly knew Bernard, I was sure that she somehow understood the situation better than I did.

RABBIT-DOG FOOD

Bernard

ON JULY 4TH, I was supposed to watch the Lions play their season opener on my dad's massive TV. But when Jasmine called and invited me for Peace Warrior, I jumped at the opportunity to see my gorgeous hippie friend. It had been almost two weeks since my last visit to her place, and even by my standards, life had gone way off the rails. I was only showering every few days—usually when my mom said something like, "The family room smells like a bachelor pad." I wasn't even motivated to make headway in Peace Warrior. I'd spent most of the last week—since I'd made the questionable decision to turn down dinner with Stephanie and Jonathan—in bed or watching movies.

My dad and Bruno had been trying to get me out for a hike. They'd made a habit of doing the Grouse Grind every second evening—which, from what I've heard, isn't so much a hike as a form of masochistic vertical torture. They never suggested that I actually *climb* the Grind with them—they pitied my physical condition too much to suggest that. They just asked if I would take the gondola up and join them for their cool-down walk at the top, then have a beer at the lodge before riding back down.

Even an awesome view and a free beer couldn't get me out of the house. The longer I waited for Jasmine to call—and the more I realized that I'd probably stopped Stephanie from ever calling again—the less I felt like getting out of bed.

Then Jasmine phoned. She apologized for not having called sooner and said that she'd been busy with family stuff—too busy to spend time on the computer. Nicholas had been asking about me—about playing Peace Warrior again—and she'd been meaning to call me for the past week.

I had my first shower in days—I even shaved off an almost full beard—and I put on some nice jeans and another of my plaid Christmas shirts. Dad let me use his car again—he seemed happy that I'd accepted an invitation to leave the house—and Mom sponsored my social life with a hundred-dollar grant, which I used part of to pick up a bottle of wine on the way to Jasmine's place.

Jasmine smiled as she opened her door, and Nicholas greeted me enthusiastically. Jasmine introduced me to her business partner, Cassie, who had Zoey wrapped around her neck playing all shy-like.

"Hi," I said, trying to conceal that I was disappointed there was another adult present. I hoped that Cassie was planning to leave before supper, but I decided it would be rude to ask about that.

"Hi," Cassie said, smiling as she reached out to shake my hand. She was even shorter than Jasmine, with spiky black hair and pointy features. She looked like a pixie.

I handed Jasmine the bottle of wine, and Nicholas and I got straight down to starting up Peace Warrior. Nicholas wanted to go to Africa, so we had to prepare him for that. He returned from the tree-planting site in northern B.C. to Vancouver, where he booked a flight to Botswana via Johannesburg. I suggested he start in Botswana because it's safer than West Africa, where I was still working, and because it's a good place to plant things.

"What are vac—" Nicholas struggled to read the task list that told him everything he had to do before he could go to Africa.

"Vaccinations," I said. "You know, shots—needles—so you don't catch diseases."

Jasmine had been working on dinner with Cassie and Zoey, but when she heard the 'V' word she came into the living room to join our conversation. "Nicholas hasn't had any shots," she said. "I don't believe in vaccinations."

"Really?" I asked, dumbfounded. I'd heard about people not vaccinating their kids, but I hadn't met anyone who admitted to it. I thought it was crazy to not want to protect your kids from pestilence.

"Yeah," Jasmine said. "There's a lot of conflicting evidence about whether or not vaccines are effective. I'm not convinced about them, and I didn't want to subject my kids to needles at such a young age."

I wanted to tell Jasmine that I thought she was being ridiculous, but I figured that would decrease the likelihood of her wanting to spend time with me. So I shrugged as if I respected her opinion, even though I didn't. "Well, if you want to go to Africa, you need to get some vaccinations. And you'll need to take a bunch of pills, too, so you don't catch malaria."

"I guess …" Jasmine started, "I hadn't really thought about that. But it's a good learning experience." I could see that she was tormenting herself over whether to let her kid's pretend game character get a pretend needle. I wanted to say that it was just a friggin' computer game, but I could see that she was stuck on a moral dilemma.

Cassie joined us, holding hands with Zoey, who was starting to come out of her shell and smiled at me. Cassie and Jasmine debated the vaccination question for a painfully long time, and I waited while they discussed it.

Jasmine finally knelt on one knee and spoke to Nicholas as if he was old enough to plan his own healthcare strategy. "Okay, Nick, I guess it's a requirement to travel, so you have a decision to make. Do you want to get a needle—which could make you feel a bit sick now and has a small chance of making you really sick—or would you rather pick a different location that doesn't require that?"

"Does a needle hurt much?" Nicholas asked.

"Not too much," Jasmine answered. "A little pinch … can I show you?"

"Okay," Nicholas said. Jasmine pinched the top of his arm, and he yelped, "Ow!"

"How'd that feel?" Cassie asked, leaning in to join the conversation.

"It was okay," Nicholas said.

"The pinch isn't the part I'm concerned about," Jasmine said. "My concern is that when they give you a needle, they put a tiny bit of liquid into your body that's meant to help you fight off diseases … and I'm not sure if that liquid is totally safe."

Jasmine and Nicholas and Cassie kept discussing vaccines while I used all my willpower to keep my mouth shut. I thought I had as much right to an opinion as Cassie did, maybe even more since I was the Peace Warrior expert. But I decided to stay out of their debate.

Jasmine finally said to Nicholas, "Now that you understand the risks about vaccinations and malaria pills, and that you need to take them to visit Africa, what do you want to do?"

I felt like laughing as we all waited for the kid to make an educated decision about something that should have been blatantly obvious. But I sat there waiting until Nicholas said, "I want to go to Africa, even if I have to get a needle."

"Hallelujah!" I blurted, which caused both Jasmine and Cassie to stare at me. Then Jasmine suggested that she and Cassie finish making dinner while Nicholas and I prepared for his departure to Botswana.

Nicholas was really patient with trip preparation, which is only slightly less boring than waiting for buses in Peace Warrior. He was just about to board the plane to Johannesburg when Jasmine called us to the table for dinner.

Dinner was challenging. We ate kale salad with sesame seeds, raw beet and carrot salad, and some oniony bean dish that looked like the canned food my parents feed Fluffball. It seemed like a weird combination of rabbit food and dog food, but the kids ate it like it was normal. I had a hard time swallowing most of it—especially the dog food component—but I did my best to pretend I liked it. The conversation was strange, too. Jasmine obviously invited Cassie over quite a bit, so they were all familiar with one another and I was like some fifth wheel that didn't quite fit in. I wished Cassie would go home—I was hoping to have some time alone with Jasmine after her bumpkins went to bed—but I was starting to think Cassie would never leave.

"So, what do you do in the business?" I asked Cassie, trying to find something to talk about.

"What do you mean?" she asked.

"Like, your part of the work."

"Oh, I'm a social worker."

"How do you help Jasmine with her art?"

Cassie looked puzzled. "Well, I'm certainly not the creative one, but I help her sell at markets."

"Oh yeah?" I said, unable to think of anything else to ask.

After dinner, Nicholas and I spent another half hour or so on Peace Warrior before Jasmine made him turn off the computer and get ready for bed.

"Thanks so much for doing this," Jasmine said, as if she was ready for me to go home.

It didn't seem like Cassie was in any hurry to leave, and her presence made it hard for me to connect with Jasmine, so I made up a story about friends asking me to join them at JR's Sports Bar. I was secretly hoping Jasmine would ask me to stay and Cassie would leave instead, but Jasmine just said, "Oh, that sounds fun." She said it half-heartedly, and I realized that someone who eats rabbit-dog food and drinks Scooby-Doo tea and doesn't vaccinate her kids probably doesn't have much interest in sports bars.

I reluctantly put on my shoes and yelled goodnight to Nicholas, who appeared from his bedroom in his pyjamas and waved at me. I shook Cassie's hand while she held Zoey in her other arm, and then I gave Jasmine a hug and thanked her for dinner.

Walking away, I felt confused. I wanted to turn around and ask Jasmine if *we* could go for dinner sometime, just her and me, but I wasn't sure if she was attracted to me—and I was still conflicted about my own feelings, too. So I just got into the car and started to drive home.

About halfway home, I decided to go to JR's Sports Bar after all—on my own, which I'd never done before. I was still starving after the rabbit-dog-food experience, and I wasn't ready to face a family interrogation about my love life.

I parked the car and went into JR's. I had an inkling that one beer would lead to six, which I couldn't afford, so I ordered a meat lover's pizza and hot chocolate. I was proud of myself for making such a responsible choice.

My pizza—a heart-attack-on-a-plate consisting of ground beef, bacon, ham and pepperoni smothered in mozzarella—offered some solace as I watched replays of the Lions being soundly thumped by the Ottawa Redblacks. It was the first time in memory that I'd missed watching a season opener, and I wondered why I'd skipped a football game to hang out with a bunch of vegan hippies. But as I downed a whole pizza and chatted with Melanie—my super-cute waitress who was wearing a distractingly sexy kilt-skirt—I cheered up significantly.

Melanie was flirtatious, and she had the uber-attractive quality of being a female Lions fan. When I found out that she had been part of the Felions cheerleading squad the previous year, I was able to name-drop about knowing Tracy Spencer—which cemented her interest in lingering at my table. We discussed the Lions' challenges, and then laughed together at a series of sports bloopers.

After an hour or so flirt-chatting with Melanie, I was feeling overwhelmed with confusion about the beautiful half of humanity. She had an unexpected rush of new customers, and I came down with a case of gut-rot from eating my entire pizza, so I paid my bill, left her an excessive tip, and waved before leaving the bar. She winked and blew me a kiss, which, if it hadn't been for my aching gut, might have caused me to stay until closing time.

I was glad that nobody else was up when I got home. I took some Pepto-Bismol and lay down, hoping that sleep would help me understand women better. But I couldn't sleep—I kept thinking about Jasmine and Stephanie and Melanie, and waiting for my stomach to settle. I even recalled my snogging session with Tamara ... and I felt a hint of regret for not letting my childhood crush seduce me when I had the chance.

SOMPIN' STUPID

Arnie

LORETTA TWIRLED IN FRONT OF ME IN HER BABY BLUE DRESS. I scanned her from top to bottom, from her button nose to her bare feet. She was modelling the dress she would wear to our first wedding together, and I was wondering how I'd managed to find such a perfect partner. Almost thirty years of waiting, of believing that I might never meet someone who made me feel that way or who felt the same about me. And then—Loretta. When I'd least expected her, discussing weddings with my best friend at the International House of Pancakes. Loretta.

"Would you dance with this?" she said.

"Uh-huh," I nodded.

"And then bring me back to your place and make mad, passionate love to me?"

"Uh-huh," I nodded again.

"Practice makes perfect," she smiled.

I reached out to pull her in, just as my cell phone rang.

"Nonononono," she said, using a pillow from the couch to smother the phone.

"But I'm on call," I groaned, reaching over to dig the phone out from underneath the pillow.

She scrunched her face.

"Maybe it's nothing." I picked up the phone and saw that it

was a blocked number. "Could be my boss though."

I tapped answer and said, "Hello." I could hear a lot of noise in the background—it sounded like traffic. "Hello?" I repeated.

"Arnie," Bernard slurred. "Anitaride."

"What? Where are you?"

"JR's. I … needaride."

"You're drunk."

"I did sompin' stupid."

"What did you do?"

All I could hear was background noise.

"Bernard, what did you do?" I asked again.

"Tellyalater. I need you to come … get me."

I glanced up at Loretta, whose brow was creased in concern. "Catch a cab, man," I said to Bernard.

"I got no money," he said, barely audible.

"How—who's phone is this?"

He didn't answer.

I wanted to talk my way out of picking up my drunk friend, but he sounded barely conscious. He'd already spoiled my moment with Loretta, so I looked at her with an expression that said, "I've gotta go," and she replied with a resigned nod.

"Okay, man," I said. "I'll be right there."

When I pulled into the parking lot of JR's Sports Bar, I spotted Bernard sitting slouched against the side of the building. I parked in a nearby stall and walked over to him. It was a warm July evening, the sun just beginning to set even though it was after nine PM.

"Bernard," I said, nudging him. He turned his head up and half-opened his eyes, looking like he didn't recognize me. "B-man," I added, "Let's go."

It had been a long time since I'd seen Bernard in this condition. And although he was always up for a social bender, I'd never known him to go out on solo drinking binges.

I dragged Bernard into my Civic, buckled him in, and started driving to his house. Then the caretaker part of me kicked in, and I turned toward my house instead. Loretta had gone home—she hadn't seemed mad; she never seemed mad—and I figured I wouldn't be called into work now that I'd survived shift change without a call.

Once I coaxed Bernard into my basement suite, I force-fed him a glass of water. Then I literally held him up in the bathroom for a pee before settling him on my couch with a blanket and a pillow. It was familiar territory—a bit of a niche that I'd found nursing drunks back to health at the hospital. More than a few of the local alcoholics knew me by name.

I dialed Bernard's house, and Blanche answered on the first ring. I told her the basics about Bernard's state, and where I'd found him.

"I assumed he was out with you," she said. "Or maybe ... that girl he's been seeing."

"Jasmine?" I said.

"Yeah."

"I know he went over to her place on Saturday. That's the last I heard. I haven't seen him ..." I hadn't reached out to Bernard in almost a week. I'd thought about him lots, but I hadn't wanted to call him. We'd had brief flashes of friendship lately, but mostly we were drifting in different directions—me toward a fulfilling life with Loretta, and Bernard toward ... I wasn't quite sure.

"Do you want us to come and get him?" Blanche asked.

"It's okay. He's already asleep."

"Well, I know he's in good hands," she said, but I could hear the worry in her voice. Then she added, "They never stop being your little boys, Arnie. No matter how big they get. Thanks for being there for Bernie. He needs us more than ever."

THE WHOLE STORY

Bernard

THAT WAS POSITIVELY, IRREFUTABLY, WITHOUT A DOUBT, *the* worst hangover I'd ever had. And that was saying something.

As my eyes fought to overcome the crud holding them shut, Arnie kept insisting that I drink herbal tea. About halfway through my first cup of the wretched stuff, the stomach part of my hangover kicked in. I barely made it to his bathroom before I had to barf, then I had only seconds to slam down the seat and switch ends. I sat on the toilet forever, wondering if I might die there. The previous evening came back to me in fragments, like I was putting together one of those 1000-piece puzzles that my dad tortures us with every Christmas.

My decision to drive over to Jasmine's house again set off a series of events that I wished I could forget. My libido had been consuming me for days, tantalizing me with visions of Jasmine and Stephanie and Tamara and kilt-skirt Melanie. As the week wore on, Jasmine danced to the forefront of my mind, consuming an ever-larger part of me. I envisioned her soft skin, her sexy little eyebrow ring, and the limber body she hid under baggy hippie clothes. I heard her gravelly voice—the soulful way she sang along to Motown classics. And I smelled her natural hippie scent—like she herself was made of cloves and nutmeg and cinnamon.

Jasmine hadn't called me all week, so I drove out to New Westminster on Thursday and knocked on her door at dinner time. I had no idea what I was going to say. I just wanted to see her.

Cassie answered the door, and Jasmine appeared shortly after, wrapping her arms around Cassie like a lover would do.

"Hi, Bernard," Jasmine said, peering out from behind Cassie. "What's up?"

I was speechless. Everything Jasmine had said to me went through my head in rapid fire, connecting dots in the worst possible way. Cassie tipped her head onto Jasmine's, and the lightbulb went on. "She's not your *business* partner, is she?"

Jasmine straightened and looked at me like I was clueless. "Business partner?"

"Yeah," I said. "When you told me you had a partner, I thought…"

Jasmine's eyes widened to the size of cue balls. "Oh … you thought … and you were …"

"Yeah, …" I said, "but …" Cassie's pixie face puckered into an *I'm-sorry-for-whatever-I've-done* expression, while Jasmine stood there with an awkward smile. "You're … rug lickers!"

Jasmine's whole face collapsed. "*What* did you just say?"

"Rug lickers. You know—carpet munchers … muff divers. You're—lesbians?!"

Jasmine and Cassie frowned at each other with mouths agape, as if my revelation of their lesbianism was even bigger news to them than it was to me. Then Jasmine locked onto me with laser-beam eyes and said, "I know what a lesbian is, Bernard. But I think you missed a few homophobic slurs. How about todger dodgers, or dykes, or—"

"Bean flickers," Cassie added. "Oh, and I *love* it when people call me a butch."

"Why don't you just call me a nigger while you're at it?" Jasmine said, spit flying like venom from her angry tongue. "No need to limit your bigotry to my sexual orientation."

I could feel myself shrinking to a fraction of my usual size. "Jesus, I didn't ... I just meant—"

Jasmine interrupted me before I could defend myself. "What century are you from, Bernard?"

I slouched into myself, wanting to disappear. "But you have kids. And you were married."

"Oh, Bernard," Jasmine sighed. "There's a lot of grey in this world. But I guess you haven't reached that level of consciousness yet. Maybe if they added some sexual diversity to that game you're so enamoured with ..."

We all stood in silence until I found my voice again. "Never mind," I finally said. "I'm used to rejection."

We stared at each other for a moment. Then Jasmine said, "Good luck with your list, Bernard," and disappeared into her home.

Cassie remained in the doorway, her mouth twisted into a sneer of contempt. Then her eyes glazed into a gaze of pity, which felt even worse.

"B-man!" Arnie shouted, startling me back into the diarrhea-puke zone. "Do I need to break down the door?"

"No!" I shouted back. "I'm ... just ... give me a minute."

My minute was more like half an hour. My gut was still churning and my chest felt like a ball of elastics all wound together pulling toward the core. I couldn't tell if I was about to have a coronary, or if I was experiencing a real-life broken heart. To make matters worse, my head was pounding and spinning at the same time, and I felt like my conscience was partly to blame.

I knew Arnie would press me for details about my evening at JR's. I was usually happy to talk about my drunken escapades—there was typically some silver lining to focus on, something witty or brilliant that I'd managed to accomplish during my stupor—but that morning I couldn't remember anything worth redeeming about the previous night.

I didn't want to tell Arnie about my standoff with Jasmine and Cassie, or about driving to JR's on my own for the second time in a week, where I'd polished off an extra-large pizza and two pitchers of beer. Where I'd been certain that Melanie was flirting with me again. Where I'd inexplicably reached out and lifted her kilt-skirt when she leaned over to clear glasses from the table beside me. Where I'd been escorted outside by a very large Australian Bar-moose, who extracted the remaining cash from my wallet to clear my tab, then said he would mail me to Tasmania in pieces if I ever set foot in JR's again. And where I'd managed to borrow a phone from someone to call my only friend in the world ... before passing out against the side of the building like a homeless guy.

When I finally sat down at Arnie's table in front of a fresh cup of herbal tea, I didn't want to tell him anything that had happened the night before. For all the stupid things I'd done over the years—drunk or sober—I'd never felt *that* stupid. So I gave him an abridged version of the evening, skipping the skirt lift and downplaying my use of lesbian synonyms. I needed him to understand that I was the victim of yet another unfair love triangle.

Then I started to cry. Arnie crossed his arms and shook his head. His eyes pierced through me like they were reading my mind, and he said, "You told me you did something stupid. I need the whole story, Bernard. That's the only way I can help you."

RESPONSIBILITY

Arnie

SEXUAL ASSAULT. That's the term that kept spinning through my mind. Or was it harassment? In any case, Bernard had finally gone too far. As he blubbered in my kitchen, anger welled up inside of me.

He hadn't been charged, but part of me wished he had. He wasn't willing to accept responsibility for his action—he blamed it on being the victim of two love triangles, which was beyond lame. There was no excuse for what Bernard had done—certain lines can't be crossed, like punching a referee or hitting your wife. Or lifting a waitress's skirt.

Bernard's only saving grace was that he hadn't attempted to drive home afterward. I shuddered at the thought of him behind the wheel with that much alcohol in his system.

I dropped off Bernard on my way to work. As he dragged his way out of the car, obviously still hungover, I couldn't think of anything to say.

B-man leaned back into the car and said, "It's my birthday on Monday."

"Oh yeah—twenty-nine," I replied.

"Yeah. You're invited for dinner."

"Yeah? Thanks. I might have to work. I'll let you know."

Bernard nodded and closed the door, then trudged to his house with his head stooped. He looked so pathetic that a part of me wanted to feel sorry for him, but the rest of me was too angry about what he'd done to feel sympathy.

I got to Burnaby General Hospital a few minutes early for my shift, so I called Loretta from the parking lot.

"How's B-man?" she asked.

"Crappy," I replied. "The guy's a mess."

"You're a good friend."

"I guess," I said, but I wasn't sure anymore. Bernard had found so many ways to push me away—to push the whole world away. I felt a sense of duty to be there for him, but I was having a harder time finding a soft spot in my heart for the man-boy I'd shared so many experiences with.

"You're a good lover, too," Loretta said, as if she knew that I needed a change of subject. "You're very generous."

"Thanks," I replied, feeling a mild pang of jealousy at knowing that I was surely not Loretta's first lover.

"Goodbye, my love," she said, and my jealousy dissipated.

"Goodbye, my love," I replied.

Walking into work, I thought about my girlfriend's words— whether she was comparing my lovemaking skills to men from her past. I wanted to know everything about Loretta Chan, but I also feared what I might learn. By the time I reached my nursing station, I decided it didn't matter. What was important was that Loretta had chosen to be with me, and to teach me what it meant to be in love.

My thoughts drifted back to the invitation Bernard had tossed out as I dropped him off at his house. I had no desire to celebrate with someone who couldn't keep his hands to himself, so I polled my colleagues until I found a nurse who traded me his Monday night shift.

A LEGENDARY GOAL

Bernard

WE CELEBRATED MY 29TH BIRTHDAY with my mom's least inedible gluten-free cake: an almond meal and coconut creation with cream cheese icing. We had a quiet family supper—even Arnie couldn't come, because he got called into work—and then we played *Settlers of Catan*. I felt a deep sense of misery all day. It didn't help that, aside from my family, the only acknowledgments of my milestone were a few lame messages on Facebook. Arnie had posted there, and so had Stephanie—which left me feeling more sad than happy, because it made me think of all the birthdays we'd celebrated together. Even the gifts from my parents and Bruno—cards containing cash—felt like patronizing acknowledgements of my piteous financial situation.

My hangover from my night at JR's had lasted almost two days—it was *so* bad that I had to miss going to the Lions' home opener for the first time since I was four—but at least the physical part was gone in time for my birthday. My mental hangover from a night of unparalleled humiliation *still* hadn't worn off. I knew that Jasmine and Cassie, two pitchers of Kokanee, and a ridiculously short skirt had conspired against me—but I still felt weird about everything that had happened to me that night.

I didn't understand what I'd done to piss off the universe so much. I was starting to wonder if those people who believe in pre-determination were right. It's like we don't really control our actions, and we're all just floating down some crazy river without knowing which rocks we're going to hit, or which back-eddy is going to suck us underwater and take our life. It's like we each have our own path down the rapids, and the sooner we resign ourselves to the fact that we're powerless, the calmer we'll feel about everything that happens to us.

I had zero motivation to work on The List after my episode at JR's. I was sure Stephanie and Jonathan would ignore me now that I was supposedly in a relationship, and that Jasmine would never want to talk to me again—which made me sad, because even though I was disappointed that she was a lesbian, and even though her rabbit-dog food was awful and she was one of those crazy anti-vaccine people, I still thought she was a cool person. I liked listening to Motown music and talking with her, and I liked playing Peace Warrior with her kid. I'd achieved *zero status* with Jasmine—the worst possible outcome in Peace Warrior, which kills you off tragically if you get caught hurting another player.

As much as I felt stupid about misunderstanding Jasmine's romantic leanings, I felt even stupider about how I'd misinterpreted Melanie's flirtatious intentions. I was pretty sure both of those situations were emotional litmus tests—and I'd scored a pair of F-minuses.

I tried calling Arnie a few times, but he said he had to work a lot, and that he was studying for some online psychology course. When I pressed him to find a bit of time for me, he said he barely had enough time for Loretta—which made me feel completely pushed aside. He got real testy when I called her Yoko again.

I could tell that I'd been playing a lot of Peace Warrior when I saw a notification that I'd reached Top Hero status in Sierra

Leone. It's just one small country in Africa—kind of like having a hit song in Iceland—but it was still cool to be recognized like that. I got Fluffball to shake a paw, and since he'd spent so much time with me in West Africa, it almost seemed like he understood what we were celebrating.

I wondered if I should branch out to another country or go for the loftiest possible goal of *Peace Warrior Legend*—a title bestowed on less than one thousand of the 12.5 million people who play Peace Warrior. I decided to go for the latter, and I felt a weak sense of pride at my newfound ambition.

I expanded my focus from desalination along the coastline to installing wells inland. I was going to have to be super patient to gain Hero Points without using my secret sauce—the desalination units that had proven to be a unique advantage for my character. I knew that one-trick ponies didn't get to be Peace Warrior Legends, so I had to shake things up and expand my arsenal of peace weapons.

I pretty much lived in the office for a full week after my birthday. I was already on my way to reaching the third of ten mileposts required to become a Legendary Peace Warrior when I ran into the distraction that would send my whole world into a tornado.

I was hanging out in a volunteer residence in Makeni, the fourth largest city in Sierra Leone, waiting for a truck to take me to a well site in a nearby village, when my personal message window popped up. I rarely got messages—usually just notifications about my Warrior status—so it surprised me. Seeing that it was from *Stephleupagus*, I jolted forward to look closer at the screen, causing Fluffball to jump off my lap with a yip.

"I heard I might find you here," the message said.

"What's with the guest appearance?" I typed.

"I came looking for you," she wrote.

"Why?" I replied.

"Jonathan said you found someone. I'm happy for you."

I wanted to say a lot of things, but I limited myself to typing, "Thanks."

"I'd like to meet her. Will she be at my wedding?"

"We'll see," I lied.

"Could we meet sometime? Just you and me?"

I stared at the screen for a long time, unsure how to reply. Finally, I typed, "OK. When?"

"Tuesday? The Big Bean at five?"

I paused long enough to make it seem like I might have something better to do in two days. Then I typed, "OK. As long as we're not shopping for bridesmaid dresses."

After a short delay she typed, "Deal. LOL <3"

The heart symbol at the end of Steph's message sent a shock wave to the big muscle in my own chest. I suddenly felt warm, like my heart was sending out a message of love to the rest of me. I had an image of the Grinch—how his heart grew three sizes when he heard the Whos singing even though he'd stolen all their gifts—and I felt like that was happening to me. Like one symbol at the end of a message caused my whole world to shift.

I spent the rest of that night examining The List in excruciating detail. I reviewed notes, analyzed responses, researched un-contacted couples, updated The Roadmap, and started writing out the speech that I was going to impress Stephanie with before she had a chance to say *I do* for a second time.

EVERYONE LOVES STEPH

Arnie

LORETTA WANTED TO MEET STEPHANIE AND JONATHAN before she attended their wedding, so we met at a popular Italian restaurant. I had been dreading the experience, but it turned out to be fun. We laughed at stories from our childhood—especially when Jonathan and I reminisced about our most ridiculous moments with Bernard. Stephanie fished for an update about Bernard's love life—vague questions that Loretta masterfully deflected by answering with questions of her own. I'm pretty sure Stephanie left the restaurant more confused about Bernard's relationship status than she had been when she arrived.

As I drove Loretta home she said, "Jonathan was funny—and nicer than I expected."

"Wait until you spend a bit more time with him," I replied. But I had to admit that Jonathan seemed to have grown up a lot over the past couple of years. Since he got together with Stephanie, Jonathan had earned an Information Technology diploma and traded a lucrative bartending gig for a day job at Telus. I wondered if his newfound maturity was a façade to impress Stephanie—but it seemed authentic.

"I see why everyone loves Steph," Loretta said. The way she abbreviated Stephanie's name—like you speak of an old friend— told me Loretta had fallen under the same charismatic spell that

Stephanie Hansen casts on just about everyone she meets.

"Yeah," I replied. "She's a neat girl. Not entirely functional, mind you."

"Who is?" Loretta asked.

"Good point," I shrugged. "Now that you've met all three parties, what do you think about this whole Bernard-Stephanie-Jonathan mess?"

Loretta pondered my question as I stopped in front of her place on Thurston Street—a bungalow that sat like a dollhouse between the massive newer homes on either side of it. "I think ..." she finally said, "they all still love each other, but they can't figure out how to fit all that love into a triangle."

"Why do you always have amazing answers to simple questions?" I asked. "And more importantly, why can't you stay over tonight?"

"Because you'd keep me up all night, and then I wouldn't be able to get up for my breakfast shift."

"That's the idea," I said, but Loretta didn't bite. She leaned over and kissed me, then opened her door and got out of the Civic. She looked back into the car, holding a hand up to one ear like a telephone, and mouthed out the words, "Call me."

BiG BEAN REUNiON

Bernard

"So … what's up?" I asked, trying to conceal that my entire nervous system was activating at once, pressing against the insides of my skin like a billion tiny needles.

"How are you, Bernie?" Stephanie was leaning over her mug of liquid dessert at the window seat of The Big Bean, like she'd done a hundred times before, gazing into my eyes as if we were still lovers.

"Okay." I was afraid to say more, because I had too many words jumbled in my mind. I picked up my own hot chocolate and sipped on it to keep my mouth occupied.

"Jonathan said you met someone?"

I shrugged.

"I'm really happy for you." I could see tears forming in her great big saucer eyes, and I wondered if they were tears of happiness. I hoped not.

"I'm not with anybody. I just said that."

"Really? So you're not …"

"She's just a friend. A lesbian friend. Actually, I'm not even sure we're friends anymore."

"Oh." Stephanie picked up her mug and took a sip, her lips curling into a smile behind it.

"I've been pretty confused lately," I confessed.

"Me too," Stephanie said.

"How so?"

"I'm scared."

We looked at each other straight on, ignoring the bustle of the coffee shop and the traffic passing by the window. "Of what?" I asked.

Stephanie set down her hot chocolate and stared at me. I waited, but she couldn't seem to find her words.

"What are you scared of?" I repeated.

"Making a mistake," she finally said. "I never saw myself getting divorced. What if it happens again?"

"What if?" I kept what I really wanted to say—*you can't get divorced again if you don't marry the idiot*—to myself.

"It's ... Jonathan and I ... we've been struggling a bit lately. It's like we're getting too comfortable with one another. We had a nice dinner with Arnie and Loretta last night, but it kind of felt like we were already an old married couple. Sort of like it felt ... when you and I, you know ... how it feels after you've been together for a while."

"No," I said. "I don't know. I never got tired of you." Stephanie's mention of dinner with *my* friends poked me with a sliver of jealousy, but her lukewarm description of life with Jonathan gave me a morsel of hope. "Maybe you're not the marrying type," I blurted, hoping to drive a wedge of doubt into her mind—ignoring the irony that if I succeeded in shattering Steph's view of marriage, I would then have to work on rebuilding it again.

"Maybe you're right," she said, "but I hope not. I grew up idolizing marriage. I was an old-fashioned country girl who wanted what my parents had. Their marriage isn't perfect—they act more like business partners than lovers—but they've been married for thirty-five years, and they have the kind of bond that you can only build by sticking together. I've always wanted that—but I couldn't even make it to three years. Before you, my record was ten months."

Stephanie's eyes watered, and then overflowed. A tear dripped into her cup, and suddenly everything I'd been feeling about Stephanie—all the love, anger, sadness and frustration—raced to the surface and caused my entire body to tingle.

"Don't cry, Steph. That's my department."

"Nobody ever loved me like you did, Bernie—you have a heart of gold. Why did I leave you?"

"That's the question I've been asking for two-and-a-half years." It took a lot of effort to fight back my own tears as I handed Stephanie my napkin.

"You know," she said, "it's our fifth anniversary this week."

"I know." I'd been trying to ignore the milestone that should have been a huge celebration, but instead felt like a funeral. "Will you think of me on Friday, at least for a moment?"

"Of course." Steph allowed her tears to flow, and mine followed. Then I reached one hand across the table, and she clasped it firmly with both of hers.

"Happy early almost anniversary," I said, bawling.

Stephanie's teary smile felt like sunshine hitting my face on a rainy day—like a perfect paradox of happiness and sadness. "Happy early almost anniversary," she replied. "No matter where life takes us, Bernie ... always know that I love you."

MOONY

Bernard

MOTIVATED BY STEPHANIE'S EMOTIONAL BREAKDOWN, I was more determined than ever to complete The List. It was a bad time to lose my wingman—Arnie had switched a few shifts at the hospital so he could synchronize days off with Loretta—but I forged ahead on my own, determined to get through the rest of the couples myself.

Reg and Lorna were easy to interview. They'd been best friends with my parents forever, and even though they had younger kids I could never relate to, our families did a lot together while I was growing up. Like my Aunt Nancy and Uncle Chris, the only thing that surprised me about Reg and Lorna was that they had gone through some rough times during their marriage. They wouldn't say what had happened, but sometime when their kids were little they'd gone through what Lorna kept referring to as *The Crisis.* Every time she said that, Reg winced a little bit. But they'd weathered it—whatever *it* was—and they both agreed that their relationship was stronger for it. I made a mental note that maybe Stephanie and I were just going through a crisis, too—a long one that included the 'D' word, which seemed a bit extreme … but I'd watched enough movies to know that even divorced people can get back together.

My should-have-been-fifth-anniversary was an emotional tornado. I stayed in bed until almost noon, wishing Stephanie would call. When I finally got up, I sent her a Facebook message that said, "How are you today? Happy ACTUAL almost anniversary." She replied with a smiley face and a heart, and I spent the next hour or so crafting and deleting follow-up messages—eventually replying with a heart of my own, because I couldn't decide what else to say. Then I distracted myself with a marathon afternoon of Peace Warrior before channeling my emotions back into The List.

I tracked down my high-school friend, Cheyenne, on Facebook, and requested an interview. I could see that she had put on a lot of weight, and it looked like she'd been living a rough life since I'd last seen her. She seemed more like forty than twenty-nine, and her third husband, Kevin, was an equally rotund truck driver with a scraggly goatee and tattoos everywhere. I was intimidated by him—and slightly concerned that he might harbour some jealousy for the fact that Cheyenne had kissed me once in grade nine. So when she responded to my request saying they were both available to meet me the next day, I chose a public location—IHOP—to minimize my likelihood of bodily harm.

On my way to the interview, I thought about how my life might have turned out if that kiss with Cheyenne—the *first* kiss that was ever planted on me by a non-relative—had actually generated any sparks. It was cool in a moments-you'll-always-remember kind of way, but I had to admit that I was glad Cheyenne never kissed me again.

Our ninth-grade smooch didn't come up in the conversation— and it wouldn't have mattered anyway, because Kevin turned out to be a candidate for the Nicest Guy in the World contest. He was super funny and soft-spoken, and he talked a lot about his daughters from a previous marriage. I asked him questions about his first wife, too, and Cheyenne didn't mind at all. Apparently, they got along great with his former wife and her second husband—they'd even gone on camping trips and stuff to let Kevin's kids spend time with all their parents at once. I thought it sounded kind of strange—in a good way. Thinking about everything I'd done with Stephanie and Jonathan over the past couple of years, I of all people had to understand that relationships with exes could be complicated.

When I looked at The List on July 27th, I was surprised to see only two couples remaining on my A-List. I still needed to arrange a Skype call with Fiona and Marcus, so I made another mental note to do that. The other couple was Amanda and Dave Carson, whom I hadn't seen since literally *making an ass of myself* at their wedding.

Stephanie and I had been married for almost two years when we attended the Carsons' wedding, and I'd only met them a couple of times before then. Stephanie and Amanda had been good friends in Kamloops, though they'd only connected a few times since moving to Vancouver. I thought it was going to be a duty wedding—Stephanie would get to reminisce with a bunch of her high school buddies, and I would spend a lot of time on my own. But it turned out to be a blast, as I quickly learned that I'd attained stud status for marrying Stephanie Hansen. Not surprisingly, Steph had been very popular in school. We were an instant hit at the wedding, so my humour kicked in and I had a ton of fun.

Sometime around my sixth or seventh Kokanee, I mooned the entire dance floor—which earned me the nickname *Moony*. That gave me the idea to have someone draw the man in the moon on one of my butt cheeks—it took me a few tries to find someone willing to do it, but eventually some guy named Dwayne, who'd consumed at least as much alcohol as I had, agreed to get up close and personal with my hairy ass. After that, I mooned the dance floor at least a dozen more times, and I had an ass-specially fun dance when the DJ played Billy Idol's version of *Mony Mony,* which of course turned into chants of *Moony Moony*—led by my new friend, Dwayne. It was all fun and games until I tripped over a rug at the edge of the dance floor and incurred a rug-burn injury on my nose and forehead.

Over the next few days, as the skinned parts of my face scabbed over and the fog from my hangover lifted, I learned that I had offended quite a few people at the Carsons' wedding—especially Dave's family, many of whom are devout Christians. I was somewhat validated by the memory that Amanda's grandma was one of the people who had cheered me on with Moony chants. She looked like she was about ninety, and she spent most of the night standing in one place, dancing without moving her feet, smiling like a Cheshire cat, redefining awesomeness.

I had been quietly dreading my interview with Amanda and Dave the entire time I'd been working on The List. Stephanie had been ashamed of my Moony performance—my star status with others at the wedding had not gone over well with my wife. When I suggested to Steph a couple days after the wedding that we could go by the new names of Moony and *Moody,* her icy stare of death told me I'd best not talk about that wedding again. Less than eight months later, Stephanie kissed Jonathan on New Year's Eve. I'd wondered ever since if things might have turned out different if I'd kept my pants on at the Carsons' wedding.

It didn't take me long to track down Amanda on LinkedIn—the social media choice for career-driven productivity freaks, which I signed up for solely to track down people from The List. Amanda invited me to visit her and Dave in their West Vancouver mansion—which must be worth a zillion dollars, because it has a panoramic view that stretches from downtown Vancouver all the way to the gulf islands. They were already rich when they got married, but since then they'd established themselves as a true West Van power couple—Dave as an investment banker, and Amanda as a realtor selling high-end homes.

I was afraid to touch anything in the Carsons' palace—all of it looked expensive, including a bunch of perfectly re-finished antiques. Their place reminded me of rich Dr. Sloper's house in *The Heiress*—one of my favourite movies from the forties, a kind of love story chess match with Olivia de Havilland and Montgomery Clift—and I half expected a bunch of servants to make an appearance.

"Would you care for some tea?" Amanda asked as I sat down on an antique chair that was probably worth more than all my worldly possessions combined.

"Uh, no thanks," I said, afraid that I might spill it on something valuable. I thought of Sabrina McDonald and her parents' perfectly maintained home—which looked like a run-down shack compared to the Carsons' place.

"It's nice to see you," Amanda said. Dave nodded, though I didn't sense that he agreed with his wife.

"Yeah," I replied. "I don't think I've seen you since—"

"Our wedding," Dave said coldly. I looked at his smooth green shirt and sleek black pants, and I wondered how much they cost. Amanda's laugh interrupted my train of thought.

"My grandma," Amanda chortled, "was in fine form that night. The image of her chanting 'Moony, Moony' will always bring a smile to my face." I felt my own face light up at the shared memory.

"Yeah," Dave said. "She was one classy broad that night."

Amanda shot Dave a nasty look, and I remembered the feeling I'd had after their wedding—not the nauseous and embarrassed part, but the why-the-hell-did-they-get-married part. Amanda had seemed spunky and cool—someone I could enjoy hanging out with. Dave seemed like a stuffy rich kid—a tall West Van snob with a nice tux and a complete lack of personality.

"Our wedding was a lot of fun," Amanda said. "For me, anyway." She tipped her head toward Dave and said, "Not so much for Mister Serious over here ... but my grandma more than made up for his lack of enjoyment."

"Perhaps we should get down to why Bernard is here," Dave said. I felt like I was being interviewed for a servant position— Dave was sitting on a chair like mine, while Amanda sat on a fancy loveseat made of dark hardwood and embroidered cloth. I wondered for a second if Dave and Amanda ever touched one another.

"Uh, sure," I said. "I'm doing a study in relationship patterns. I just want to find out what's working well in your marriage, and what's not."

"Oh, *this* should be fun," Dave sighed.

"I'm in," Amanda said. "This has to do with you and Stephanie, right?"

"Uh, yeah," I said. "I assume you heard that we're ... taking some time apart?"

"Yeah." Amanda scrunched her face in pity. "I've reconnected with her—we meet for a walk every Saturday."

"Oh. Has she said anything about her upcoming ... you know ... ?"

"Wedding?" Amanda said. "Yeah, I'm up to speed."

"How about ... that she's having some doubts?"

Amanda nodded. "She's having pre-wedding jitters, for sure. It happens to everyone, I think. Especially the second time around."

"Huh," I said.

"This must be hard on you." Amanda's face was soft with compassion, a stark contrast to her husband's crossed arms and stone face.

"Yeah," I said directly to Amanda, trying to ignore Dave's death stare. "But I just want to understand people better, you know ... to build on for ... future relationships."

"Stephanie doesn't want to lose your friendship," Amanda said. "It means a lot to her."

I nodded, unsure how to respond.

Dave chimed in, almost cheerfully. "I have a lot of work to do. If you two are going to reminisce, I'll leave you to it."

I figured I could juice more marital advice from a boulder than I could from Dave, so I shrugged and awaited his departure. Amanda shrugged too, as if to say, "Do whatever you want," and Dave completed the shrug-fest before leaving the room. Amanda and I reverted to small talk until Dave reappeared and said, "I'm heading to the office. I'll eat downtown."

"Okay," Amanda replied as her husband slipped his shoes on and headed out the door.

"You two are pretty different," I said to Amanda, my voice settling as if I'd let out a deep breath.

"Yes, we are," she agreed.

"I don't mean to sound like a jerk, but …"

"You're wondering what I see in him?"

"Yeah."

"He's nicer than he seems. He's just a little uptight. I've been working on him for years, and believe it or not, there's been a major improvement. He's still brittle, but … under that hard shell, he's a good guy."

"Hmm," I grunted, unable to imagine Dave being anything more than an arrogant prick.

"The truth is," Amanda said, "Dave checked off most of the boxes on my list. He never swept me off my feet—romance isn't his thing—but I know he loves me, and he's …"

"A dork?" My eyes shot open as I realized I'd used my outside voice. Amanda's face hardened, and I stopped breathing. Then a smile consumed her whole face.

"Oh, my God," she said, "I see why Stephanie loves you so much."

For a second, I pondered why Amanda was so quick to forgive my technically-accurate-but-socially-questionable observation about her dorky husband. Then my mind shifted to what she'd just said. *Why Stephanie loves you …*

"You might be the most honest person I've ever met, Bernard." Amanda was still smiling. "And for the record, I thought you were a lot of fun at our wedding. Dave's family … they're a little on the conservative side."

"I noticed," I said.

"I've secretly nicknamed them the Polski Ogorkis," she said, "because they all have pickles stuck up their asses."

I laughed—snorted—and then said yes to Amanda's second offer of tea. We moved into the kitchen, which was way less stuffy than the living room, and the granite counter top didn't pose any dangerous spillage threats. We talked for an hour or more. I even admitted the real reason for my project, and I made Amanda promise not to tell Stephanie. At one point, Amanda told me she hadn't laughed so much in years. I deduced from all my questioning that she and Dave weren't really happy, but they had what she kept calling *a good life* (though the more she said it, the less I felt that she believed it). I also learned that she hated real estate, and that she would be happier living in a cottage in some small town. But Dave was lobbying for a move to Toronto, where he coveted an executive job on Bay Street.

I wondered how long Amanda could keep up the charade of happiness that she had locked into when she married Mister Serious. When I finally left, she leaned out the doorway and said, "Good luck with your project, Bernard. I don't know how it'll turn out, but … no matter what, I hope you and Steph both end up happy."

Me too, I thought. *Me too.*

THE KNIFE

Arnie

"WAY TO GO, MAN." Looking at the diagram Bernard had spread across the largest table at The Big Bean, I tried to sound enthusiastic. Bernard only had to Skype his cousin Fiona to complete the A-List—which was no small feat for a guy who never completed anything. "So, what are you calling this beauty?"

"I haven't named it yet," he said. The chart had all sixteen couples from The List on it. He had listed positive attributes in green and negative attributes in red for each couple, along with their marital status. Looking more closely, I noticed that under "Bernard and Stephanie" he had written almost entirely positive attributes, with the only negative being "Jonathan"; and for his own marital status, he had written "Crisis" instead of "Divorced." He'd added a seventeenth couple—Jonathan and Stephanie— whose list of negative attributes was long. Their positive list was empty, and their status was listed as "Delusional."

"So, what's next?"

"I might try some statistical analysis," Bernard said.

"What about all that stuff you said about pattern recognition?"

"I know, right? But I've gotta try something. I'm running out of time, and I'm having a hard time seeing any clear patterns. I even tried staring at this with my eyes crossed—like I used to do with those stupid 3D pictures you could only see if you entered some kind of altered-mind state—but nothing's come to me yet."

"So … what do you know about analysis?" I asked, feigning interest.

"I've been reading up on cluster analysis and linear regression, but I can't figure out how to group my data so it means anything. I'm kinda stumped."

"Maybe it's not that complicated. Maybe you just need to get out of your own way and let it come to you."

"I don't have time for that."

"Well, you know how much I love stats." I shuddered at the memory of the one statistics course I took at university.

"Yeah, I know, but you're the academic. Do you have any ideas at all?"

We both stared at the chart for a while, and I built up the courage to speak what was really on my mind. "Bernard," I said, "I've been thinking about what you did at JR's."

Bernard dropped his head and stared into his lap.

"You really crossed a line—"

"Shut up," he said. "I was drunk."

"That's not an acceptable—"

"I said shut up." He glanced at me briefly before looking out the window.

"I'm worried about you."

"You and everyone else," he snapped.

"Well, I had to say it. That's the kind of thing that changes how someone views you. It's not okay."

"I didn't even touch her."

"No, but you still violated her."

"Shut up, man." Bernard looked straight into my eyes and spoke with an unusually quiet voice. "Do you want the whole world to hear you? I'm not some kind of pervert, you know. I was just ... really ... drunk."

We stared at each other for a long while before I said, "We both know that doesn't justify what you did. You're better than that, Bernard. Aren't you?"

"You tell me," Bernard replied.

I wasn't surprised that B-man deflected the question back to me, and I was relieved that I had voiced what I'd come to say. I didn't have any idea what to say next, so I changed the subject. "So ... the wedding's only three weeks away."

"Yeah," Bernard said.

"Are you still planning to go—you know, assuming—?"

"Assuming I fail to stop the wedding?"

"Yeah."

"If I can't derail the wedding ahead of time, then I'll have to be there to stop it."

I cringed at the damage Bernard could do when he was actually trying to disrupt a wedding, given what I'd seen him accomplish without even meaning to.

"I might invite Sabrina," he blurted.

"The redhead with the baby?"

"Yeah," he nodded.

"Why?"

"I don't know. She's female ... she's safe date territory ... and she knows Steph. She might even be invited already, for all I know. If not, I could present her with a win-win situation—she gets a night away from her claustrophobizone, and I get to give Steph a dose of what-if-Bernie-really-did-find-someone-else."

I curled my lips together and counted to ten, allowing the words I was thinking—idiot, moron, fool—to dissolve in my head.

Then I spoke as calmly as I could. "You think it's a good idea to ask a widow out to a wedding to help you make your ex-wife jealous?"

"That's a pretty harsh way to describe it."

"Harsh ... or accurate?" I asked.

Bernard changed the subject again. "Have you seen Steph and Bozo lately?"

"Yeah," I nodded. "A couple of times."

"Huh." Bernard stared at his massive document for a long time before he blurted, "The KNIFE! I'm calling this diagram The KNowledge In Feelings Examination chart. It's about examining how people feel ... and using that knowledge to sever a relationship that wasn't meant to be. I'm sure there's a pattern in here somewhere ... I just haven't seen it yet."

"I'm at a loss," I said. "I want to help you, really help you, but I don't think ... this whole thing just seems ..."

"What are you trying to say?" Bernard asked.

"That ... I don't think trying to stop Steph's wedding is a good idea ... for anyone."

"Easy for you to say. You've got Yoko."

I fought hard to contain the stream of profanity that wanted to escape my lips. Just when I was about to say something, Bernard reached into his knapsack and pulled out a small wrapped package.

"I almost forgot," he said. "Your birthday's coming up. I know you've been busy, so ... in case I don't see you ..."

As Bernard handed the package across the table, I suddenly felt ashamed. "Thanks," I said. "I'm sorry I didn't get you anything."

"It's okay," he said, but I sensed his disappointment, and I felt like a schmuck for forgetting how much birthdays mean to Bernard Kirby.

TURNCOATS

Bernard

AUGUST 6TH, 2015—sixteen days before the wedding I planned to sabotage. I'd made no measurable headway with The List, The Roadmap or The KNIFE. I'd spoken to Arnie once since our last Big Bean chat a week earlier, and he explained on the phone that he was feeling conflicted about my wedding derailment plans because he and Loretta were starting to get cozy with Stephanie and Jonathan. Those weren't his exact words, but that was definitely the message. Once I realized Arnie's loyalties were in question, I knew I'd have to forge ahead without a wingman.

I tried plotting and grouping my data in all different ways, looking for patterns to emerge. I tried assigning numeric values to different relationship attributes—rating couples for the similarity of their values and interests; for their attitudes toward children; and for the steaminess of their relationships. (I gave Amanda and Dave a one for steaminess. Tamara and Tracy got a ten.)

The more I looked at the data—the more I sliced and diced, mapped and plotted it—the less clear it became. I was starting to wonder if love was a dark art that nobody really mastered. Many of the couples who seemed happy didn't have much in common, and some of the ones who were miserable or divorced looked like good matches. It was like the BC Lions, who looked awesome on paper, but there they were with two wins and three losses.

I'd been so preoccupied with Stephanie—and all the other stuff that happened to me because of her—that I'd hardly paid attention to the Leos' first five games. I was glad for the distraction that would come that night from painting my face orange and black, riding the Skytrain down to BC Place with my family, and yelling derogatory things at the green and gold villains from Edmonton. But I also felt sad about going to my first game of the year—sad because the fat biker dude with the handlebar moustache who'd been sitting in row 12, seat 16, for the past two years didn't belong there. That was Stephanie's seat. The one she had occupied for three amazing years, after my mom masterminded a multi-person season-ticket swap to land an extra seat in our row. In the interest of family unity, my parents had always treated Bruno and me to tickets. They added Steph's ticket as an early wedding gift, and they carried on the tradition as anniversary gifts for the next two seasons. Then, in 2013, when my mom informed the Lions that we would be reducing our ticket count to four—despite my argument that we should hold onto it for when Stephanie came back to her senses—fat biker dude swooped down like a moustached vulture and snatched the extra ticket from our grasp.

When I walked into the kitchen, Mom was already painting a lion outline on Bruno's face with black eyeliner, and Dad was waiting to fill it in with dark orange blush. I was eager to receive my face-paint mask; to feel anonymous; to pretend I was someone else for a few hours.

As my mom worked her artistic genius on my face-canvas, I thought about how much my seat at BC Place felt like home—despite my sadness about Stephanie's absence and my disdain for the guy who took her place. That seat—and the memories it evoked—was bigger than any one chapter of my life, or any relationship. For as long as I could remember, Lions games were a part of me. Even Stephanie and Jonathan and handlebar-moustache biker dude couldn't take that away from me.

When I climbed into the Jetta wearing my prized Lui Passaglia jersey, I felt excited—maybe even happy. My belly was temporarily placated with borderline-edible gluten-free pizza, and I was looking forward to downing a greasy burger at the game.

As we parked the car and walked to the Skytrain, my family reminisced about Lions highlights from the past, especially their 1994 Grey Cup win, when Lui kicked his way into my eight-year-old heart with a last-second field goal. It was almost as if I'd never met a beautiful woman who had become part of our football family and then deserted us. Almost like I was a kid again, and my parents were taking me to watch the game with my little brother—except now I was old enough to drink beer, which made it extra awesome.

We rode the Skytrain to Stadium Station, then walked up Beatty Street and turned onto Terry Fox Pavilion. Pausing to look at the four statues of one of Canada's greatest heroes, tears formed in my eyes. Dad had told me the story of Terry Fox when I was a little bumpkin: about how he ran the equivalent of a marathon a day for 143 days—on one leg—and then died of the cancer that had claimed his other leg. The Terry Fox statues have always reminded me not to forget stuff that's important.

I caught up with my family in one of the line-ups for the entrance gate. I had my game face on, and I could feel the electricity of the gathering crowd. That's when I saw the turncoats standing in the line beside us.

It wasn't just that I saw them there, *together*; it was the way they were carrying on, laughing like there was some big joke that

I wasn't part of—or maybe I was the butt of, for all I knew. Arnie even put his arm around Jonathan and patted him on the back, like they were the closest of friends—like I didn't matter, even though I was the reason they'd gotten to know each other in the first place. Loretta and Stephanie looked all chummy, too, and the whole scene made my insides churn.

"Bernie!" Stephanie called out when she saw me looking at her happy foursome, "I thought we might see you here."

"Hi, B-man," Loretta said, grinning from ear to ear.

Arnie and Jonathan both said, "Hey," so I joined the monosyllabic male greeting ritual with a "Hey" of my own.

Then my parents joined in the fray, making it seem like some grand reunion. Next thing I knew, the four traitors were standing in our line with us.

Once we got inside the gate, my dad said, "It's nice to see you all—and to meet you, Loretta. We've heard so much about you from Bernard."

Loretta beamed and said, "It's nice to meet your whole pride."

Mom and Dad looked at each other, confused by their first exposure to a Loretta-ism. Loretta pointed at my face and said, "The makeup. You Kirby boys look very ... feline."

Stephanie made a fake sad face and said to my mom, "I miss your face paint—and I miss you guys, too. You're still like family to me."

"We had a lot of good times," Mom replied half-heartedly.

After a bit of silent group awkwardness, the four of them turned and headed to find their seats.

I was in a trance while I bought a burger and beer. I couldn't stop thinking about how comfortable my former friends looked together. The least they could have done was tell me they were going.

When Travis Lulay hit Emmanuel Arceneaux for a Lions touch-down three minutes into the game, I downed the last half of my first beer and started into my second. My mood was buoyed as I got into watching the game. Then, just before the first quarter ended, some sadistic, demented stadium employee decided it was a good time to project a Kiss Cam on the giant screen in the middle of the field.

At first it was just stupid. Most of the couples pecked like birds, a few of them blushed like flamingos, and one older couple revved up the crowd by performing an impressively dextrous dip. When the dementoid cameraman focused on two people who looked aghast at being chosen—I think they might have been twins—the whole stadium groaned uneasily.

Then it happened. Jonathan and Stephanie appeared on the big screen, as if they'd been waiting for that moment. They stood up in front of twenty thousand people, and Jonathan dipped Stephanie like they'd been planning it—like they'd *wanted* to put on a show, just to crush the last remaining scraps of my dignity. He leaned down and gave her a huge, open-mouthed kiss. The camera lingered on them for what seemed like an hour as they sucked face. I'm sure I even saw some tongue, which is *way* out of bounds for Kiss Cam protocol. When they finally unlocked their faces and stood up, they looked at the camera with messed up hair and guilty smiles—like they'd just had sex. The crowd roared as if the Lions had won the Grey Cup, and I bolted from my seat.

Bruno tugged my arm and said, "Bernard," but I pulled away and squeezed past handlebar-moustache biker dude, who stood up to let me pass.

As I stormed up the stairs, the enormous stadium—which usually felt cavernous and empty with less than half its seats filled—was closing in on me. I gasped for air as I climbed the last few steps and walked into the concourse, brooding about Stephanie and Jonathan's kiss. *Hadn't she told me that she was unsure about their wedding? And that she missed me?* She didn't seem unsure of anything as she put on the biggest, baddest Kiss Cam show I'd ever seen.

I walked laps around the concourse for the rest of the first half. Dad and Bruno found me—they were walking in the opposite direction, looking for me—but after a brief fatherly lecture disguised as sympathy, I told them I didn't want to talk and continued my lap-walking. I lost count of my beer consumption—I used up the cash I'd brought with me, then stopped at an ATM to withdraw the last of my birthday funds.

I had passed through rage and sadness, but something shifted in me when I saw the throngs of people coming up for halftime. I pushed my bitterly jaded body through the crowd and returned to my seat, where my mom looked very relieved to see me.

"Bernard," Mom said, "I know …" She couldn't find any more words. How *could* she know? My dad had been her first serious boyfriend—they'd *always* been together. She didn't have the first clue what it was like to have your heart ripped out of your chest repeatedly. And she certainly didn't know what it was like to see your ex-wife kissing her scumbag of a fiancée on the Kiss Cam in front of twenty thousand people.

Looking away from my mom, I locked eyes with Bruno. I was starting to see double. "Sorry bro," he said. Even though we aren't particularly close, Bruno has always had a reassuring effect on me. Right then, he gave me exactly the look I needed.

The beer really caught up with me by the end of halftime, and when the Lions scored a touchdown early in the third quarter to bring them within six points of the Eskimos, I got all riled up and started rallying the crowd around me.

I started with chants of "Go Lions Go!" and "Leeeooooos!" Then I repeated some of my favourite cheers from when I was younger, back when two crazy guys wearing pyjamas with lion tails united the crowd with ridiculous sayings.

I got a few people going with: "Go Esks Go! Go Esks Go! Around the track and out the back, Go Esks Go!" Then I moved onto: "Cigarette ashes, cigarette butts; We've got the Eskimos by the nuts! Pull, team, puuuuullllllll!"

I glanced at my family and could see that they were getting uncomfortable with my antics, but with every chant I was growing less concerned about what anyone thought of me. If Stephanie and Jonathan could act out a soft-core porno on the big screen, I could do whatever I wanted to get the crowd going.

Late in the third quarter, my buzz reached its peak. I rose from my seat and turned to face the crowd above me. Like a conductor, I waved my arms in what I remember as a graceful act (though Bruno told me later that I looked like a buzzard in flight). Then I sang at the top of my lungs:

I'd rather be a Lion than a fucking Eskimo
I'd rather be a Lion than a fucking Eskimo
I'd rather be a Lion than a fucking Eskimo
'Cause Eskimos suck balls ...

Bruno tried to pull me down by my arm, but I refused to budge. Then my mom reached over and tapped me on the shoulder, and I remember my dad saying "Ber-nard!" with his most assertive voice. But I tuned out my family and kept singing.

Some guy above me yelled, "Sit down, fat boy! There's kids here." That only made me sing louder, which apparently wasn't well received by most of the people in our section.

The next thing I remember was being escorted up the stairway by two security guards. I didn't fight them—all my energy had been used up thinking hateful thoughts about my former friends—but I kept on singing. The security guards were gentle with me, and Bruno said that by the time I got to the concourse I was barely muttering the song.

Then I barfed—right in mid-stride, all over myself and on one of the security guard's shoes. My memory of what happened after that is spotty, but I recall sitting in front of the stadium with my mom while Bruno went to get water and paper towels. And I remember that my dad didn't come with us—he stayed to watch the game, no doubt brooding about what a loser his eldest son had become.

Mom and Bruno made me drink a full bottle of water, and they cleaned me up as best they could while I stared at the Terry Fox statues and cried. I'd never been able to look at those statues without feeling guilty for having two legs and a body that isn't riddled with cancer. But that day, Terry Fox made me feel like a worthless piece of crap.

NOT HOME

Arnie

"Hi, Arnie," Blanche said. "I'm supposed to tell you he's not home."

"Still, huh?"

"Yes. He's hardly emerged from his bedroom in three days."

"Well, tell him I called, will you?"

"I will. For a guy who thinks everyone hates him, he sure gets a lot of phone calls."

"Yeah," I sighed. It was a coordinated effort—both Stephanie and Jonathan had also attempted to reach Bernard multiple times since the Kiss Cam disaster.

I said goodbye to Blanche and went to sit beside Loretta, who was sipping a cup of tea on my couch. Resting my arm on her knees, I said, "I tried."

"I know," she replied. "Keep trying."

"For how long?"

"As long as it takes, silly." Then she tipped her head toward the gift Bernard had given me, which was sitting on my coffee table. "Are you going to open it?"

I picked up the gift, feeling a strange combination of appreciation and resentment. It wasn't like *I'd* kissed Stephanie on the Jumbotron, so why wouldn't he talk to me—on my birthday, no less?

I looked at the gift again—it was slightly larger than my hand, rectangular and mostly flat. I peeled away the wrapping paper and two layers of tissue, and was stunned to find Bernard's framed, autographed picture of Doug Flutie in a BC Lions jersey.

"Who's that?" Loretta asked.

"Only the greatest player to ever wear a Lions jersey," I said. "Bernard got this when he was about six—before I even met him. I ogled it a few times over the years, and he knew I loved it. I can't believe ..." I was truly speechless that Bernard would part with such a treasured keepsake.

"He's a good guy," Loretta said.

"Yeah. I sometimes forget that. I know he doesn't have much money right now, so I guess ... man, I feel like such a jerk."

"Why?"

"I didn't even get him a birthday gift. And I've been feeling so frustrated with him. I've even been questioning whether he's as good a person as I've always thought he was."

Loretta smiled and said, "He's a better person with you as a best friend."

THESE BREASTS

Bernard

IF I BELIEVED IN GOD, I would have thanked Him for the call I received on August 10th.

For the first few days after the Kiss Cam debacle, I abandoned all hope of stopping Steph and Jonathan's wedding. I didn't feel like I could ever be happy again. On the fourth day of my hangover that wouldn't go away, I still had little appetite and no desire to leave my bedroom. Mom kept bringing me food, which I pecked away at, but after a few failed attempts she stopped trying to get me to talk.

Then Sabrina McDonald called.

Despite strict orders to tell anyone who called that I wasn't home, Mom demonstrated amazing intuition when she knocked on my door and said, "Bernard ... someone from your list is on the phone. Sabrina."

I had thought about Sabrina a few times since the day I'd interviewed her, but I never expected *her* to call *me*. I hesitated for a minute, then opened the door and reached out my hand. Mom gave me the phone and said, "You're welcome."

I closed the door and put the phone to my face. "Sabrina? What's up?"

"Hi, Bernard. I just wanted someone to talk to," she replied. "A real conversation, you know? I can only go so far with my parents. They're ... well, you met them ..."

"Anal retentive?"

"Yeah," she laughed. "I like talking to you. You're so forthright."

"A little too forthright for some people's liking."

"Well, you opened me up when you came to visit. It was therapeutic."

"Huh," I said. "Could you tell that to my friend Arnie?"

Sabrina laughed again, and the discussion got really comfortable. Before long I was telling her all about my plan to win back Stephanie, and I even told her about the Kiss Cam episode. She kept me talking for an hour or more—it was like I imagined confession would be, except that I was talking to an attractive woman instead of a supposedly-celibate old dude in a penguin suit. I told Sabrina about the Vegreville Egg, about the Carsons' wedding, and about the time I launched myself off the stage at the Roxy. I told her about kissing Tamara; about falling for a lesbian; about dress shopping with Stephanie. I told Sabrina so many things that I wouldn't normally have admitted to anyone—especially to a girl.

When Mikey woke up from a nap, I could hear him crying in the background. Sabrina said, "Well, my little man's calling for my breast," and then she teased, *"you guys* ... you start so young."

I felt something stir within my loins, and for the first time I was a bit nervous about what I might say to Sabrina. I just laughed and said, "Yeah."

"Thanks for this," Sabrina said. "I really needed a friend today."

"Me too," I agreed, taking solace from the fact that someone else was feeling as lonely as I was.

Mikey had stopped crying, so it was a bit awkward—as if neither of us wanted to stop talking, but we both felt that we were supposed to. "I guess I'd better go," Sabrina said.

"Hey," I replied, trying to keep the conversation going just a little longer, "were you invited to Stephanie's wedding?"

"No," she replied. "I haven't talked to her since I moved to Fort Mac. We just kind of … grew apart."

"Would you go with me?" I blurted. "It's on the 22nd."

Sabrina was silent for a long time. Then she said, "I don't know. It would be nice to see Steph … but …"

"Never mind," I said. "It's a crazy idea. I just thought … it would be nice to have company. Especially if they go ahead with the whole *I do* thing." It was the first time I'd admitted that Stephanie and Jonathan might actually get married—and that I might not be able to stop it.

Sabrina took a long time to reply. Finally she said, "I'll think about it. With Mikey … I mean, if I did go, I wouldn't be able to stay out late. These breasts, you know … they're in high demand."

"I'm sure they are," I said. "Well, just let me know."

After we said goodbye and hung up, I had a shower—my first in four days—and joined my parents at the dinner table.

PEACE OFFERING

Arnie

BERNARD WAS SURPRISINGLY CHEERFUL when I dropped by his house on my way to work.

"What's this?" he asked when I handed him the envelope at his front door.

"A very belated birthday gift. I decided it was better late than never."

"Uh, thanks. Feels like a peace offering."

"I guess it is. Open it—it's self-explanatory."

Bernard opened the envelope, pulled out a Big Bean gift certificate, and then read the card I'd written—which explained that my gift included the ear of a good friend. I knew that Bernard had very little money, and I hoped that personalizing an otherwise lame gift would mean something to him.

"Thanks," he said. "Have time to come in for a bit?"

"No, I have to work. I just wanted to drop this off ... and say thanks for the Flutie picture. I know how much that picture means to you. I'll take good care of it."

"Yeah, no biggie," Bernard said. But I knew that it was a big deal—for him and for our friendship.

"Let's use that gift certificate soon," I said. "I'm overdue for an update."

"About what?" Bernard asked.

"The List … your emotional well-being … everything. I'm just wondering where you're at these days."

"I dunno," he said. "I think I'm suffering from a case of blender-brain."

"That's understandable," I replied. "So, what's your next step?"

Bernard shook his head. "I have no friggin' clue. I'm waiting for a sign ... or for an anvil to fall on my head and put me out of my female-induced misery."

"I hope the sign arrives first."

"Thanks," Bernard said.

The levity of our conversation left me feeling lighter than I'd felt in weeks.

THE RESUME

Bernard

AFTER ARNIE DROPPED BY WITH A BELATED BIRTHDAY GIFT, my dad came into the office where I was playing Peace Warrior with Fluffball.

"Hey, Scout," Dad said, leaning over the back of my chair to watch me dig a well, "I might have a job opportunity for you."

I stopped moving my fingers on the keyboard, and my Warrior stopped digging. "What kind of job?" I asked.

"A bit of this and that. Various office work."

"Like, filing and stuff?"

"Yeah, and some data entry. Maybe even a bit of bookkeeping once you're up to speed."

"Huh." I moved my fingers again, pretending to focus on my game.

"Our office manager is overloaded," he said, "and my boss has been really happy with Bruno, so he thought—"

"I'm not Bruno."

"I know," Dad sighed. "I'm not comparing you. I just … I'd like to see you …"

"Get a life?"

"Don't start with me, son," he said. "We're not helping you by feeding and housing you while you sit on your butt all day, or by loaning you money whenever you need it. It's time for you to get back on your own two feet."

"You want me to pay rent?" I asked, focusing again on the hole my Warrior was digging.

"That would be a start," he replied.

"Bruno never had to pay rent."

"He was going to school full time," Dad said, his voice rising. "Your brother moved out at twenty-two—and got a full-time job. Bernard … you're twenty-nine years old."

"I know how old I am," I said, kicking myself for comparing myself to my incomparable sibling.

"Do you?" He let the question hang, and it felt like he'd stunned me with a Taser. My own dad—who had mostly stayed out of my problems, except for the occasional lecture—was now piling on, adding his name to the list of people suggesting that I'd never grown up. I'd been married, for Chrissake, and it wasn't my fault that I'd been abandoned. I tried to ignore my hurt feelings and focus on my Warrior, who had finished digging and was ready to construct the well.

Dad broke the silence. "Look, I'm here for you … and I'm offering you an opportunity." He set a sheet of paper on the edge of the desk and added, "If you're interested, I'd like to take your resume in by Friday. Your mom's a whiz with that stuff … I'm sure she'd help."

"Okay," I said, still staring at the screen. "Thanks."

I thought about the job opportunity for the rest of the day. Nobody mentioned it at supper, but it sat there like an elephant between my dad and me. After dinner, I stayed up late trying to work on my resume, and it caused me to do some soul searching. That was probably Dad's real reason for suggesting the job—he has a way of injecting lessons and messages into things. I felt like the job opportunity was one of those lesson-messages, and I was a bit stoked about it.

I've always liked my dad's office—it's funky, and there's a couple of super cute women there. I'd been jealous of Bruno for following in Dad's footsteps, especially because he got to see Trina Bergenheim—the office manager who would be my boss if I got the job—on a daily basis. Trina was in her late thirties and had three kids, but she'd worked for the company forever and I'd had a crush on her since I was thirteen—long before she became a hot mama. I had to admit that the thought of working with Trina Bergenheim was a big motivator to dust off my resume.

The problem was that my resume sucked. I'd lasted six weeks as an assistant paperboy when I was fourteen, before repeated sleep-ins got me fired. I tried retail three times—my longest stint being two months at a discount shoe store, where I got sacked for missing three shifts in a row. I endured almost four months in the grease pit at Dairy Queen, until I referred to an obese customer as a carnivorous brute for ordering a quintuple bacon cheeseburger and two large milkshakes. (That firing was really unfair, because I'd totally meant it as a compliment.) I made it through two-and-a-half shifts selling video games, where I was apparently expected to do more than demonstrate my Xbox skills. And although my recent five-month stint at White Spot was a personal record for employment duration, even that micro-success hardly felt like a springboard for career advancement.

My education was equally spotty. I'd done okay in high school, but post-secondary was a whole different story. I made it through half a semester of Computer Systems Technology, which required way more exertion than I'd bargained for. I dropped out of Marketing because the sadistic program scheduler made me use my friggin' alarm clock *three days a week*. And I tried some writing courses when Stephanie urged me to channel my creative awesomeness into prose. I dropped my first two attempts at literature—journalism and poetry—because they turned out to be long on drudgery and short on amusement. But I was signed up to start a sci-fi short story course—which was totally up my alley—when Stephanie dropped the bomb about her lust-crush on Jonathan. I had a severe dip in motivation after that and didn't even bother to show up for the first class.

I went to bed feeling crappy about my resume, convinced that my chances of landing the job at my dad's firm were slim to none. I overslept the next day, and I might have given up on my resume altogether if it hadn't been for another phone call from Sabrina McDonald. She just called to chat again, which was cool, because there wasn't exactly a line-up of attractive women who called me to chat. She'd been having a tough week, thanks to Mikey falling into a nocturnal vampire sleep pattern. She seemed a bit sad at first, but she was laughing by the end of our conversation, and we agreed to talk again soon. I almost asked her again about Stephanie's wedding, but I decided not to, and she didn't mention it either.

After talking to Sabrina, I asked my mom for help on the resume. Dad was right about mom having serious skills in the art of self-promotion. Within a couple of hours, I had a resume and a cover letter that made it sound like my inability to hold down a job was a positive. My cover letter mentioned stuff like "breadth of knowledge" and "a wide variety of skills." On my resume, we consolidated a few of my least productive jobs into a section of impressive-looking bullet points under the heading *Other Experience.* By the time we were done, I felt a trace of optimism that thanks to Mom's wording, Dad's influence as a senior architect, and Bruno's demonstration of Kirby offspring success, I might have a chance to work for Trina Bergenheim.

Mom and I were savouring a well-earned lemonade on the back porch when the phone rang. Feeling encouraged by my resume and still warm from the call with Sabrina, I jumped up and ran to the phone, answering it with a jovial, "Y'ello."

"Hi, Bernie."

I was so shocked to hear Stephanie's voice that I froze solid. In the week since the Kiss Cam event, Steph had gone in and out of my mind like a strobe light—one second she was all I could think about, and the next moment it was like she'd been erased from my memory. Sitting on the porch drinking lemonade with my mom, I'd temporarily forgotten that Stephanie Hansen existed. Then, with one "Hi, Bernie," it was like everything that happened between Steph and me came back in a flash of light, reminding me that in nine days my ex-best friend was planning to marry the love of my life and dash all the hopes and dreams that I'd shared with her.

"Bernie," she said again in her softest voice, the one that never failed to melt my heart, "are you okay?"

"I don't know," I said.

"I'm sorry. The game ... I wasn't thinking."

"Yeah," I muttered.

I heard Stephanie breathing, but neither of us spoke for a while. Then she said, "What are you up to on Saturday night?"

"I dunno," I said. "There's an early Lions game on TV, but nothing after that. Why?"

"It's my stagette," Stephanie said. "Jonathan and I are joining forces for a Jack-and-Jill. We'd like to have you there—we both would—if you're up for it."

"I dunno," I said again.

"You and me," she said, "we've had quite a history together."

"Uh-huh."

"It's pretty cool that we've been able to remain friends, isn't it?"

I didn't say anything.

"Bernie?" she said, almost too sweetly.

"Yeah?"

"I really want you there on Saturday. We're going to the Roxy, and ... we have so many good memories there ..."

I waited for her to continue.

"I still want you in my life, Bernie. You've always ..."

"What? What have I always?"

"I don't know," she said. "I can't describe it. But I like knowing that you're there. So, how about Saturday?"

I clenched my jaw as I contemplated a reply, trying not to say something I would regret. I was angry at Stephanie for everything she'd done to me, and yet I still yearned for her—at times more than ever. Feeling more confused than any person should have to feel, I said, "I'll see ... I want to be there, and I don't."

"Well, think about it," Stephanie said. "It would mean a lot to me."

"Okay," I replied. Then we said goodbye and I stood there holding the phone, my brain like a slate of concrete, unable to hold a cohesive thought.

Eventually, I returned to the patio in an attempt to recapture the peaceful mindset I'd had before Stephanie called. But I felt completely messed up. Sabrina had started my day on a positive note, and my mom had pumped me up with her resume-building skills. Then the call from Steph hit me like a punch in the gut, and the idea that I could live a meaningful existence without her vanished in an instant.

AIDING AND ABETTING

Arnie

"YOU THINK THIS IS A GOOD IDEA?" I asked Loretta as we drove to Bernard's house to pick him up for the Jack-and-Jill party.

"Of course not," she said.

"Then why are we ..."

"Aiding and abetting a potential wedding thief?"

"Yeah."

"Because," Loretta said, "he has to figure this out for himself. They all do."

"You mean ... you think it's a good idea to put them together in a room—a room with alcohol and a lot of shared history—a week before the wedding?"

"No," she said.

"Then why are we?"

"Because they've already made so many bad choices that this seems almost ... so wrong that it's right."

"You don't always make sense, you know."

"I know," Loretta beamed. "Isn't that part of why you love me?"

I smiled and replied, "Yeah, it is."

199

THE ROXY

Bernard

AFTER I WATCHED THE LIONS GET CRUSHED by the Hamilton Tiger-Cats, Arnie and Loretta picked me up to head downtown. My family lobbied me to skip the festivities, but I had already squandered too many hours that could have been spent derailing Stephanie and Jonathan's wedding. With only a week to go, I could no longer waste a single opportunity to get between them.

I fretted a bit when we walked through the door of the Roxy, praying that none of the bouncers would recognize me from my flying Foo Fighter incident a year earlier. I exhaled in relief when I made it to the heart of the venue, where Stephanie and Jonathan were sitting with two couples I didn't know—and Tamara, who was flying solo while Tracy held the Leo's clipboard in Hamilton.

The table was already littered with empty glasses, and the group was talking loudly about wedding stuff, which made me want to puke. They were all wearing idiotic accessories—the girls donning leopard-coloured cat ears while the guys wore clip-on bowties of all different colours.

Jonathan handed a blue bowtie to Arnie while Stephanie placed a set of leopard ears on Loretta's head. Then Jonathan held up a pink bowtie to my face and said, "Hey, it's your shade."

"Huh," I grunted, taking the bowtie and trying not to let his smile distract me from my mission.

"I'm glad you're here," Jonathan added, and despite the sincerity of his voice—or maybe because of it—I felt my heart harden.

"Wouldn't miss it," I said coldly, stiffening in determination.

I had to stay focused, which meant I couldn't drink myself into oblivion. I didn't have much money, anyway—I'd talked Mom into loaning me another sixty bucks for the night, against my dad's wishes—so I had to be very strategic about my alcohol consumption. I decided to pretend I was a designated driver, requesting free ginger ale from a waitress with tattoos all over her shoulder and neck.

When the house band started, most of our group bolted for the dance floor.

"Come on," Tamara yelled over the music and gently grabbed my wrist. She looked radiant, in a plain way. Like Grace Kelly—the kind of natural beauty who could take your breath away without any help from the makeup department.

Despite Tamara's allure, I didn't know if I was capable of dancing without alcoholic lubrication, so I said, "I'm not up for it yet."

Tamara gave me a gloomy smile before saying "Okay" and heading out to join her friends. I felt kinda funny knowing that Tamara Spencer was sad to be turned down by *me* for a dance.

I became the group's de facto table-sitter—which gave me a good perch for watching the dance-floor action. I'd never experienced the Roxy without booze—it was like an out-of-body experience, being the only sober guy in a group of drunk people. But there was something oddly intoxicating about it—maybe it was the sugar buzz. Whatever it was, I kinda liked the feeling of sobriety. So I kept ordering ginger ales from tattoo chick while the rest of my so-called friends consumed a wide range of alcohol and partied like there was something to celebrate.

I sat and watched and pondered my next move. Stephanie and Jonathan both disappeared into the mob—separately—for long stretches of time, maximizing their opportunities to flirt with as many different people as possible. Tamara joined me at the table more than anyone else, though it was too loud to really talk. She finally dragged me onto the dance floor while Arnie and Loretta took over table-sitting duties to stare at one another with googly eyes.

Without a dose of liquid courage, my moves were half-hearted. Sobriety didn't lend itself to the kind of dancing I was known for, but I still didn't want to have a drink. There was a small part of me that feared becoming the guy who climbed up on stage and hijacked a Foo Fighters song. I was worried that if I did anything remotely questionable, one of the bouncers *would* recognize me and kick my ass out of the bar.

When a song I didn't know started to play, I turned to walk off the dance floor. Tamara came with me.

"How are you doing, Bernie?" Tamara asked, yelling into my ear to be heard over the music.

"I'm okay," I yelled back.

"I know this is hard for you." I could feel her hair brushing against my neck, and it felt good to be so close to her.

"I guess," I said. I realized then that I had felt kind of numb all night. With all the loud music and lights and people screeching, I was experiencing sensory overload. I felt the whole place vibrating to the boom-boom-boom of the sub-woofer. Even my sense of smell was overwhelmed by the strange concoction of alcohol, sweat and romance that wafted through the room. "I need some air," I said.

"That makes two of us," Tamara replied.

Right then, Stephanie appeared at the table. She stumbled into me with a clumsy attempt at a hug. I stood up, wrapped my arms around her, and held on tight.

"Bernie," she slur-yelled. "Where have you been?"

"Here," I replied.

"I've missed you," she spat into my ear. "My Ber-nie."

Sober Bernard wasn't sure how to deal with drunk Stephanie. In all the years I'd partied with her, I'd always been at least as drunk as her.

Stephanie rested her head on my shoulder, her leopard-cat ears tickling my ear, and said, "Why'd I leave you, Bernie? You were good to me."

I hoped that Tamara couldn't hear anything Steph was saying, because I was actually embarrassed by the whole scene.

"I still love you," Steph said. "You know that … right?"

The song stopped, and she was still draped all over me. My own arms dropped to my side. I pulled away from her and said, "Then why are you marrying *him*?"

Steph looked at me and smiled weakly, saying nothing. The leopard-cat ears sat at an angle on her head, amplifying her intoxication.

The next song began—*Shout*—and brought with it memories of so many fun nights at the Roxy. Steph and I had always danced like maniacs to the Isley Brothers classic.

She leaned into me and yelled, "You *have* to dance with me. It's *our* song."

I raised my voice to speak over the music. "I can't. I can't stay here and watch you go home with *him* again."

I stepped back and looked at Stephanie—really looked at her—imperfections and all. Her eyes were droopy, her cheeks had fallen, and the thick layer of foundation on her face made her look like a doll—a very drunk doll. Clumsily, she raised her hand and placed it on my face.

I turned away, Steph's fingers brushing against my neck as I broke her spell and put some distance between us.

I tipped my head toward Tamara, then looked back at Stephanie and attempted to smile before walking away. The band was in full swing playing *our* song as I headed through the door, past the bouncers and onto the sidewalk.

I looked at the lineup for the Roxy and saw a bunch of dolled-up kids. I was ten years older than some of the people in the lineup—and there *I* was, sober and single, heading home to my childhood bed. Just as I started to lament about my status as a Roxy elder, I heard a familiar voice.

"Bernie!" Tamara said. "Are you okay?"

"Hey," I replied, happy for the company of a fellow old-timer.

"Tough night, huh?"

I nodded.

"At least we don't have to deal with hangovers tomorrow." Tamara reached over and removed the pink bowtie that I'd forgotten I was wearing.

"You're sober, too?" I asked.

"Yeah. I've been drinking cranberry-and-soda all night." She leaned in close to me and said, "I haven't told anyone other than my family yet, but ... I'm pregnant."

"You're *what?*" I felt a warm sensation building in my chest. Even though years of crushes and one failed reverse seduction suggested I should have felt a shard of jealousy, I only felt happiness for Tamara and Tracy. A wide smile formed as I wrapped my arms around her. "That's awesome," I said before releasing her from my overly enthusiastic hug. "I'm sorry. I hope … I mean, you're …"

"It's okay, Bernie." Tamara laughed. "I'm only two-and-a-half months. She's tiny—and well-protected."

"She?"

"Actually, I don't know. I'm calling her a she for now. I don't really care, but … I've had my fill of football gear and stinky socks."

"Girls can play football. Remember Tina 'The Tank' Harris? She scared me away from football forever."

"Shame on me," Tamara said. "You're right. I guess I'm just reliving my youth—it wasn't easy being the twin sister of the school's top jock."

"I'll bet. What ever happened to Teddy?"

"Would you believe that he's a math teacher in Kelowna—with three kids under three?"

"Wow." I was surprised that I didn't already know that—surprised that I'd never asked, and nobody had ever told me.

"Hey, would you grab a shawarma with me? I'm"—Tamara looked down at her belly—"*we're* famished!"

"Sure," I replied.

"You want this?" Tamara held up the pink bowtie.

"Nah. I'm not really collecting souvenirs from Stephanie and what's-his-name's engagement."

Tamara laughed, stuffed the bowtie into her small black purse, and started to walk down Granville Street. As we strolled past bright lights, drunkards and homeless people, my sadness at the state of the world—and at my own tragic love life—was balanced by happiness for Tamara.

"Wait a minute," I said, stopping to look at her. "Are you sure the baby's … you know … his?"

She looked at me sheepishly. "Yeah. We're not as wild as you might think. It's more of a philosophy than a lifestyle … and in any case, I'm feeling rather maternal these days."

"Huh," I said, trying to pretend I could understand Tamara and Tracy's complicated relationship. I had always been a one-girl kind of guy. Marriage was simple in my mind—you married someone you loved and settled down with them for the rest of your life. Unfortunately, Stephanie hadn't received that memo.

Tamara led me into a funky little Lebanese cafe, where we ordered shawarmas just before the waiter locked the doors. He told us to take our time while he cleaned up, so we relaxed over an awesome meal and reminisced about childhood. Tamara told me more about Teddy, who had shed his massive ego once he got to university and found that he was no longer the strongest or the fastest at anything. Then we talked about Stephanie and Jonathan. Tamara wasn't convinced about them, but she said they suited each other, and I sort of understood what she meant.

We could have talked all night, and I wondered why we hadn't been closer when we were kids. I guess my crush—and her brother—had always stood in the way of thoughtful conversation. There at my new favourite restaurant on Granville Street, feeling more sober and mature than I'd ever felt on a Saturday night downtown, I was glad to know her as a friend.

Tamara offered to pay for my shawarma, and I didn't argue—since I was on parental assistance and she still had a few months of dual-income-no-kids prosperity. Then she drove me all the way out to Burnaby. I felt super content—until her car pulled away and I was left alone on the sidewalk, forced to recall that Stephanie and Jonathan were well on their way to another night of drunken fiancée sex.

Feeling a strange mixture of joy and sadness, I wasn't ready to go to bed, so I logged onto the computer to play Peace Warrior. I noticed a Skype message from Fiona—I'd finally gotten around to messaging her earlier that day—saying that she was available for a call. It was already morning in Switzerland, so I went ahead and dialed my favourite cousin.

"Bernieeeee!" Fiona bellowed as her face lit up my screen. "How *are* you? I haven't seen you in forever!"

We caught up on how our families were doing, then Fiona gave me a rundown of all the countries she'd visited since moving to Europe. I'd almost forgotten how great it was to talk to my closest cousin. I'd seen a lot of Fiona during my childhood, as our moms had been super-close sister-friends during our early years. Even though Fiona lived in Kamloops and I lived in Burnaby—and our visits became less frequent once we hit our teenage years—Fiona and I always enjoyed our time together.

"So cuz, I've gotta ask—" Fiona said, moving from small talk to more meaty discussion, "—how go your wedding sabotage plans?"

"What the—how'd you know?" I hadn't said a *word* about winning back Steph in my Skype text.

"Oh, come on," Fiona laughed. "What's a girl supposed to do when she's stuck in a new country with no friends and an over-worked husband? Why, call her best friend, of course."

"You've been talking to Stephanie?"

"Almost every day," Fiona said. "I've been getting a play-by-play of her wedding plans—*and* your mischievous activities."

"What does she know?" I asked.

"The million-dollar question is—what *doesn't* she know? Let's see … you're trying to win her back by asking her friends a lot of questions about marriage—and you've talked to a few of them. But Steph's not sure what you're planning."

"Oh, man," I said, unsure whether I should be delighted or dismayed that Stephanie was onto me. "Guess I suck donkey balls at being a private investigator."

"Now *there's* a visual," Fiona groaned. "You weren't really trying to keep it a secret, were you?"

"I dunno. I thought so. Maybe not."

"Well, Steph's flattered."

"That's good," I said, "but ... she's still planning to marry *him* next week. Right?"

"Yeah," Fiona said. "That's the plan. I'm ... supposed to be there, but ..."

"But what?"

"I'm playing the overseas excuse. Between you and me, I'm having a hard time with this whole Stephanie-Jonathan thing."

"I know, right? What does *he* have that I don't—I mean, *other* than a job and a car, and his own place ... and great hair ... and ... okay, maybe the putz has a *few* things going for him."

Fiona sighed. "I don't know what Stephanie really wants. Her love life has been a train wreck in progress since kindergarten. I've gotta tell you ... when I found out you two had hooked up at our wedding ... don't take this the wrong way, but ... I didn't give you a week."

"Why?" I asked.

"I knew Stephanie was going to be a heartbreaker when she kissed Todd Hunter on Valentine's Day—when we were five. The poor guy didn't know what to do. He brought her Valentine's chocolates for weeks, but she never kissed him again ... and he harboured a crush on her into high school.

"Then there was Geordie Milton in grade one. And Brendan Schmoltz ... and Davie Getzler ... and ... well, you get the picture."

"She kissed them all?"

"Yeah—every year she picked a new Valentine to kiss—and not like their moms did, I'll tell you. She was messing something fierce with all those confused little boy-brains, which were still trying to figure out if girls were gross or delicious. Then all hell broke loose in grade seven."

"What happened in grade seven?"

"It was like that song, *Jar of Hearts*—as if Steph was collecting hearts from every little boy in Juniper Ridge Elementary, stringing them along, never quite letting any of them go ... and then their hormones caught up ... which led to the Valentine's Day Rumble of 1997."

"The Valentine's Day Rumble?"

"Yeah—there was an all-out brawl in an alleyway down the street from our school. It started with two boys contesting Stephanie. One of them—Kenny Buckthorn—was a real tough little cowboy kid, scrappy as a bulldog, and he had the other boy—Warren Davidson—in a headlock. After Warren screamed 'Uncle!' he looked over at Stephanie and said it was all her fault, which Steph's lonely hearts club took exception to. They circled Warren, and then his friends came in to save him. It was like a rugby scrum. There's no telling how ugly it might have gotten if Principal Ryerson hadn't caught wind and found us all in the alleyway." Fiona broke out into laughter. "It was total mayhem—all caused by *your* ex-wife."

"Man," I said. It made me think of Teddy Turnbull and his band of bullies, and all the shit I'd had to endure in my mid-school years. "What happened after that? With Steph, I mean ..."

"She kept growing her heart collection ... right up until she met you. Honestly, I was worried for you. But you two lasted a week, then two, then a month ... there was something different about you and Steph. You had so much fun together—she was truly in love. Eventually, I convinced myself that you really were destined to be together."

"That's what I thought. I still do."

"I know," Fiona said. "It hurt me when she left you. It felt like I should have warned you—but I don't think you would have listened."

"Probably not," I agreed.

"You know, cuz," Fiona continued, "I know what you want me to tell you. But you're too good a person to wait around for Stephanie. She's my best friend, and underneath her dysfunctional love life she has a heart of gold—"

"Then why does she do it?"

"I don't know," Fiona said, "but I would guess that it's an overcompensation of sorts—Steph wasn't exactly bathed in affection as a child. I mean, Earl's a softie at heart, but even Steph has a hard time cracking that rawhide skin he wears around. And Bonnie is all business. She's practical and fair ... but I think she lacked whatever chromosome it is that makes a mother dote over her child. Don't get me wrong ... she's a good person. But she's about as warm as a snow cone."

"Huh," I grunted. I couldn't argue with a word Fiona had said. "So, where do you think that leaves me and Steph?"

"I think ..." Fiona stopped to gather her thoughts. "I don't know, cuz ... I think Steph liked the *idea* of being in a long-term relationship, but the *reality* was too much for her. I'm not sure she'll ever truly settle down, Bernie. To be completely honest ... I think you need to move on."

"Easy for you to say," I snorted.

"It's not easy for me to say—not in the least. I'm talking about my cousin and one of my best friends."

"Yeah, but you're over there in fairy-tale land—happily married, livin' the dream—while I'm here in the heartless reality of divorce, being emotionally crushed by *your* best friend."

"Oh, Bernie," Fiona said, "you think *my* life's perfect? My husband is a workaholic, and I don't have a work visa—so both my marriage and career are stuck in neutral."

"But you're travelling all over Europe. That's a pretty awesome place to be stuck in neutral."

"Yeah—alone! Even when Marcus travels with me, I hardly see him—he's meeting with clients from early morning 'til after I'm asleep. You think I'm not lonely? Try walking down the Champs-Élysées on your own while your husband wines and dines French bankers. Oh, and I *loved* my solo gondola ride through Venice."

"Really? You did a gondola ride *on your own?* That *is* torture. I didn't know … I thought … it seems like you two have it all."

"Don't get me wrong. We are blessed," Fiona sighed, "But it's still hard work. I love Marcus, and I know he loves me. I want to have his babies and grow old with him. But right now, I need to let him live his dream, and trust that he'll support me when I need to live mine. In the meantime, I'm making the most of my opportunity to see Europe. It's the gap year I never took after high school."

"Huh," I said. Fiona's words made me remember how much Stephanie and I had enjoyed each other's company—and how much we still did, if wedding-dress shopping was any indication. "You know," I said, "I think Steph just needs to realize how good we had it—and I have a feeling she's going to figure that out before she makes the biggest mistake of her life."

Fiona sighed. "I'll never understand you two. Who am I to say you're not meant to be together? I just ... don't want to see you get hurt again."

"Do you think Steph still loves me?" I asked.

"Of course," Fiona said. "I *know* she does. That's half the problem. Just ... tread carefully, Bernie. Stephanie is a minefield. I should have told you that years ago."

TWIST OF FATE

Arnie

I'M STILL PIECING TOGETHER EXACTLY WHAT HAPPENED at the Roxy. I may never fully understand it.

I don't usually have more than two or three drinks. But dancing with Loretta, celebrating the forthcoming nuptials of two people who were becoming our closest couple friends, I lost count of my alcohol consumption. Even Loretta was tipsy—the first time I saw her drink more than a glass of wine—and Jonathan and Steph were half-cut before the band took the stage.

It was strange to watch Bernard brood at the table while I celebrated—he's usually the dancer, while I sit and watch everyone else have fun. And seeing Stephanie drape herself all over him was uncomfortable, to say the least. But Jonathan ... I still can't believe it ...

Jonathan was having a blast, savouring his groom-to-be status, dancing with every woman in sight. It was all fun and games until he got cozy with the supermodel blonde who was completely tanked. It didn't feel right ... the fun atmosphere started to take on that closing-time edge that I usually try to avoid, and Jonathan was acting like his old, womanizing self. If I hadn't been having so much fun with Loretta—if I hadn't been so drunk myself—I might have been able to head him off at the pass. But I couldn't. I just watched it happen in slow-motion ... and even when it happened, I still thought it would all turn out okay ... until I got the call from Steph.

HEMORRHAGE

Bernard

I SAT WITH THE PHONE IN MY HAND and looked at Fluffball lying on my bed. His expressive little face told me that he probably understood my feelings better than I did.

Brain surgery. That's all I'd heard at first. Arnie said a bunch of medical jargon that I didn't understand, especially in my groggy early-morning state. But he got my attention with brain surgery. After that, he slowed down and explained the situation in English. Not long after I'd left the Roxy, Jonathan got cozy with the girlfriend of a 'roid monkey, who decked him without warning. Jonathan's head hit a table and he collapsed on the floor, sending the dance floor into pandemonium. The paramedics arrived quickly, stitched a gash over Jonathan's eye, and sent him home with Stephanie, putting an emphatic end to their Jack-and-Jill party.

In the middle of the night, Jonathan got up complaining of a wicked headache. Stephanie thought he was just drunk, but when she got up to pee and found him lying on the floor, she called 911. Next thing she knew, they were in the emergency ward, wheeling Jonathan in for a CT scan … then into surgery for a brain hemorrhage. He was still in surgery when she called Arnie—hoping for some nursing advice that would magically make things better. Once he talked her down a bit, he hung up and called me.

217

Images of Jonathan came into my mind like fireworks. Memories of playing soccer in elementary school; of throwing snowballs at cars on Kingsway from our expertly hidden snow fort; of walking the scenic route past the houses of girls we liked in junior high; of watching classic movies with my parents—Jonathan's willingness to sit through *Gone With the Wind* scored him a lot of friendship points. I had almost forgotten how many happy memories Jonathan and I had created when we were kids.

There were bad times too, like when I discovered that it was Jonathan who suggested the invite-Bernie-to-the-popular-kids-party bet to the Turnbull twins back in grade nine; when he asked Tamara for the last dance at our end-of-year social in grade ten; whenever he drove with an unhealthy dose of denial about his own alcohol consumption, leaving me to cab it on my own. And then there was that little issue of stealing my wife.

Thinking about Jonathan being in surgery for a brain hemorrhage, and about Stephanie sitting in the waiting room with his mom and Dale, was like putting all my memories and feelings in a blender and turning it to frappé.

Buried within my overwhelming sense of nostalgia, there was an infinitesimal part of me that wondered if this was the break I'd been waiting for with Stephanie. If there was some ideal level of brain-injuredness that would let Jonathan lead a functional life while losing just enough of his sickening charm to push Stephanie back to me. I knew it was a horribly selfish thought, and I wondered if I could ever be satisfied winning Stephanie's heart back because of Jonathan's misfortune—so I tried to push the stubborn nugget of evil optimism out of my mind.

I set down the phone and spoke to my dog. "We want him to be okay ... don't we, Fluffball?"

JOHN WAYNE

Arnie

EVEN THOUGH I SPEND HALF MY WAKING HOURS IN A HOSPITAL, it felt surreal sitting in the waiting room of Vancouver General, wondering if Jonathan would ever regain consciousness. Loretta took the day off work to wait with me, and Bernard caught a ride with us. Jonathan's mom, Vivien, and her partner, Dale, paced restlessly. I wondered if his real dad would show up, and if so, what he'd be like. I didn't know anything about Jonathan's real dad.

Stephanie appeared and disappeared from the room repeatedly, her anxiety putting everyone a little more on edge. I knew that Bernard had a burning desire to console her, but even he seemed to understand that she was inconsolable. We all left Steph to sort out her feelings while we struggled with our own.

In the hours since Stephanie called me for support and advice, I had relived my entire friendship with Jonathan Donaldson. It surprised me to realize how much I had grown to care about him. Over the past few weeks, the four of us—Jonathan, Stephanie, Loretta and I—had grown closer than I ever could have expected. My heart ached at the realization that my newfound friendship with Jonathan might be cut short.

The atmosphere shifted noticeably when Earl and Bonnie Hansen arrived. It was as if the sheriff and his wife had ridden in on horseback to save the day. Earl John Wayne Hansen looked as much the cowboy as I had ever seen him, and Bonnie was the perfect ranch wife with her red-and-white-checkered shirt, blue jeans, and white cowgirl boots. Earl removed his hat as he entered the room, and Stephanie launched herself at her dad the moment he arrived. He held onto her for at least ten seconds before passing her to her mom, where Steph received a brief pat on the back before Bonnie's arms shot to her sides. Earl glanced around the room and nodded at each of us, pausing for a moment before tipping his head to Bernard.

I've always had a hard time connecting Stephanie to her upbringing. Steph has embraced city life—she is the consummate urbanite. But there in the hospital, waiting to learn the fate of her fiancée, I saw a glimpse of the little girl who grew up on a cattle ranch east of Kamloops.

We waited a full two hours after the Hansens' arrival for the doctor to appear—two stressful hours filled with the murmur of quiet conversation. I sat beside Loretta and held her hand. When the surgeon finally walked down the hall toward us, the entire room went quiet. Vivien and Dale approached the doctor, and Stephanie got up to join them. I couldn't hear what the doctor said—he spoke quietly, and his three listeners hung on every word, nodding frequently.

Finally, the surgeon retreated into an office down the hall. Jonathan's mom turned and said, "He's out of surgery. Now we just have to wait."

Over the next few minutes, we learned through fragmented discussion with Jonathan's family that he had suffered an intraventricular hemorrhage, which had led to a brain herniation. Simply put, he had suffered a much greater injury than we had realized when he hit his head—possibly due to a second impact on the dance floor—which led to bleeding and swelling of the brain. In the doctor's words, Jonathan was lucky to have survived the night. The surgeon relieved the pressure and contained the bleeding, but Jonathan's recovery was very much uncertain.

When Stephanie's mom cleared her throat, everyone turned their attention toward her. "It's uncomfortable to ask this," she said, "but did the surgeon say anything about brain damage?"

Jonathan's mom nodded. "That's what they're worried about. His vitals are stable, but they don't know how much damage has been done."

Once it set in that there would be no immediate answers about Jonathan's fate, Loretta and I decided to head home. I turned to Bernard and said, "You ready to go?"

"In a minute," he replied. Then he walked over to Stephanie and whispered something to her. She hadn't spoken since listening to the surgeon—her usual bubbly personality was nowhere to be found—but whatever Bernard said made her crack a weak smile and throw her arms around him. I thought Stephanie might never let Bernard go. When she finally did, he nodded to the rest of the people in the room, pausing when he looked at Earl, then tipping his head the same way Earl had to him. It was like a showdown, but a respectful one—like two former foes who just wanted the best for the girl they loved more than anyone else in the world.

OH, BERNIE

Bernard

TWO DAYS AFTER JONATHAN'S SURGERY, I was awoken at the god-awful time of eight-thirty AM by a relentlessly ringing handset that I'd left in my room the night before. It rang to voice mail the first time, but when it rang again I conceded that my mom obviously wasn't available to answer the phone—so I gave in and picked it up.

It was Stephanie. The second I heard her voice, I snapped to full consciousness. She said that she'd phoned me for support because she knew I was likely to be at home. I let that subtle insult roll off me and listened as she told me that Jonathan was still being held in an induced coma. Then she repeated what Arnie had already told me the night before—that Jonathan's vitals were stable, but the doctor warned of brain damage and a long recovery when, or if, he regained consciousness.

My call with Steph was more monologue than dialogue. I wasn't sure what to say, so I mostly listened and grunted. She'd decided to take stress leave from her job, even though her parents and Arnie suggested that work would provide a good distraction. Her parents had headed back to Kamloops at sunrise to tend to their ranch, and she couldn't handle being alone. Steph told me she was missing Jonathan dearly … and her parents … and me, too.

I was super conflicted about Jonathan. I wanted him to be okay, but I still wanted Stephanie to leave him. Since the accident, I hadn't admitted those feelings to anyone—not to Arnie or my parents, not even to Fluffball. It was hard enough to admit them to myself. I certainly wasn't about to tell Stephanie how I felt, so I just let my thoughts mix with her words, responding from time to time so she would know I was listening.

After Steph talked my ear off for ten or fifteen minutes, she asked if I would come over to her place. *Her* place that used to be *our* place, which was now *their* place. I hadn't been there since January 5th, 2013—the day Stephanie returned from her three-night extramarital affair with Jonathan. I'd waited there loyally during her absence, keeping myself busy by cleaning. I'd even scrubbed the toilet for the first time ever, determined to impress my wife when she came to her senses and returned to me. When she finally came back, she didn't seem to notice all the work I'd done; she just told me that she needed some space to think about our relationship. I pleaded and cried, but she got stone-faced serious and told me the best thing I could do to save our marriage was to leave her alone for a while. So I called the only person I could bear to tell—Arnie— and the next thing I knew he was driving a hollowed-out version of me to Burnaby, where I turned up unannounced on my parents' doorstep with one suitcase that I'd packed in a daze. That day, I tried to convince myself that I would be back where I belonged in no time. But within two weeks, the rest of my stuff showed up at my parents' house in a small stack of boxes that Jonathan dropped off when I wasn't home.

Two-and-a-half years later, I still wasn't sure if I could face seeing *our* place that had become *their* place. But when Stephanie cried into the phone and said, "I need you, Bernie," I wasn't about to let her down. I showered and dressed, looked up transit options, and then headed downstairs to grab a cereal bar and hoof it to the bus. I still found no sign of my mom, and my dad's car keys were on the kitchen table—he must've taken transit or cycled to work—so I grabbed the keys and raced to the car. Then I drove west, determined to exorcise one of my fiercest demons—returning to the place that I had called home for the happiest days of my life.

When I pulled up to the curb, Stephanie was waiting in front of the house. The morning sun was beating down and the garden was in full bloom. The grass was brown, as it always was by August, and the yard smelled just the way I remembered from my summers living there—like flowers and warm air and Stephanie. Standing under the giant maple tree that covered half the front yard, my ex-wife looked stunning—even though her cheeks were red from crying.

"Oh, Bernie," she said, throwing her arms around my neck and squeezing me close to her. "Why is life so complicated?"

"I wish I knew," I replied, wrapping my arms around her back. "Thanks for coming."

"Yeah, of course." I was half aware of Stephanie's body, which was pressed tightly against mine, and half distracted by the big blue house that I used to call home. My mind filled with memories of the years Stephanie and I had spent together on West 26th Avenue: of picnicking on the front lawn on the first sunny day of spring; of walking to the coffee shop on Dunbar Street—which I did a lot, especially while Stephanie was working and I was between jobs; of weekend love strolls along Jericho Beach; of Stephanie climbing on top of me on our couch; of loving my wife in a way that she could never quite reciprocate; of knowing that each time I made love to her could be the last, because on some level I always knew that I was not good enough for Stephanie Hansen.

I felt tears begin to form. Despite my best effort to stop them, they dripped, then flowed, from the corners of my eyes. Stephanie joined me in a symphony of waterworks, and I wondered if she thought I was crying for Jonathan. In fact, I was crying for everything I had lost the day she told me our marriage was over.

Steph sat down cross-legged on the crunchy summer grass, inviting me with her eyes to sit beside her.

"We sure shared some good times here, didn't we?" she said, and I was glad to hear that she was also thinking about us—about our own shared history.

"Yeah," I replied as a random memory popped into my head. "Remember the first time you showed me Wreck Beach?"

Stephanie's lips curled upward, and she raised her eyebrows knowingly at my reference to Vancouver's famous nudist beach. "Oh yeah," she said. "You were so shy ... which was unusual for you. I liked seeing you shy ... it was fun to tease you as I peeled away my clothing piece-by-piece. And then ... you were suddenly naked, like you went from terrified to full monty within a split second."

"Well, I didn't have to worry about anyone looking at me," I said. "Not with you standing there in all your naked glory."

"You always were sweet," Stephanie said, sadness tinging both her voice and her smile.

"You always were gorgeous," I replied. Then Stephanie shuffled her butt away from me and laid down with her head in my lap. After a few moments, I dared to reach down and run my fingers through her long hair, picking out dried grass as I went.

Stephanie laid her hand on my leg, just below the end of my

shorts, and started to caress my knee. Then I felt her pinky-tip touch the inside of my thigh, just a couple inches above my knee, and my whole body stirred. If I hadn't known Stephanie as well as I did, I would have assumed that I was overreacting. But I knew better—I'd learned early in my romantic life with Stephanie that her lightest touches were her most potent. Sitting there on that front lawn, covered in dry grass and filled with too much emotion to bear, I was no match for the feather-light touch of Stephanie's pinky finger.

The minutes that followed were blurry and muddled—like I was drunk, even though I hadn't sipped a drop of alcohol. I remember helping each other get up and walking around the back of the house with arms around each other's waists, sharing a strange concoction of emotions—grief, friendship, love, lust—as we fumbled through her doorway—*our* doorway—and collapsed on the couch where we had made love countless times during our life together.

As Stephanie ripped off her shirt and bra, pressing her breasts into my face, I froze. The familiarity of that moment—of Stephanie driving me the way she drove our lives—struck me like a semi-truck. Stephanie had always driven, always taken what she needed while I took what she gave me. There had never been a doubt that Stephanie's satisfaction came first—as she whispered at me to lick her ear, yelled at me to touch her breasts, ordered me to please her. Sometimes I'd wondered what our landlords thought—if the quiet older couple from Malta got excited by Stephanie's screams, or if they were reciting the rosary while we sinned in their basement. But for the most part I hadn't cared, so long as Stephanie was on top of me, making me feel like a man.

Sitting there in a familiar position, in *our* place that had become *their* place, Stephanie's passion felt wrong. My body was ready—it had been since the moment Steph's pinky grazed my thigh. But my mind struggled to catch up. Before I could figure out what I was feeling, my shorts were around my ankles and Stephanie was pounding me into the couch. One second she was saying, "Oh, Bernie," and the next she was swearing like I'd never heard her curse. I was trying to focus on Stephanie—to focus on the moment—but I couldn't. The louder she yelled, the guiltier I felt. I wanted to tell her to stop, but I couldn't. I just sat there like a statue.

Then I thought of Sabrina McDonald.

I'd never thought of anyone else when I was making love to Stephanie. I tried to chase the image of Sabrina from my mind— she was just a friend I talked to on the phone—but I couldn't. As Stephanie's screams became louder, images of Sabrina grew stronger. I began to imagine that *she* was the one on top of me, and then ... I envisioned rolling her over and making long, slow love to her ... looking into her green eyes and running my fingers through her red hair. My body wasn't even moving—it was like the only thing happening between Steph and me was friction— and my mind had seen a whole different version of what my future could look like.

I felt my voice forming within. It rose from the pit of my stomach and built its way up my throat to the back of my mouth. Just as the word reached my lips, Stephanie squeezed me so hard I thought she might break me. As I yelled "No!" she yelled, "Yes! Yes! Yes!" Then she collapsed into me, wrapping her arms around my head and suffocating me with her breast and shoulder. "Oh, Bernie," she said. Then she began to sob, weeping almost as loudly as she had screamed.

OH, BERNARD

Bernard

DRIVING BACK TO BURNABY, my head was as cloudy as the sky was blue. When I reached Boundary Road, I turned left and realized I was no longer heading for home.

I was trying to understand my feelings for Sabrina. I hadn't thought of her romantically until Stephanie was sitting on top of me. Or maybe I had, and I just hadn't admitted it. I hardly knew her—and I'd hardly even noticed how beautiful she was when I'd interviewed her, because I'd been so determined to win Stephanie back. But when Sabrina and I talked on the phone, it was so comfortable. Like it was with Tamara, except … different.

Sabrina's mom greeted me at the door and showed me into her living room, where Sabrina was nursing Mikey. I suddenly felt that I'd made a mistake—that I should have gone home and gathered my thoughts before talking to another human being—especially one I was attracted to.

"Hi, Bernard," Sabrina said, smiling over at me as I sat down on the couch. "This is a surprise. What's up?"

"I'm …" Nothing was coming out. I'm sure there were at least a thousand words in my mind, but none of them made sense.

Sabrina's expression turned serious as she shifted in her seat, causing Mikey to pull away from her. I felt uncomfortable at the sight of her breast, and I forced myself to look down at my feet.

"Do you want to go somewhere to talk?" she asked.

"Yeah," I nodded.

"I'll ask my mom to hang with Mikey."

Sabrina left the room and was gone for a few minutes. When she returned, we headed out to the Jetta. It was awkward and comfortable at the same time. I decided to open her door for her, which caused her to smile and say, "Thank you, sir."

I climbed in the Jetta and started to drive, not sure where I was heading. I turned east on Hastings Street and thought of an idea. "Wanna go for a stroll at Barnet Marine Park?"

Sabrina lit up at my suggestion. "I'd love that. I haven't been there in years."

I tried to gather my thoughts to say something intelligible, but it was Sabrina who spoke first. "Thanks for rescuing me."

"From what?" I asked.

"From another afternoon pretending to enjoy living with my parents."

"Oh, man, can I ever relate to that. I'm in the third year of my second childhood—and it friggin' sucks."

"I'm not sure I could survive three years," Sabrina said.

"Are you going back to Fort Mac?"

"I don't know. There's not much for me there. I have more support down here, and I don't think I'll go back to work until Mikey's a bit older."

"It would be good if you stayed." I wasn't sure what else to say—I didn't want to tell her that I could use a friend, because I hoped there was more potential than that. But I didn't want to say that I saw potential, either. So, I held my tongue and said nothing.

"I'm glad to hear that from someone other than my parents," Sabrina said. "So ... why did you drop by today? I sense that you're dealing with something ..."

"Confusion," I replied. "I'm feeling a boatload of confusion. Let's see ... where to start ..."

I opened my mouth and a bunch of words came out—about the Roxy and the hospital and not knowing if Jonathan would be okay. Every so often, Sabrina would say something like "Oh, my God!" or "That's awful."

My motor-mouth was still in full gear when I pulled into the parking lot. I turned off the car and said, "And then I went to Steph's house, to console her, and ... if there's a hell, I've reserved my room there."

Sabrina didn't say anything, so I kept talking. "I've spent the last few years hating Jonathan Donaldson. I've actually wished him dead on more than one occasion. And now he's lying in a hospital bed, unconscious, and I hate him ... but I love him, too. He was one of my best friends for most of my life, and we had a lot of great times together. And then he stole my wife, which was totally in character because he's selfish. But it was also Stephanie's fault, 'cause she can be a selfish bitch, too."

I couldn't believe I had called Stephanie a selfish bitch. I looked over at Sabrina, who smiled like she understood. She didn't say anything, so I continued.

"All I've wanted was to win Stephanie back. She was the only person who made me feel good about myself—at least I thought she did. When I was with her, people looked at me like I must have done something special to land a woman like her. And I always wondered how that happened, why she was with me when she could have had just about any guy she wanted. I thought I was living in some fairy tale—like I was Shrek or The Beast or something, and she was the only woman who'd ever known the real me.

"Ever since Steph left me, I've felt like my happiness was dependent on her. Then, last weekend at her Jack-and-Jill party, something happened. While drunk Stephanie was slurring words into my sober ear, a little voice told me that if I really wanted to, I could win her back. That was the first time I ever questioned if I really *wanted* her back. Then the thought vaporized, and I tried to forget about it … and next thing I knew Jonathan was in a hospital and I was at *our* house that had become *their* house, and Stephanie was sitting on top of *me*, and … I found myself thinking about *you*.

"That's it. That's what I'm trying to say … that I … have feelings … for you."

Sabrina's face shifted, and I knew the look right away—the sad smile and puffy cheeks and Bambi eyes. It's as if every woman has the same expression that says *I like you as a friend, but …*

I looked down at the steering wheel, and we sat in silence for a very long time. Then Sabrina said, "Oh, Bernard …"

CUTE TOGETHER

Arnie

"You don't know where he is?"

"No," Sabrina said. "Oh, Arnie, I feel so bad."

"It wasn't your fault. If anything, it was mine." I sat down at my kitchen table and switched the phone to my other ear.

"I just wanted to help ..."

"I know," I said. "It seemed harmless. Look, thanks for trying. I thought ... actually, I don't know what I thought. I just figured a bit of company ..."

"Me too," she said. "And ... I like him. Just ... not, well, I don't know ... not now, anyway."

Neither of us said a word. We sat on opposite ends of a phone call, thinking about how we'd teamed up to add another layer of crush to Bernard's spirit. When I'd tracked down Sabrina following the Kiss Cam incident—thanks to a bit of undercover List investigation from Blanche—I'd justified it as being for him. But if I was honest, I had to admit that my motives were partly selfish. I'd thought that if I could find Bernard another friend, maybe that would appease my guilt for spending so little time with him. When Bernard mentioned inviting Sabrina to Steph's wedding, I thought she was safe friend material. Or did I? I was beginning to doubt both my judgment and my intentions.

"So," I said, "what happened after you told him you weren't

interested?"

"We got out of the car and walked along the inlet. He spilled out his heart to me—said he'd been attracted to me since the day we met, even though it took him a while to see that through his feelings for Stephanie."

"Oh," I said. "I probably should have seen that coming."

"Me too," she agreed. "I mean, I *do* like him. He's funny, and we have a lot in common. Our phone calls are so comfortable. He just … has some growing up to do. And me, I'm still a mess. We'd be an atrocious pair."

"So were Bernard and Stephanie," I said. "But they were cute together."

"I'll bet," she said.

"So, what happened next?"

"Bernard got really down and started to mutter things about having no real friends left. That's when I told him that you and I had talked—I was trying to point out what a good friend you were to contact me—but it came out wrong, like you'd put me up to it. I kept digging a deeper hole, until finally he said we should go. Then he drove me home without saying a word. When he stopped in front of my parents' place, he looked at me blankly and said, 'Well, bye.'"

"And then?"

"Then I got out, and he peeled off down the road and raced around the corner. That's when I thought I'd better call you."

END OF THE ROAD

Bernard

ONCE SABRINA RIPPED OUT THE REMAINDER OF MY HEART, I drove until I found myself on Lougheed Highway, passing the site of one of my lowest moments—JR's Sports Bar. I spewed profanities over my shoulder, intent on continuing my aimless joyride into emotional oblivion.

Without warning, my subconscious launched an assault from within, spearing my brain with scenes from *My Name is Earl*—an awesomely funny TV series about a guy who discovers karma and sets out to right every wrong he ever committed. My conscience rose like a stomach full of alcohol at the end of a drinking binge, dredging up a moment I'd fully intended to forget.

I pulled a fast U-turn at the corner, causing the doofus behind me to lean on his horn like a vigilante traffic officer. I flew back to the previous intersection, where my second U-turn—which might have stretched the yellow light just a tad—caused an orchestra of angry horns. I kicked the accelerator to put some space between me and the honkers, completing my double-U-turn loop by squealing into JR's parking lot.

I slammed the Jetta to a halt across two stalls and briefly debated if double parking was a cardinal sin. Before I could tangle myself in an ethical dilemma—or talk myself out of executing my hastily devised plan—I got out of the car, straightened my back, and entered the premises with an unusually high degree of moral conviction. I scanned the room for kilt-skirt Melanie and silently prayed that some almighty karmic being would ensure that the Aussie Bar-moose who'd kicked me out last time was off shift.

I spotted Melanie delivering a tray of drinks on the other side of the room. Then I turned my head and locked eyes with Bar-moose, who was standing behind the bar, forming an almost perfect triangle between the three of us.

"I told *you* to stay away from here," Bar-moose bellowed with his powerful accent, which scared me almost as much as his redwood-sized biceps. "I believe I have an appointment with the post office," he added, reminding me of his threat to mail me—in pieces—to Tasmania.

I took one step toward Melanie, and Bar-moose bolted toward the end of the bar closest to her. I realized there was no way I could get to her before Bar-moose reached me, so I stopped and shouted, "Melanie!"

Melanie spun around—I must have yelled louder than I meant to, because a large drink flew off her tray, smashed onto a table, exploded into a million pieces and sprayed a customer in a business suit. I looked at the suit-clad customer, then at Melanie, then at Bar-moose—everyone had frozen solid—and I realized my ill-conceived idea could have used a bit more planning.

I'm not quite clear what happened after that. I remember the customer in the suit standing up with a look of indignation, and I remember Bar-moose running in my direction. I remember charging through the door so hard that it jarred my shoulder, then fumbling for my car keys. I remember hitting the panic button— which in hindsight was probably the right thing to do, even though it was totally an accident—and then somehow making it into the driver's seat of my dad's Jetta in time to slam my door before Bar-moose rammed it. I must have pressed the lock button before he found the door handle, though I have no recollection of doing so. He looked like a rabid pit bull as he tried in vain to open my door while I struggled to start the car—wishing like frig for a normal key instead of the plastic knobby thing that didn't want to mate with its matching dashboard genital. I finally got the male knobby thing into the female holey thing, kicked the car into reverse, and left Bar-moose standing in a rage. As I jammed the car into drive and peeled toward the parking lot exit, I saw kilt-skirt Melanie in the doorway of JR's, looking at the car chase that me and her freakish bartender were engaged in. I froze for a split second—long enough to realize that I was no longer in immediate danger of being ripped to shreds by a raging lunatic—and I hit the brakes hard. I rolled down the passenger window halfway and yelled, "I'm sorry!"

I glanced back at Bar-moose—who started to run with impressive speed for an oversized mammal—and I dared one last glance at Melanie through the half-open window. She cracked a smile as I kicked the accelerator and launched the Jetta onto Lougheed Highway, causing another long, loud honk. I braced for a crash that never came. Then I drove along Lougheed as if nothing had happened, trying to ignore the guy who pulled up beside me and scolded my peripheral vision with a wide range of animated motions.

The road-rager cut in front of me and maxed out the acceleration of his Ford Focus, disappearing into the distance with the power and pitch of a ride-on lawn mower. I took stock of my recent activities and realized that my past fifteen minutes had probably not improved my karmic bank balance—but it felt good to know that I had apologized to Melanie.

My heart rate gradually slowed from hummingbird to rabbit-trying-to-outrun-a-fox, and it eventually dipped into human range. Reaching over my shoulder to put on my seatbelt, I thought about Melanie's smile and everything it might have told me. I wondered how many times she'd been harassed by horny drunkards, and if any guy before me had risked his life to apologize. I wondered if she *had* been flirting with me, even if it was mostly to increase her tip. I wondered if her employer gave her a choice whether to wear the skimpy kilt-skirt that made her look so sexy. I wondered what sequence of drunken brain farts had given me the idea that I should try and see underneath it. And I realized that Arnie was right—there are some lines you just can't cross.

The emotional ping-pong that followed my near-death experience at JR's took me on a meandering drive through Burnaby, over the Second Narrows Bridge, through West Vancouver toward the Sea-to-Sky Highway. I started out feeling oddly elated about Melanie's smile, but by the time the friggin' gas light came on just before the exit to Horseshoe Bay, my cerebral vortex had spun itself into another whirlpool of romantic ineptitude.

I pulled into Horseshoe Bay and found a two-hour parking spot on the street. There was a ferry docked at the terminal, and I still had fifty-five dollars of parental grant funding, so I briefly considered taking the ferry to wherever it was going. But my indecision was crippling, so it pulled away while I sat there pondering my next step.

Watching my escape-from-reality vessel leave the cove, I was struck by another realization—that in my haste to see Stephanie, I had forgotten about my job interview. No wonder the Jetta was at home—Dad had left it for me to drive to my interview.

"Shit!" I said out loud, wanting to blame my dad for going to work without leaving me a note about the interview. I knew it was lame to want a scapegoat for my own stupidity, because most unemployed humans would remember something as important as a job interview. But I desperately wanted to blame someone—anyone—for everything that had happened to me lately. My head fell against the steering wheel, and I felt like the world's biggest loser.

I had a sudden craving for alcohol—the same feeling I'd had the night Jasmine and Cassie humiliated me. I ignored the warning bells in my head—the flashing reminders of how *that* night had turned out. Trusting my newfound understanding of allowable customer-server interactions, I followed my craving to a barstool in the Troller Pub.

The bartender slid a coaster in front of me and said, "What can I get for you, sweetie?" She was about my age, a bit pudgy with a cheerful smile and a dusty blonde bob.

My mind drifted. Visions of Stephanie using me on her couch—*our* couch—mixed with images of Sabrina's scrunched up face admitting that she'd been assigned to cheer me up by Arnie—mixed with anxious memories of my narrow escape from JR's.

"Sweetie?" The bartender shifted her head to catch my vacant gaze. "Are you okay?"

"I don't know," I said. Then I forced myself to focus. "What's on special?"

"The Warty Toad."

"Sounds toxic."

"It's a strong brew ... and it's only five bucks. Good value for the money."

"Okay," I said, choosing quick inebriation over my usual preference for lighter beer.

The mirror behind the bar reflected the small bay surrounded by jagged peaks against the afternoon sun. It felt cruel to be looking at such a romantic scene while I wallowed in emotional purgatory.

The bartender set my beer down and said, "You sure you're okay?" I sensed that she was one of those telepathic chicks who reads other peoples' feelings. Rather than make her use those talents, I launched into a lengthy response.

"Yeah," I said. "I'm friggin' awesome. I'm broke … unemployed … divorced … I live with my parents … my *former* best friend is in a coma … my *supposed* best friend set me up for emotional disappointment … so I guess that means my *real* best friend is a toy poodle. And … I just about died at the hands of a crazy bartender today, trying to apologize to a waitress for mistreating her—I probably shouldn't have told you that last part—and I almost caused two accidents by driving like a *Fast and Furious* stunt double." I wanted to spill out everything to the nice bartender—to tell her all about the six years of highs and lows that I'd experienced at the hands of Stephanie Hansen. But my whole history caved in on me, and I slumped into my barstool.

"Oh, sweetie," the bartender said. "Sounds like a tough day."

I realized I was falling into a familiar trap—believing my server cared about me. I wiped the dampness that was starting to form in my eyes, and I felt my skin thicken. "I'm fine," I said. "I just needed to vent. I won't bore you with a slow-motion replay of my own personal blooper reel."

She assured me I wasn't boring her, but I could feel my heart hardening, so I said, "I just need to be left alone."

"Okay. Let me know if I can get you anything."

I nodded, stared down at the Warty Toad, and said, "I'll have another of these, please." Then I downed the rest of the tar-like substance in my glass.

As I chugged another pint of horribly strong beer, I felt a seed of self-loathing expand within me, and I knew that my feelings were finally catching up with my actions du jour. I recognized the emotion that I'd spent much of my life suppressing—the same feeling I'd felt when my mom found out I'd stolen a bubble-gum hamburger from Danny's Corner Store when I was eight. The same feeling I'd felt whenever I brought my report card home and had to face my dad's look of disappointment. The same feeling I'd felt every time I woke up with a hangover following a drunken Bernie episode. They were all different flavours of the same emotion.

Sitting in the Troller Pub drinking sludge-beer, a lifetime of missteps came back to me in layers, rising up to consume me. It was like I'd been depositing shame in a bank account since I was a kid, and the vault had finally overflowed. I couldn't stop thinking about all the stupid things I'd said and done.

I felt my eyes well again as I lifted my glass and finished the second Warty Toad. When the nice bartender came back to check on me, I was trying hard to contain my tears, which made them work even harder to escape.

"Oh, sweetie," she said, leaning her elbows on the bar and placing her head in her hands.

"I'm sorry," I said.

"For what?" she asked.

"For everything I ever did to anyone—which is a lot of stuff to a lot of people. Too much to ever make up for. It's not like my life is a sitcom, and I can make things right one episode at a time—and besides, for everything I do right, I seem to do at least two things wrong." I pointed at my glass and said, "Could I have another, please?"

"How about a water?" she asked. "Those Toads are really potent."

"Just one more?" I asked.

"Promise me you're not driving?" she said.

I slapped my dad's car keys on the bar. "Promise," I replied.

As I chugged my third Warty Toad, I realized I was not only at the end of *the* road—the last mainland stop on the Trans-Canada Highway—I was at the end of *my* road. I had spent more than six years of my life wanting only one thing—to be with Stephanie Hansen. Once I discovered that I might have a chance to win her back, I wasn't sure that was the life I wanted anymore. My dad always said that you can't go back—that you need to keep moving forward. He'd told me in one of his countless lectures that he'd quit a skookum job—leading adventure tours all around the province—when he and Mom decided to have me. He said that although he missed that job, there was no way he'd go back to that lifestyle once he had a family.

When I tried to order a fourth beer, my nice bartender said something about serving me responsibly and offered me any non-alcoholic beverage on the house. Even though my head was starting to fog up, I felt the need for more liquid therapy. So I paid my bill and got up to continue my solo pub crawl.

Walking out of the Troller, I looked out at the ocean and had the strangest feeling that I wanted to march into it and disappear. It was a blank, hollow feeling, devoid of emotion—and yet it was as powerful as anything I'd ever felt. I wondered how far I could make myself walk, and how cold the ocean would feel. Then I wondered if I could sleep through drowning … and how long it would take my family to notice me missing.

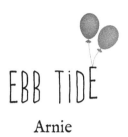

EBB TIDE

Arnie

DRIVING TO BERNARD'S HOUSE AFTER MY DAYSHIFT, I was deeply worried about my best friend. On my morning break, I found a message from Blanche trying to track down Bernard to remind him about his job interview. I didn't think much of it—I just chalked it up to another irresponsible B-man moment. But when I spoke to Blanche during my lunch hour and she still hadn't heard from Bernard after he'd missed the interview, I began to share her concern. Then, when I found Sabrina's message and returned her call during my afternoon break, I really started to worry. But it wasn't until I caught up with Stephanie at the end of my shift that I fully understood the situation.

"I shouldn't have ... oh, Arnie," Stephanie said, "I hope I didn't make things worse."

"What do you mean?"

"I sent him some mixed messages."

"That's nothing new."

"No, this was ... different. We were both emotional, and we just ... it was like ..."

"How was this time different?"

The line went silent. Then she said, "I'm worried about him. And I'm already so worried about Jonathan. Oh, Arnie, why is this happening to me?"

"I don't know," I replied, feeling uneasy about Stephanie's choice of words. "I'll call you when I find him. Do the same for me, okay?"

"Okay," she sighed, her voice pleading with me to solve her emotional jigsaw puzzle—even though I didn't have all the pieces.

"Steph," I said, "is there something you want to tell me?"

"Oh Arnie … I had sex with him. I just couldn't help myself."

The Kirbys' foreheads were etched with stress lines. Nobody had heard anything from Bernard since he'd left Sabrina's house.

"Where have you tried?" I asked.

"Bruno called from The Big Bean," Mr. Kirby said. "No luck there, or at Boston Pizza."

"I checked IHOP," I said, then I filled them in on my conversations with Sabrina and Stephanie—except the part about Bernard and Stephanie sleeping together. I hoped I wouldn't need to share that part of the story with anyone.

"How about Tamara?" Blanche asked.

"I didn't think of her," I said. "She's a strong possibility … but I don't have her number."

"Maybe he saved it on my phone." Mr. Kirby hurried to his office, while Blanche went to get her research notes for The List.

"Found it," Blanche said a moment later, re-entering the kitchen and picking up the telephone. She called Tamara, who said that she hadn't seen Bernard since the Roxy party. A short time later the phone rang again, and Blanche answered.

"Hi, son," she said. "Uh-huh … he did? What time?"

As Blanche hung up the phone again, Mr. Kirby rushed into the kitchen and said, "I think I might have her number."

"We're two steps ahead," Blanche said. "That was Bruno

calling from JR's. Apparently, Bernard showed up there this afternoon and created a scene, trying to apologize to a waitress for something he'd done last time he was there."

My face must have dropped, because Blanche took one look at me and said, "I assume this has to do with that night you took care of him."

I was unsure what to say about Bernard's experience at JR's. I decided not to say anything—I just nodded and said, "Yeah, probably." I was shocked to hear the words 'Bernard' and 'apologize' in the same sentence—and I wondered what kind of scene Bernard had created this time.

The three of us were stumped—and growing more worried by the minute. Bruno came over, adding to our collective stress by telling us that Bernard had almost caused a pile-up on Lougheed Highway when he peeled out of JR's parking lot after raising a commotion.

Evening dragged on, and there was still no sign of Bernard. We sat in the Kirbys' kitchen, Blanche calling each of the people on Bernard's List—none of whom had seen or heard from him— and reporting him missing to the Burnaby RCMP. The police took her seriously, but they could offer no reassurances about finding Bernard if he didn't want to be found.

"What about Vivien Donaldson?" Mr. Kirby said. "Did you call her?"

Blanche shook her head and picked up the phone, dialing a number that must have been etched in her memory for decades. After a minute she said, "Hi, Vivien. It's Blanche. I know you have enough on your mind already—we're thinking about you all the time. But we're also … I'm just wondering … if you've seen Bernard today. We're trying to track him down. If you hear from him, could you please give me a call?" Blanche put down the phone and let out a deep sigh.

As darkness fell and worry turned to despair, Mr. Kirby's cell phone rang. He picked it up and spoke in simple terms—"Uh-huh … yes … okay"—and I could tell he was onto something. As soon as he hung up the phone, he blurted, "That was West Van Towing. The Jetta was parked in Horseshoe Bay all afternoon and they've towed it to their lot." He shook his head and added, "What the hell was he doing in Horseshoe Bay?"

"Does he know anyone on Vancouver Island?" I asked, thinking of the village's main feature, a ferry terminal.

"Not that I know of," Mr. Kirby said. "Blanche, can you call BC Ferries and give an update to the RCMP? And Arnie—can you drive?"

"Sure," I said. "Let's—"

"I can take you," Bruno said, standing up from the table, where he'd been sitting in a trance until the towing company called.

"Why don't you stay with your mom?" Mr. Kirby replied, grabbing his coat off a kitchen chair. "In case there are other leads—it might be best if we divide and conquer."

"Okay," Bruno said, but I could tell that he was every bit as stressed as his parents—and wanted to find some way to help.

Mr. Kirby and I were just about to walk out the door when their landline rang again. We paused to listen while Blanche answered it.

"Hello," she answered excitedly. Then her face softened and she said, "Oh, hi, Vivien. How are you?"

As Blanche listened to Jonathan's mom, I thought about the value of friendship. Though our parents didn't hang out together, they shared a bond that had been cemented by years of concern about their sons. In some ways, our parents—who only talked when something was amiss with their children—were the oldest of friends because of us.

Mr. Kirby and Bruno and I stood like statues, waiting for Blanche to show some kind of reaction to whatever Vivien Donaldson was telling her. Then she pursed her lips and squinted, and her eyes began to water.

We decided to drive straight to Horseshoe Bay, rather than stopping to pick up the Jetta. We rode along the Upper Levels Highway in an uncomfortable silence. Although we'd never talked much, Karl Kirby and I got along fine—but the emotion of the day was too much for either of us to put into words.

When we arrived in Horseshoe Bay, most of the restaurants and stores were closed. We talked to the staff at the ferry terminal, and the barista at Blenz, before going into the Troller Pub. Mr. Kirby showed the bartender a picture of Bernard on his phone.

"No, sorry," the bartender said, "I haven't seen him. I'll check with someone who was here earlier." He hollered over to a nearby waitress, who came over and looked at the phone.

"No, I don't recognize him," the waitress said. She turned to head toward the kitchen, then spun around and pointed behind the bar. "I forgot—there's some keys under there. I meant to mention them when you came on shift. Trudy said some guy left them with her this afternoon, then walked out and didn't return."

The bartender reached under the bar and picked up a set of keys, setting them down on the counter with a *VW* symbol face-up. I looked at Mr. Kirby and saw the colour drain from his face.

We took the keys and headed out of the Troller, then checked the only other restaurant that was still open—Subway—to no avail.

Mr. Kirby and I agreed that Bernard had most likely caught a ferry to one of the three destinations reached from Horseshoe Bay, but we decided to do a detailed sweep of the village in case he had passed out somewhere. We walked around the few blocks that comprised the village, checking back alleys, nooks and crannies—then split up to scan the seaside—Mr. Kirby taking the sidewalk route and me searching the rocky beach. The moon was barely a sliver in the sky, so we had to rely on the faint light coming from a series of pathway lamps. As I hustled along toward a long wooden dock, I saw the outline of a human-sized lump beneath the huge wood pilings, only feet from the water. I moved faster. I could tell by the wet rocks and the fresh seaweed on the beach that the tide was going out.

My fast walk turned into a run, and when I caught a glimpse of Bernard's checkered Bermuda shorts, I yelled out, "He's here! Under the dock! He's ..." I couldn't complete the sentence. My friend—my best friend—was an unmoving mass.

SHOWDOWN

Arnie

"I AM WAITING FOR YOU, VIZZINI," Bernard slurred, sitting up halfway as I shook him.

"Bernard," I said. "It's me, Arnie."

"Fezzik?" He looked at me momentarily, then slouched back onto the beach. "Fuck, my head hurts."

"Son," Mr. Kirby said, "I'm here, too."

Bernard forced his eyes open and said, "Father, you're alive." Then he passed out again.

Mr. Kirby looked at me, and even in the dim glow of the lamps I could see that he was confused.

"*The Princess Bride*," I said. "He thinks he's Inigo Montoya."

"Ah," Mr. Kirby replied, still looking baffled.

"It's too new," Bernard mumbled.

"What do you mean?" I said.

"It's too new," Bernard said more clearly. "My dad doesn't know any films made after 1960."

Mr. Kirby said, "You'll have to bring me up to date. But first, let's get you moving."

Bernard tried to sit up, then slid back into a heap, looking like a drunken hobo. There was enough light to see that he was covered in seaweed, and he smelled as bad as he looked—a blend of alcohol and sea life wafting from his clothing and pores.

"Come on, son," Mr. Kirby said. "We need to get you home."

"I don't wanna go home," Bernard replied.

"Where do you want to go?" his dad asked.

"I dunno … maybe I should become homeless. Live the simple life."

"Don't be ridiculous," Mr. Kirby said. "Let's go sort this out at home."

"Fuck home," Bernard said, finally managing to prop himself up on his elbows.

Mr. Kirby stiffened and stood up. Then he walked a few paces, took out his phone and tapped his finger angrily against the screen.

"Hi," he said, holding his phone against his ear. "We found him. Drunk, of course—but otherwise unscathed. You can call off the search party." After a brief pause he added, "You tell me. He said he wants to be homeless, and I'm half inclined to support that ambition."

Mr. Kirby came back over and knelt beside Bernard. I could tell that he was trying hard to contain his anger. "Son, come on, we need to take you home."

"I don't want to go home," Bernard said.

"Where the hell do you want to go?"

"Forward."

Mr. Kirby took a deep breath, then said, "That's a start."

"I don't know how," Bernard said. "I don't know what forward looks like."

Mr. Kirby was still agitated—his movements were jerky, and even his breathing seemed forced as he searched for words. "You scared the heck out of us," he finally said. "Not like that's anything new … but you took it to a different level this time. And I heard about your antics at JR's, too. Come on, son ... let's go sort out your life at home."

"No," Bernard said firmly.

"No?!" Karl Kirby said, his voice rising. "You steal my car, skip an interview ... drink yourself half to death ... practically drown yourself ... cause us to call out a search party to look for you ... then have the gall to say 'no' when I offer to take you home?"

"Yeah." Bernard anchored himself into the rocky beach. "I appreciate your concern"—his voice was anything but thankful—"and now I'd appreciate you leaving me here to rot. I don't need your pity. I've already had enough of that for one lifetime."

Mr. Kirby turned to me. "Come on, Arnie. Apparently, Bernard doesn't need our help."

Mr. Kirby started to walk down the beach, and I felt pulled in two directions. Part of me knew that he was right—that we couldn't help Bernard if he wasn't willing to accept our efforts— but I couldn't imagine leaving him on the beach. What if he passed out again and drowned? It seemed that he had come close to that already.

I crouched down and said, "Look, man, we just want to help you."

"I don't need your help."

"I beg to differ."

Bernard turned back toward the ocean and spoke like he meant to be heard. "I'm not blaming you. It's me and my dad. We have nothing in common, and"—his volume jumped another notch—"he says he wants me to grow up, but he still treats me like a kid."

Mr. Kirby stopped, then turned around and walked back to crouch beside us. "What did you just say?" he asked Bernard.

"I said you still treat me like a kid."

"Well, you act like one."

"Maybe I wouldn't act like one if you didn't treat me like one."

"Maybe I wouldn't treat you like one if you didn't act like one."

Mr. Kirby plopped down onto his butt and crossed his legs, settling on the beach beside B-man. I froze with indecision, unsure if I should stay there or let them settle their differences one-on-one. My thighs ached from crouching, so I made a decision and sat down beside them. Nobody spoke for ages, and I noticed the sounds around me—the gentle lapping of water and a light breeze in the trees.

"Sorry I took your car," Bernard finally said.

Mr. Kirby took a moment to reply. "It's okay ... son ... we just need to figure out what forward means for you." He placed a hand on Bernard's shoulder, and I felt the tension between them evaporate.

"And the interview," Bernard sighed, "I forgot about it."

"I'm sure there'll be other job opportunities," Mr. Kirby said.

"I don't know if I could work there anyway," Bernard replied. "You and Bruno ... you have so much in common. I'd be a third wheel. I'm tired of being a third wheel."

"That's what you think? That you're a third wheel?"

"Yeah."

"Huh," Mr. Kirby muttered. "Well, you may not be into architecture or hiking or small batch brewing, but ... I'm sure your brother feels left out, too ... when you and I listen to golden oldies or watch classic films."

"He hates them, doesn't he?"

"Yup. So does your mom."

"No!?" Bernard's face dropped in shock. I found it cool how

much expression I could see—like the darkness and the contrast brought out more emotion than I ever would have noticed in daylight.

"Yup," Mr. Kirby said. "She thinks they're ridiculous."

"But she ..."

"—tolerates them because she loves us."

"She does love football though, right?"

"Not really."

"You mean ... it's all been a lie?"

"No, son, not a lie. Just ... love. Nothing gives your mother more joy than seeing her family happy."

"Huh." B-man shook his arms and brushed some of the seaweed off his clothes.

"Look, Bernard." Mr. Kirby removed his hand from B-man's shoulder. "I know we don't always seem close, and I've challenged you a lot ... but it's because I know what you're capable of. You don't give yourself enough credit, and then you play the clown card and—"

"I don't want another sermon," Bernard said, his voice stiffening. "We were making headway there for a moment."

His dad nodded and said, "Okay. Just know ... I've always been there for you, and I still am."

"I know," Bernard said. He seemed way more sober than he had been when we found him. It felt like the right time to share the news I'd been carrying with me.

"We have an update about Jonathan," I added.

"What about him?" Bernard asked.

"They brought him out of the coma this afternoon, and ... he's talking. The doctor said he has a long recovery ahead, but ... so far so good."

It took Bernard a while to process the news about Jonathan. I watched his face shift like a mood ring, twisting and scrunching its way through a range of emotions. Then all his muscles relaxed and he said, "That's awesome. That's really awesome."

J-MAN

Bernard

"B-MAN," JONATHAN SAID.

"J-man," I replied, walking over and sitting beside his hospital bed. Calling Jonathan J-man took me way back ... to our friendship ... to our childhood. Before Arnie joined the fray—before *The Gruesome Twosome* became *The Three Amigos*—back when it was just *J-man* and *B-man*. We'd stopped using our nicknames when we became rivals for the same girl. We'd stopped doing a lot of things then. "You look ..." I said, "well, I've gotta be honest. You look like one of Frankenstein's creations—but it's good to see you awake."

"I can always trust you to call it like you see it," he said. "Nobody else is honest enough to comment on my lobotomy bandages."

"You're still better looking than me." Although his head was bandaged and his voice sounded tired, I found it hard to believe the man I was talking to had been through brain surgery and a coma in the week since I'd seen him on the dance floor of the Roxy.

"I don't feel so great," he said, "but they told me that's to be expected. My head hurts and I feel nauseous most of the time, probably from the meds—but at least I'm on this side of the ground."

"I'm glad you are." I had thought about Jonathan almost nonstop in the few days since I'd learned he was out of the coma. As I'd nursed myself out of another brutal hangover from my solo pub crawl in Horseshoe Bay, I'd relived my entire history of friendship—and foeship—with Jonathan Donaldson. I realized that for everything he'd put me through, Jonathan *had* been a great friend for most of my life. Sitting on the beach under the pier, my own head pounding from too many high-octane sludge beers—capped off by two-for-one *She Ran Over My Heart with a Bulldozer* shooters for old times' sake at the pub down the street from the Troller—I'd finally understood how badly I wanted Jonathan to pull through this ordeal.

"So," J-man said, "Are we still … friends?"

"Yeah," I replied. "You have a hell of a knack for testing a friendship, though. You steal my wife and *then* get me to feel sorry for you. What's next?"

Jonathan cracked a weak smile. "Stop it, man. It hurts to laugh. You're dangerous in my state."

"Always the class clown, right?"

"Always," Jonathan replied.

I looked at the clock on the wall and saw that it was noon—two hours before Jonathan and Stephanie were scheduled to be wed. "That's a nice gown you're wearing. Still planning to tie the knot today?"

"No," he said—I already knew they'd postponed the wedding, but I let him blabber on about it anyway. "I suggested it. I'm still totally committed to marrying Steph, but she's had a lot to process, and she—well, she's just not ready. This has been really hard on her."

Always about Steph, I thought, but for once I kept my deliberations to myself. "I'll bet," I said instead.

"I know I said it before," Jonathan began, "but … I really am sorry."

"I am, too."

"For what?"

"Just ... everything." I wondered if Stephanie would tell Jonathan about our morning on their couch. I kind of hoped she would—someday. Arnie told me that Steph had admitted it to him when they were searching for me. He'd been super cool about it, telling me that grief causes people to do crazy things.

Sitting beside Jonathan's bed, my shame about having sex with Stephanie faded away. It felt like closure—like I understood something new about the greyness of morality. It didn't make sense at all, and yet it did—in a you-stole-my-wife-and-then-she-slept-with-me-one-last-time-while-you-were-in-a-coma-but-now-you're-back-and-it-won't-happen-again kind of way.

I wrapped up my visit with Jonathan—we both had a lot to say, but no need to say it then—and I passed through the sterile hallways out into the bright sunshine of a late August afternoon. A late August afternoon when one of my best friends was supposed to marry my ex-wife. I felt no joy that the wedding I had intended to derail was postponed indefinitely—but I felt a faint and undefinable sense of hope ... for myself, for Jonathan, and for a lifelong friendship that had been to hell and back.

ABOUT-FACE

Arnie

BERNARD'S ABOUT-FACE WAS REFRESHING, but also a bit discon-
certing. It was great to see my friend acting like an adult for a
change, but my optimism was tempered by years of experience
with B-man. Despite his assurances that he no longer planned to
derail Stephanie and Jonathan's wedding, I couldn't help feeling a
vague sense of concern about Bernard's new, improved attitude.

The wedding was delayed by almost three months to allow
Jonathan to recover. During that time, Bernard busied himself in
unusually productive ways—helping his family build a new deck
and working part-time for his dad's architectural firm, which had
given Bernard a second chance for an interview. And the project
that was at the root of my wedding angst: a secretive undertak-
ing that Bernard would not share with anyone. He spent hours
working in his bedroom, with frequent visits to his dad's shop
in the garage and some mystery trips—he wouldn't even tell his
mom where he was going—to pick up supplies.

Every time I asked Bernard about Stephanie and Jonathan—
to gauge his mental state—he just smiled and said something like,
"New plan, man. New plan." He wouldn't elaborate, no matter
how hard I pried.

"What do you think it is?" Blanche asked when I called during
one of his outings.

"I don't know. He just calls it a research and development project."

"And he tells you not to worry?" she asked.

"Yeah."

"Which ... makes you worry?"

"Yeah."

"Me too. He did give me one clue," she said. "When I pressed him a few days ago he said, 'What would Gregory Peck do?' I have no idea what movie he was talking about—he wouldn't tell me that."

"Why do you think he's being so secretive?" I asked.

"I wish I knew," Blanche said. "But then, I've always wished I could understand him better. Do you recall the roof fort?"

"How could I forget?"

"Well, I remember when that was happening—even though I didn't realize it was happening—Bernard seemed happier than usual. Something about working toward a goal, toward ... anything. He's spent most of his life floundering, waiting for others to make him happy. And that project, even though it infuriated me, I must admit that it gave me a deep admiration for my son, and a sense of hope that he was going to make something of his life."

"I know what you mean," I said. "I always thought Bernard was destined for greatness. Maybe it just hasn't found him yet."

Blanche paused for a long time. "I like that. I just want him to be happy. I've always worried that we might have broken his spirit. With all the times we said, 'Don't do this, Bernard,' or, 'Don't do that, Bernard,' I wonder if we stifled his creativity too much. But he was such a handful ..."

"Yeah," I laughed. "He still is."

"What do we do with him now?"

"I don't know. Let him build his new roof fort—or whatever it is—and see where it leads?"

"Yes, Arnie," Blanche said, "I think we'll just have to let him work this out, and be there to offer a hand if he needs one. Just like we always have."

CONSTRUCTIVE JUICES

Bernard

HELPING MY PARENTS BUILD THE BACK DECK got my constructive juices flowing, and hanging around the architects at my dad's firm gave me a kick in the pants to create something awesome.

I started out with a simple idea, but I quickly learned that implementation would be harder than it looked. Twice I abandoned the project, frustrated by my inability to get from concept to reality. But on my third attempt I rose to the occasion, allowing the project to consume me. From that point on, I spent every spare moment working on it. Even when I was doing other things, my mind wandered to designing the most amazing creation I had ever imagined.

Fluffball visited me frequently. Mostly he sat there and stared at me—his tiny poodle head tracking my every move like a fuzzy bobble-head doll. Everyone was asking about the project, but I refused to tell them anything—so I talked to my dog *a lot* during my weeks of research and development. I think the real reason I kept my project a secret was that I wasn't convinced I could actually finish it. I'd had a lifetime of false starts, and I was determined to prove to myself—if not everyone around me—that I could complete something.

As I was putting the finishing touches on a finicky part of the project, I poked my finger with a sharp piece of wire, causing me to spew a stream of profanities. I shoved my injured digit into my mouth, and Fluffball tilted his head in the way that cute little dogs say, "Are you okay?"

"You're the best," I said to my half-pint pooch. Then I waved my hand at my almost-finished creation. "What do you think, little dude?"

Fluffball studied my invention like it was the Mona Lisa. Then he looked at me again, and I could swear he was smiling—like he was giving me his paw-stamp of approval.

"Yeah," I said. "It is pretty friggin' impressive, isn't it?"

WHO'S THE SNEAKY ONE?

Arnie

Blanche and I had embraced The List out of a shared sense that it might provide Bernard a form of therapy. We also shared a common faith that Bernard would never see it through—that he would burn out along the way and find something else to focus on, as he always seemed to do. But as Stephanie and Jonathan's wedding approached, Bernard once again started asking questions about all the weddings he'd attended.

Bernard's attractions to Jasmine and Sabrina offered promising glimpses into a life beyond Stephanie, but his renewed interest in The List—coupled with his focus on the secret project—unsettled everyone around him.

One day in late October, I called Sabrina to see if she'd heard from Bernard.

"Yeah," she said. "He called me a couple weeks ago. He wanted to ask me about my marriage again. And he apologized for leaving in a huff last time I saw him."

"He asked about your marriage? I don't want to pry, but ... I'm trying to figure out what he's up to."

"He asked me for a quote about married life, and if I could tell him one thing about my marriage that inspired me. One thing I wouldn't change."

"And ...?"

"I don't remember my exact words, but I said that even though my marriage was a disaster, I wouldn't change a thing about how my life unfolded. Because, if I did ... then I wouldn't have Mikey."

One by one, I tracked down most of the people from The List. Prakash and Meera. Jerry and Jordan. Jasmine. Tamara. Joey and Cecilia. I was becoming as obsessed with Bernard's secrecy as he was about his project. I'm not sure why I kept digging or what I hoped to achieve. I was convinced that I had to solve the mystery, and that I might need to save Stephanie and Jonathan's second attempt at a wedding from B-man's meddling.

I compared notes with Blanche a little more than a week before Stephanie and Jonathan's rescheduled November wedding. I was quite sure that Bernard had re-contacted every one of the couples on The List—right down to his former Aunt Shirley and his Aunt Aggie's widower, Leonard, who was still enjoying the elderly high life in Palm Springs.

I flopped down on my couch beside Loretta. "He's reached out to every one of them," I said. "And I still don't know what he's up to."

"What's he been asking them?"

"He seems to be fishing for soundbites about their marriages."

Loretta grinned as if she knew something I didn't.

"What are you smiling at?" I said.

"I think it's cute. Go on ... what else did you learn, Sherlock?"

"He wants to know one thing they wouldn't change if they could—even the ones whose marriages failed."

"Have you asked B-man about your findings—since you started spying on him?"

"God, no," I said. "I asked them all to swear they won't tell him I called. They all get it on some level—we all share a kind of unspoken understanding about B-man."

"So, you're conspiring now," she said. "Sneaky."

"Who's the sneaky one?" I said. "If Bernard would just tell us all what he's up to …"

"Why do you need to know?" she asked.

"To save him from himself."

"You think he needs saving?"

"I … well, he needs … he's … come on, you know Bernard."

"Yeah," Loretta said. "He's one of a kind—aren't we all? Maybe it's time the world accepted him for who he is."

THE SHOE BOX

Bernard

"You're not going?" Arnie said, his face twisted in confusion.

I glanced down at my sweatpants and t-shirt. "Do I look like I'm dressed for a wedding?"

"No, but …" Arnie turned to Loretta, and she smirked at him.

"You two look awesome," I said. "Super stellar."

"So, when did you decide?" Arnie still looked puzzled.

"A few days ago. I called Steph to let her know I wouldn't be there."

"What did she say?"

"Not much. I just told her it was best if I wasn't there, and I explained why. I think she understood."

"What made you change your mind?"

"Well, let's see … residual jealousy, for one. And in case you haven't noticed, I have a history of binge drinking at weddings."

"Yeah, I kind of noticed that."

"My dad's been teaching me about the value of one good pint. I've been limiting my alcoholic intake to a pint with our coworkers every Friday. Let's face it … if I go to the wedding—at least *this* wedding—I'll have to get warmed up with a bottle of wine, which will lead to a dozen cans of horse piss … I'll probably start a game of *Where's Uncle Bob?* … then I'll do something catastrophically stupid, and Earl John Wayne Hansen will finally snap."

"Oh," Arnie said, "that sounds really ..."

"Wise?" I asked.

"I was going to say mature."

"I *am* thinking of moving out of Neverland. Not yet, but ... one day."

Arnie nodded, and we all stood in silence for a few seconds.

"Hey, I want you to deliver this, okay?" I handed Arnie the shoe box that I had wrapped with as much care as I'd ever given anything. Even though I'd written *fragile* all over it, I added, "Please be careful with it, and make sure it gets to them."

"It's not a bomb, is it?" Arnie asked, causing Loretta to giggle.

"Not exactly," I said, "but I am hoping it'll make an impact."

"Hmm," Arnie said. "Just tell me it's not going to embarrass me."

"I can't promise that," I replied. "You're pretty easy to embarrass."

Loretta giggled again, and Arnie said, "You sure you don't want to deliver this yourself?"

"Surer than sure. I'm starting to understand some things I didn't use to understand."

Arnie turned to Loretta, who raised her eyebrows to say that *she* understood what I meant about understanding. Then he looked back at me and nodded. "Okay. But ... why didn't you tell me you weren't going?"

"I dunno," I said. "I wanted you to deliver this anyway, and since you've been following me around, I thought I might toy with you a little."

"Wha—who told you that?"

"Do I look like a snitch?" I enjoyed watching Arnie sweat for a moment before saying, "Nobody told me. I overheard you talking to my mom a while back. She thought I was out, but I'd come back into the house to get my wallet. Oh, and that Gregory Peck movie my mom mentioned to you ... it was *Roman Holiday*. It's about taking the high road."

"Oh," Arnie said. "So much for my career as a secret agent. You know I was just looking out for you, right?"

"I know," I said. "You've *always* had my back."

T︁HE G︁IFT

Arnie

S︁TEPHANIE AND J︁ONATHAN'S WEDDING was a small, informal affair at the Roundhouse Community Centre, an historical site that used to be the main train hub in downtown Vancouver. Unlike her large Catholic wedding to Bernard, Stephanie chose a marriage commissioner and a simple, non-religious ceremony for her second wedding.

It was a nice day for mid-November, so Loretta and I slipped out of the reception at dusk to walk along the False Creek waterfront. When we reached the water, we found Earl looking out at the yachts parked in Quayside Marina.

"Hi, Mr. Hansen," I said.

Stephanie's dad turned to face me, and even in the dim light of a late fall afternoon I could read emotion all over his cowboy face. "Oh, hi, Arnie," he said.

"Sorry if I interrupted you."

"Not at all." He turned back to face the boats. "I was just admiring the luxury of this place."

"Congratulations on the wedding."

"Thanks," he said.

"It's a blessing that Jonathan … well, that this wedding was able to happen."

"Yeah." He nodded in our direction, then said, "I don't think

I've met your friend."

"Oh, this is Loretta. Loretta … Earl Hansen."

Earl and Loretta exchanged greetings, then we stood in silence until I said, "I know Bernard wasn't the easiest guy to have as a son-in-law. I hope you have a better relationship with Jonathan."

Earl smiled and said, "I was hard on that boy, but his heart was in the right place."

"Yeah," I agreed. "It usually is."

"Now his brain, on the other hand …"

Loretta and I both chuckled.

"Hey," Earl said, "you tell that boy that as much as he drove us crazy, we kind of miss him. Maybe someday, if he's passing through the Thompson Country, he might drop by for a coffee."

I smiled at the thought of B-man dropping in on his former in-laws. "Yeah," I said. "I'll let him know."

On the morning after the wedding, Loretta and I went to Stephanie's house for the gift opening. I was dying to see Bernard's gift.

"What do you think it is?" Loretta asked as I drove west on King Edward Avenue.

"I don't know. Maybe he had Tracy get all the Lions to autograph a football."

She looked at me doubtfully.

"Well, it's the right size to be one."

The nice fall weather had continued, so we sat out in Stephanie and Jonathan's backyard—the same yard we'd sat in five years earlier for Stephanie and Bernard to open their gifts—and I felt like I was watching a rerun with a different lead male.

Stephanie and Jonathan cooed at their gifts—mostly cards with cash, as they had requested—plus a painting, a plant, and a few bottles of wine. When they got to Bernard's gift, I stiffened in anticipation.

Stephanie handed the wrapping to Jonathan, then lifted the top off the shoe box and peered inside. "Wow," she said.

"Wow," Jonathan echoed.

The two of them looked like they were handling a newborn. Jonathan held the box and Stephanie reached inside. Everyone who was there—about twenty of us in total—held our breath as Stephanie lifted the gift from the box. Then we all exhaled in unison.

I had never seen a more beautiful gift. The pattern of gold, black and white triangles was an impressive reproduction of the egg that Bernard had cursed during our trip to Saskatchewan.

"Look at the inscriptions," Jonathan said, breaking the silence. "There's a whole bunch of them."

From across the lawn, it dawned on me that they must be quotes from the couples Bernard had interviewed. He had turned his research project—the project that began as an effort to sabotage a wedding—into a tribute to marriage. Even without being there, B-man had stolen the show.

When it was our turn to view the egg, I counted the inscriptions. Seventeen. Then I started reading them aloud to Loretta: "Never miss a goodnight kiss"; "Grandparenthood is the pinnacle of wedded bliss"; "1 + 1 is more than 2. Start saving now!"; "Commitment is greater than loneliness"; "Don't strive for perfection"; "Before you know it, you're old and grey ... so when in doubt, smile and stay."

I paused to ponder who had contributed each of those quotes, and Loretta picked up where I left off. "Even in darkness, there is light," she said.

"I'll bet that was Sabrina," I guessed, turning the egg into a game.

"Dance until the lights go out."

"Maybe … Len and Aggie."

"Love is eternal."

"I wonder if that's Bernard's … him and Stephanie."

After we went through all the other inscriptions, Loretta read the only one with a label. "Love and life are fragile. Cherish them both and handle with care. Stephanie and Jonathan, November 14, 2015."

Loretta looked at me and beamed.

"Did you know about the egg?" I asked. "You always seem to know things."

She shook her head and said, "No. I just know his heart. It's a good one, like yours."

I knew then that I was going to marry Loretta Chan.

July, 2016

CHARLES DE GAULLE

Bernard

A LITTLE GIRL, NO MORE THAN FIVE YEARS OLD, looks up at an old black woman and says in a strong English accent, "Mummy, why are some people dark?"

The mother's eyes widen in horror, but the woman smiles gently and says to the girl, "Why are you so small?"

"People come in all different colours," the mother says. "And shapes … and sizes, too. That's one of the things that makes humans so amazing."

I'm overwhelmed as I scribble details into my journal, taking in the scene in Charles de Gaulle Airport. I've flown before but never to somewhere this far away, and never on my own. I'm enamoured with the whole experience and still blissed out from the surprise send-off party my parents threw for me before my overnight flight from Vancouver to Paris. I wish I'd gotten more sleep on the flight, but I couldn't resist all-you-can-drink ginger ale and an *Iron Man* movie marathon.

I'm pretty amazed by the sequence of events that led me here. On the day of Stephanie and Jonathan's wedding, I logged on to play Peace Warrior. I saw the picture I'd set as my splash screen—of the little girl sitting on a beach in Sierra Leone—and it got me thinking about doing something real with my life. I made Legend status on the game that day. From there, a perfect storm of opportunity and support spiraled together like a happy tornado, pushing me toward a goal that I couldn't have even imagined a year ago.

And yet, here I am, waiting for a flight to take me from Paris to Freetown, to a place that never gets colder than 15 degrees Celsius. Waiting to see a whole different world. My dad's firm sponsored my application to volunteer for a well-installation project with the Pure Water Foundation, and his colleagues—*my* colleagues—worked with me during lunch hours to apply for the role of Assistant Project Engineer. My gorgeous and brilliant boss, Trina Bergenheim, helped me incorporate what I learned about Sierra Leone—from a video game—into a cover letter that made it seem like I'd been there.

The whole project will last less than a month—my return flight allowing a few days' jetlag buffer before Arnie and Loretta's wedding at the end of August—but I'm super stoked about getting to see Africa for real. I've grown a lot this past year—and shrunk a little too, thanks to a few changes in the lifestyle department (hot chocolate addiction notwithstanding). I arrived a little late to this whole grown-up thing, but I'm beginning to embrace it.

If I've learned anything since my last binge drinking episode in Horseshoe Bay—I call it my rock-bottom-strewn-with-seaweed day—it's that I am the master of my own happiness. Once I figured that out, other stuff that used to be hard—like showing up for work on time—started to get easier. I still hate my alarm clock, but I now accept that it serves a useful purpose.

I'm looking forward to trying college again this fall—I signed up for the Building Design and Architectural CAD program at BCIT. If that goes well, there's potential for longer-term employment with my dad's firm. With *my* firm, that is.

I've developed a strong friendship with Tamara and Tracy. I'm starting to understand that their whole polyamory thing really is about loving people, not just about lust or sex—but I'm still a bit flummoxed by the whole idea. These days they're pretty focused on loving their little girl, Penelope, who might be the cutest parasite in the world. Tamara is an awesome mom, and Tracy's Buddha-like patience serves him well as a dad. Patience has helped Tracy at work, too—he finally rose to backup quarterback this year—and as much as I envy his unfair combination of super-human traits, I have great admiration for his long path to semi-stardom.

Speaking of patience, Sabrina and I are taking our own long and winding road to building some sort of relationship. I don't really know what we are—kind of more-than-friends-but-less-than-lovers-who-may-or-may-not-ever-enter-into-a-romantic-relationship. We hang out a lot, and I've grown very attached to little Mikey. Sabrina and I hold hands sometimes, but we haven't tried to kiss or anything. We've both been through too much emotional turmoil these past couple of years to have any chance of being a functional couple. Yet, anyway.

One of my favourite activities is playing Peace Warrior with Jasmine's son, Nicholas. After my meltdown last August, I phoned Jasmine to apologize for calling her names, and to my surprise that was all it took to get back in her good books—well, that and a willingness to accept a much-needed education about diversity and labelling. She and Cassie are really cool to philosophize with, although we've had some heated debates about food and global warming and whether the Edmonton Eskimos should be forced to change their team name to something less racially sensitive. But mostly we get along great. They even supported my decision to go ahead with real vaccinations for my trip. Oh, and they got engaged last month. I'm looking forward to experiencing my first ever same-sex wedding, now that I understand that people are people ... love is love ... and Uncle Bob can be an uncle or an aunt or whatever they want to be called ... so long as I can call them Bob. The only thing I'm not looking forward to is the vegan atrocity they will no doubt commit when it comes to dessert. I might have to pack my own cake to fully appreciate their nuptials.

I'm still working to master the word *sorry*. It doesn't roll off the tongue the way I'd like it to, but each time I apologize for something, I peel away a thin layer from the lifetime of stupid things I've said and done. I'm sure my karmic debt is still substantial, but I feel like I'm slowly chipping away at the principal.

As for Stephanie and Jonathan, they're only eight months into their marriage and they're already six months pregnant. Jonathan still isn't a hundred percent—he has trouble driving at night, and he has a harder time focusing than he used to—but overall, he seems to be doing well. I don't see much of them, but when I do, it's surprisingly comfortable. They seem happy together, and that actually makes me happy, too. I'm looking forward to seeing what kind of offspring they create; I have a hunch their bumpkin will be both beautiful and dramatic.

My cousin Fiona, who recently moved back to Vancouver, accidentally spilled the beans to me at my send-off party that if Steph and Jonathan have a boy, they're planning to name him Earl Bernard Donaldson. I'm deeply touched, but I figure if they're going to name a baby after me, they might as well call him Cupid. After all, in a strange and roundabout kind of way, that's who I turned out to be.

ACKNOWLEDGEMENTS

IT TRULY TAKES A COMMUNITY TO PUBLISH A BOOK.

My gratitude starts and ends with my amazing-in-so-many-ways wife (and editor), Sheila, who consistently provides exactly the right blend of support and constructive criticism required to bring a book to fruition.

I receive tremendous motivation from my teenage children on a daily basis. Iris, a prolific reader and reviewer of Young Adult fiction, inspires me with her love of books and her insightful reflections on the words she reads. Simon, an author in his own right with two books under his belt and a third on the way, inspires me with his dedication to the writing craft.

To those who read earlier versions of this manuscript—Rolf Reynolds, Kylie Hutchinson, Karl Rebner, Christy Leslie, Lenni Porter and Robert MacDonald—your honest and thorough feedback was invaluable. You pushed me to delve deeper into the minds of my characters, and your collective input shaped the arc of this story more than you might realize.

To Kristin Summers of Redbat Design, thank you for sharing your gift of visual creativity—and exceeding my expectations with a cover that perfectly represents the words within it.

To my proofreaders—Mary Haggeman and Mike Wilson—I appreciate your eyes for detail and your thoughtful feedback regarding the nuances of wordsmithing.

To my parents, whose children put them through three weddings in three years back in the 1980s, I am thankful for fifty-six years (and counting) of modeling commitment on many levels.

To my extended family and friends who have given me so many wedding experiences to draw on for this book, I thank you for an abundant source of content and inspiration.

And finally, thanks to you for reading this book! I hope you enjoyed my exploration into the wacky and wondrous world of weddings.

If you wish to follow my blog or learn about future projects that I am working on, visit me at www.markofwords.com or e-mail me at markofwords@gmail.com.

ABOUT THE AUTHOR

MARK CAMERON has travelled a long and varied road to authorship. After a twenty-year career in the software industry, Mark left the tech sector in 2011 and turned his attention toward his lifelong passion for the written word.

During his journey to self-acceptance as a writer, Mark has dabbled in various and sundry work-like practices in an attempt to pretend he has a "real" job—including business and technical consulting; book design; publishing; experiential tourism; and managing a co-working office. He has also reignited his commitment to community by volunteering with a car co-operative, a seniors village, an Art Farm (yes, really), and the many activities that his kids take an interest in.

Mark lives on the Sunshine Coast of British Columbia with his wife, Sheila, and two homeschooled teenagers. *17 Weddings* is his second book. His debut novel, *Goodnight Sunshine*, was longlisted for the inaugural Whistler Independent Book Awards in 2016.

CPSIA information can be obtained
at www.ICGtesting.com
Printed in the USA
LVHW111935301018
595373LV00001B/3/P